Dove Strong

Dove Strong Trilogy
#1

Erin Lorence

Dove Strong
COPYRIGHT 2019 by Erin Lorence

Contact Information: titleadmin@pelicanbookgroup.com

All scripture quotations, unless otherwise indicated, are taken from the Holy Bible, New International Version[(R)] NIV[(R)] Copyright 1973, 1978, 1984, 2011 by Biblica, Inc.™ Used by permission of Zondervan. All rights reserved worldwide. www.zondervan.com

Cover Art by *Nicola Martinez*

Watershed Books, a division of Pelican Ventures, LLC
www.pelicanbookgroup.com PO Box 1738 *Aztec, NM * 87410

Watershed Books praise and splash logo is a trademark of Pelican Ventures, LLC

Publishing History
First Watershed Edition, 2019
Paperback Edition ISBN 978-1-5223-0118-9
Electronic Edition ISBN 978-1-5223-0117-2
Published in the United States of America

Dedication

To my husband and best friend, Brian.
*I never would have succeeded without your love
and fierce support.*

Dove Strong Trilogy

Dove Strong
Fanatic Surviving
Sent Rising

1

I had two choices.

Either ignore my brother, Gilead. Or knock him out of the tree.

Then, the limb under my feet tried to buck me off.

"Quit it." I snatched at an iffy branch near my ears while widening my stance.

How dumb of me not to have acted quicker. So what if a major reason I was about to risk my life trekking across the enemy's territory was to save my brother's? It would be kind of pointless if I killed Gilead now. But at least he wouldn't be here, twenty feet in the air, annoying me.

The shaking lessened some, but I still grappled with the branches next to me.

"So help me, Gilead, I will tell Grandpa if you break my neck. What's more, breaking my neck won't help my survival rate for the trip. I'll jump when it's time, and it's not time yet, so go home."

As the shaking eased off, I squinted through the sunlit greenery at my brother.

A foot taller than me, he perched on nearby limbs in the shade at the oak's trunk with one foot still planted on my branch. His arm, one that could haul me over his shoulder without trying, gestured at a limb below us. It was the first step in a climb down into dead bushes and the water I'd soon land in.

A scream echoed overhead.

We both ignored it. Gilead tried to bully me out of the tree with his dagger eyes. And I pretended he'd reharnessed and taken the zip line back home.

Another scream. Only blue jays scuffling for territory in the foliage. Birds speckled the forest's canopy and summer sky. Everywhere except *down there*. In all the hours I'd watched, nothing feathered had touched that oblong of water.

Yeah. That water definitely had something off about it.

I sniffed again but still didn't catch any telltale stink from the giant, freak puddle in the middle of a waist-high bunch of grass. Only the ho-hum smell of baking pine needles and sun-scorched dirt.

According to my brother it was a pond—and the best entrance point into our neighbors' underground home.

The leaves next to my shoes quivered again. A threat.

"Climb down then, Dove, and run for it. Since you're too scared to jump."

I glanced over. His chosen limb seemed sturdy enough for any job. A lot like him.

"It's safe." He spoke through a jaw that had been clenched for the last six months. His frustration bled through the reassurance of his words. Frustration that *I'd* been called for this journey. Me. Not him.

"And you've got speed now...well, for a girl. For sixteen...I mean, they're far enough away that they won't catch you if you run flat out like I've taught you." His tone melted to clover honey. "Don't be scared, lil' Dove Bird."

He was goading me with...what? My supposed

fear of those stupid dogs?

"*Tchah*." I stayed focused. "Genius plan, Gilead—"

"They always are."

"If I run, I lead those beasts to the Braes' door. And every Heathen in Oregon will know where they live. Nice." My eyes flickered to a shadowed spot between some half-buried boulders at the pond's farthest edge—the Braes' hidden entrance—before returning to the too quiet puddle...pond.

"Or I could throw you?"

Wooroo. Wooroooooooo.

The hounds hunted far enough away, although they sounded more excited now, which probably meant they'd caught my family's scent.

Maybe they were under our home's maple trees, balancing on their hind legs. Clawing at the rippled bark and baying up at my grandpa who'd use the buckets of water if he got fed up with it.

No. Scratch that. Today he'd keep them from Gilead and me—no doubt baiting them, holding them there.

A home built in the tree canopy—like ours—was pretty safe, even if not hidden. A home carved out from the ground like the Braes'...

No way would I lead the beasts there. I clenched my fists at the pure evilness of the idea.

There was only one way I wouldn't leave a scent trail for the enemies' dogs to track. And that was straight down from this providential, jutting branch into the suspicious water below. I'd reach the entrance from there.

"You're killing me, Dove. We're losing light, and I'm worn. And you're sun damaged if you think I'm going to camp out here all night while you gape at the water. Plus, I'll have to check the zip lines all over again in the morning if vandals mess with them. No joking. I'm gone."

I released my breath and raised a hand at the trunk. "See you, brother."

But he slumped against its bark with crossed arms instead of reaching for the harness. It dangled from the taut wire that stretched to a pine's trunk, a stone's toss away.

I shrugged off my disappointment. A stupid reaction. I might never see my only brother again because...well...no one promised I'd make it back. But I'd received his half hug and rundown on staying alive back when the sun was high. He was free to fly back home. I wished he would.

"Dove—"

I thrust my palm outwards. It was the sound I'd waited for—an abnormal hush as the wind died. The whispering leaves became moth wings. The screaming jays muted.

Then came the clear directive from Heaven.

Have faith.

The oak branch groaned behind me, and Gilead's commands retreated into the sky. "Eyes on target. Feet together. Chin down. You will come back to us."

Rushing air. Painful water. Gasping—lots of gasping. The next terrible minute of my life blurred. But in the end, three things stood out.

I jumped.

I sank.

And I drowned.

2

I drowned, but I didn't die. Not all the way.

Dying would've been giving up.

Dying would've been easier.

I'd expected a jolt on surface impact...but not for my eyeballs to sizzle in their sockets. The water jammed up my nose became a fire trail. And proof.

The unruffled pond...no bugs...no birds.

Poison.

I flapped my arms and scissor-kicked my legs. I did it the way Gilead trained me a million years ago, when I wasn't drowning in poison.

Another wave of panic twisted my gut when I imagined the invisible Enemy stepping out from the bushes, eager to play his favorite game with me: Time to Torture the Christian.

My splayed fingers broke the water's surface. Sharp grass materialized under them. And the fragile stalks broke before I tasted air.

I kicked, lunged up, and grabbed another handful. Again, it disintegrated. I made a third attempt. Failure.

He laughed—a being a thousand times more powerful than me, a breakable, human girl.

My feet sank into the boggy bottom and stuck. *No, no, no,* my slow-firing brain objected. *My calling. Grandma's dream. I had to reach the mountain. The Council. To save my family...Gilead...some others. I couldn't die.*

~*~

I awoke in a tomb. When I lurched up and smacked my head against packed dirt, a shovelful showered my face. I shielded my eyes in the impenetrable darkness.

But I could sit, so I guessed I wasn't dead. And since I wasn't up a tree, Gilead hadn't done the saving.

My hand leaped to the waist of my pants under my tunic and patted around until the papers there crackled inside their protective plastic. I let it fall. Both prayer results. I hadn't lost my family's and our neighbor's votes for peace regarding the war. The votes God had commissioned me to deliver to the Council.

Grit coated my tongue and teeth, so I spat between mouthfuls of soupy air. I felt around, discovering my loss. My backpack—the one I'd been wearing. It was gone.

My eyes ached while my nose cringed, rejecting the intense earth smell that carried hints of other stuff. Decaying leaves. Animal fur. Burnt wax. I eased onto my knees like my arthritic grandma would. *Sky alive*, I hurt. Groping in blind arcs, I searched for the burnt candle whose odor filled the space...but I ended up knocking into cool metal that rolled.

I snatched up the flashlight. My cold thumb jammed down with still enough life to trigger the heat sensor. An ultraviolet circle flared—a tiny sun in a world that'd never known light. Tears rushed into my eyes, but I squinted around them.

I crouched in a dugout—a large burrow that a

giant rabbit might hunker down in for the winter. The hard earth I'd knocked into created the walls, ceiling, and floor.

My backpack!

As I scrambled for it, better air wafted through a half-circle wall opening, brushing the sweat on my temples. The breeze carried a muffled snatch of a song. A voice.

My haphazard flashlight hit on a single word scratched high on the wall.

Shalom. B.

Beneath it, a crooked dirt arrow pointed to the tunnel's opening.

Shalom. The familiar greeting of Christians written in Amhebran, the relaxed form of Hebrew we spoke as well as English.

And the *B*.

Well, that was brainless enough. *B* for Brae. And proof I crouched in the right place.

Perfect. I'd go now. I'd follow this arrow, locate these Braes, and find out who I'd be traveling with so I could get on with this suicidal mission.

I continued to crouch in the dirt, gripping my pack. The battle in the poisoned water. I'd lost...*no.* Somehow, I'd won.

I closed my eyes and held my breath.

Lord?

Yes, my Best Friend was present. Here to protect and guide. He hadn't abandoned me—as if I doubted for a moment He would.

A light tap of pressure, like a kiss, landed on my forehead above the line of freckles there.

I found my feet, and invisible arms began to nudge me forward.

I swallowed hard, gripped the smooth light, shouldered my pack, and allowed myself to be prodded into the pitch-black tunnel ahead.

~*~

Mealworms. A whole mess of them.

A hiss from the corner distracted me from the half-filled bowl. Another drip from the skewered, charred meat hit the embers with a hiss, and my stomach twisted.

I leaned against the stump, which served as a table in the center of this fire-lit burrow, and picked out a crispy-brown larva from the woven bowl. The toasted skin crackled between my fingers when I crushed it. A musty tang hit my nostrils. Horrible.

I smiled. Eating bugs was hardcore survival. This Brae family was tough. And toughness was as crucial to survival as a beating heart in my own family.

A muted murmur wafted from behind. As I pivoted with a stumble, a different one answered from a partly hidden tunnel opening. I plunged into it, leaving the grubs and dripping meat behind. Ahead, someone began to laugh.

Goosebumps pricked my arms. No sane person could be so glad in this human-sized rodent home.

Maybe these people weren't tough. Maybe they were crazy.

3

A blast of brightness bludgeoned me back into the tunnel's shadows. After a few seconds, I peeked through my fingers, forcing my pupils to adjust.

Fighting my wobbly knees, I strode out into the fake, blue light flooding the dirt. The space expanded before me like a flat desert or farmer's field, except with a bumpy dirt ceiling so low I had to duck.

I passed the topsy lantern on the ground and zeroed in on the Mr. Brae from my memories, now kneeling and jamming the pointy end of a wooden spear into the ceiling. As he repeated this senseless activity, a trickle of dirt showered his upturned, cheek-splitting grin.

I jolted and froze.

I hadn't seen this bearded face in six years—not since a year after the last Council meeting when I'd perched on a fir branch next to our garden.

At ten years old, I'd been fascinated by Mr. Brae. The crow-black of his hair. The ashy-whiteness of his cheeks. His bulky patchwork clothes. And his tears.

A man crying. How funny.

My dad's hand had rested on his shuddering back while moonlit drops had traveled down the paleness into the wild beard. And when Mr. Brae had opened his swimming eyes, I'd seen the grief. The torment of loss.

So now, six years later, I forced myself forward. And told myself not to be weirded out because Mr. Brae had recovered so well from his son's death.

Get a grip, Dove. People smile.

"I'm up now, sir. Who's the messenger coming with me? Because we need to get going." I braced myself for those haunting eyes. But Mr. Brae remained focused on his ceiling and his half-buried pole.

Without warning, enough dirt to bury a toddler rained down. I lurched backwards.

"Whoo, baby doll!" Through the grit storm, his eyebrows zinged up to his hairline in excitement. The enormous, skewered potato waved back and forth before my eyes. "Did you ever see such a beauty, Dove? Hello, my beautiful baby."

He didn't mean me. He meant the vegetable he rubbed against his bearded cheek.

Unexpected hands from behind yanked me back. "Better keep out of his way. You'll do better with me."

The boy I shook off was crow-haired too. Younger than Gilead, it appeared—around my age—and with half my brother's muscles.

After hesitating, I followed his bare feet toward a heap of soil that pressed against the ceiling. The cleanish areas on the backs of the boy's hands glowed pale with a bluish, bruised tinge. My own were too sun-stained to reflect the fake light.

Two specks-of-girls with Mr. Brae's eyes dug at the mound's base. One of them pulled out an odd-shaped dirt clump.

Thud. She tossed the earthy object into a cracked bucket. Some sort of vegetable, maybe.

Not one of them, OK God? Please don't have called one of them to come with me on this trek. I'd rather swallow every mealworm in this place than drag a whiny little kid across the world with me to the Council.

"You can't communicate with my dad when he's harvesting. But me, I can tell you anything you need to know." The boy stared at me, forgetting to blink. But it didn't matter. Although I *did* care about the way he rubbed his dirt-stained palms together, promising great plans in store for me. For *us*.

Or him, God, I aimed at Heaven. *Not him. If You truly love me, God. Please, please. Don't have called him.*

"So? You pulled through OK? Got your bag and flashlight?"

I was alive and holding both. I blinked.

Skink-boy's eyes traveled in that same rude way from my blonde hair to my woven shoes. "Good."

Skink.

Why did the comparison of him to that lizard pop into my head? Well, skinks are smallish...as far as reptiles go. They don't blink. And young ones are blue marked.

I bit my curling lip, dirt gritting on my teeth. "Good enough. But how about some water?"

"Water? You want more water? What we left you wasn't enough? Or wasn't good enough?"

Was he personally offended by my thirst? "Not *more* water. Water. I haven't had any yet."

Still, he made no move to round up some—didn't even drop a hint about where to find it. "It was good stuff, you know. None of that poisoned crud I saved you from."

I crossed my arms. "Listen. I'm not dumb. Or blind. There was no water. Not a cup. Not a wet puddle on the ground. None. Nada."

"Not my fault, not my fault. Hey! Worm!"

The runt of the tiny diggers, who'd been spying, froze with her twig-like arms tensed.

"Whatever happened to that water you were supposed to leave our guest, Worm? You think she's part scrub bush—doesn't need to drink for weeks? Yeah, you better run."

He kicked a dirt clod that exploded against the tattered fur racing for the tunnel's entrance.

Oh, yeah. Skinks bite.

"Twinsies, Micah!"

Mr. Brae's shout caused me to slap a hand over my prayer result papers.

He held up what looked like a weird, *V*-shaped potato. It was actually conjoined twin potatoes. "Have you ever seen anything like it? I'll call this half Micah and that side Melody. But don't think because they're your namesakes you two get to hog the potato to yourselves."

He waggled a finger and set the potato in his bucket as if it were an egg. He lunged at the ceiling with his pole.

His son—Micah—leaned closer. "I know about you. You're Dove Strong. Your Uncle Saul went with my brother to the Council last time. So. Did he—your uncle—ever turn up?"

"No-pe." I let the *p* pop in the silence. "Dead." We'd never had physical proof of this, but it was our obvious conclusion to why he'd never returned home from his journey. The same one I was about to take.

"Er...well. And...and how's your father, Dove?" His skinny chest puffed out, and he became all-knowing again. "Your dad's Jonah Strong. Yeah, I know all about him too. Terrifying when crossed. Commands wasps to fight for him. See? I'm not so clueless. And I'll bet—"

"Dead." My dad would be dead three years in October. Shot by a trespassing vandal he'd confronted.

I waited for Micah to finish stuttering. "My cousin had a pet raccoon once named Berry. It's dead too, if you want to ask about it. Buried it under a pine."

His toe twisted in the dirt. "It's not my fault I didn't know...about your dad. I'm never allowed out. So, what?" His large eyes narrowed. "It's like you and a bunch of kids swinging around in the trees, then?"

"Don't be a lamebrain. My mom's fine. And my aunt and grandparents. Enough with the interrogation. I need to get going. So tell me—who's been called to go to the Council?"

Skink boy blinked. And then glared past his dad at a woman and girl on the other side of the space—his mom and sister, no doubt, and perhaps Melody. His twin and the potato's other namesake, since she seemed about his size. Both mom and daughter prodded the ceiling with sticks like Mr. Brae, only less excited-like.

"We—my dad and I—haven't...a hundred percent decided yet. It's complicated...lots of things to consider about who should go."

Another obstacle. And all I needed was to be out of here.

My cheeks ignited like torches. Hot waves pulled at my body, filling my muscles with strength. Making them swell until I was sure I loomed huge and terrifying—like Gilead. For the first time since I opened my eyes underground, I didn't tremble like a newborn calf attempting to walk.

"You haven't decided? You—your family—has known for seven years—has had seven years to pray for God's direction! For His answer. *His* answer, not yours. The decision of who's traveling with me isn't yours to make. It's God's. So don't say *you* haven't decided. At least..."

Calm down, deep breath.

I obeyed myself so I didn't explode like the kicked dirt clod. I relaxed my clenched fingers, which oddly still showed up skinny and weak as clover stalks. "Have any of you paid enough attention to hear God's answer about peace?"

He stayed silent, but I didn't bother to clarify. Even cut off down here in these tunnels, he had to know I referred to *the Reclaim*—the hearsay about a future war between Christ's followers and Satan's. A battle to reclaim America.

No, it'd be more than a mere battle if it happened.

It'd be a bloodbath.

Those of us who didn't believe that God had promised this war—which was every person I knew except my bloodthirsty brother Gilead—referred to the Reclaim as *the Rumor*. Because that's what it was.

The Rumor. Unbiblical. No heavenly signs supporting it. But it got respect since it was almost as ancient as my grandparents, who were alive when it cropped up over sixty years ago—right after all true Christians were exiled from pagan American society.

In my mind, this proved that the Rumor—or *OK, fine*...the Reclaim—was a lie. Or, more kindly put, a dream. Fabricated by some of our people who weren't satisfied with their lives. Christians determined to make something better of their futures here on earth.

But even those of us who scoffed at the Reclaim still prayed for God's clear direction for peace...or for whatever else He wanted. Because every seven years,

God chose a member from each Christian household to make the risky trek through the Enemy's territory to his or her nearest Council, most often hidden on a mountain. For us, we hiked to Mount Jefferson—sixty miles from home as the crow flies, according to my grandpa.

This year, God had appointed me.

I'd become one messenger of hundreds...or even thousands...starting a journey for one of the fifty Councils meeting in our country. On September fifteenth, a month from now, the Councils would tally our nation's votes. After coming to a consensus, they'd announce the new decision. Unite and reclaim our land by force? Or peace.

Of course, the decision was peace. It had always been peace. It would always be peace.

Why did God appoint messengers every seven years? Perhaps He knew if He didn't allow that consistent seven-year timeframe to address taking back the land, the least content of us would have taken measures into our own hands long ago.

For sure, the idea of the Reclaim squashed the amount of random violence cropping up on our side. It kept our revolutionists patient and preoccupied, busy crossing their fingers and dreaming of a different future.

Micah snatched up a spear from the soil. "Yeah. Peace."

He harpooned a nearby parsnip on the ground, and it burst open revealing its frosty center. Before I could grab it to suck out the moisture, he'd kicked both fragments at the dirt-clump pile.

Seven more years of hiding. Of letting the devil's workers dump poison and garbage on our doorsteps while we stood by and watched. In this past year, Gilead had destroyed more of his junkyard tinkering projects than he'd completed in fits just like Micah's.

Something nudged my arm. A mud-caked, rusty can jammed into my open fingers. Water sloshed over its dented brim.

I gulped it all and clamped my lips against the wave of nausea. The water giver detoured to her vegetable pile, avoiding her brother who murdered the ceiling with his spear.

4

When my shadow blocked her light, Micah's mom didn't pause in her methodical hunt for crops—unlike the girl next to her, who froze with her stick midair and stared.

Those eyes...I'd seen them a million times before—in the faces of baby mule deer. Each time, they'd whispered the same panicked question as hers. *Run away or stay close to Mama?*

I turned my back on them. "Mrs. Brae, I've got to get out of here. And since God hasn't called any of you to make this journey, I'll carry your result to the Council. I'm delivering another neighbor's result, since no one in his family's been called either. One more isn't a big deal. It's nothing to me."

Mrs. Brae's back stiffened. Then she eased down her spear until it supported her weight like a walking staff. Relief pulled her cheeks' hollows into a smile.

I could almost hear her silent relief, *Hallelujah. Send the doomed neighbor girl into Satan's realm. Spare the Brae family.*

"We've new neighbors?" At my elbow, Mr. Brae smeared his forehead with a black rag, beamed, and waited for my response.

"Yes, sir." I folded my arms across my queasy stomach. "The Joyners. They're tree dwellers like my family—moved onto the north end of our property a few years ago. William—I mean, Mr. Joyner—felt God was telling him and his wife to stay home this time around. Their baby girl isn't quite a month old yet."

Mr. Brae ran his fingers across the earth sky. "William...William...Will. Little Willie. Wee Willie Winkie runs through the town. Upstairs and downstairs in his nightgown—"

"He was a friend of my dad's from jail."

He gaped. Right. He wouldn't have known about my dad's arrest.

But having to tell the whole story about how my dad had been convicted of environmental terrorism for burning trash forever dumped on our land by Satan's minions—*blah, blah, blah*—was downright tiring.

I went with the four-second version. "Dad got a year for burning tires."

Mrs. Brae clasped her hands. "Nehemiah. She's offering to deliver our prayer result for us."

He hummed while reaching into the bucket at her feet. The onion he'd found rustled in his fingers. There was a crunch, followed by a sharp smell. "I've got ears, Emily. I heard. But one wee skinny girl carrying three results? Satan would be on her faster than a rattler on a bunny. Every demon in Oregon...oh, baby doll! He'll hunt her with a vengeance that won't stop 'til she's dead."

I squared my shoulders instead of flinching. *Like he won't be trying anyway.*

"No." He took another dripping bite. "We must be fair and give Dovie here a fighting chance. I've decided now. Melody will carry ours."

The girl with deer eyes squeaked. Mrs. Brae closed hers. I glared.

"No!" Micah hurtled over piles, his spear clenched

in his fist. Chest heaving, he snatched the onion from his dad. It disappeared into the shadows with the faintest thud.

"No. Dad. I'm supposed to be the one. Remember? Me. Me, Micah. Not her." He thrust his harvesting stick at the girl who'd buried her face in her pants.

"No!" Mr. Brae's roar made me stumble back. He grimaced at his empty palm. "I will not lose my last son! If God is sparing the Strongs their son, then He will spare ours too!"

The fury evaporated…a thunderstorm passing, leaving behind rainbows and blue sky. He cocked his head, beaming, and stretched a wavering hand in the air above his daughter's head. "Melody. Daughter. I appoint you official Brae messenger. You, my squirrel, will scamper along with Dovie and deliver our family's result. Which I will jot down momentarily."

Melody ignored the high five and remained on the ground like the cast out onion.

Why didn't she speak up and either accept her commission or reject it? Wimpy mouse.

I cleared my burning throat to refuse to travel with her since she hadn't been called. To announce I'd go alone. That it didn't matter I was sixteen and a girl. And that it wouldn't matter if I carried a hundred prayer answers or none at all. I hadn't been chosen for my strength…or for what I knew about surviving in the world. Otherwise, Gilead or my grandpa would be here in the Brae's home now. I'd been selected for my gift—my unique connection with the Spirit. I'd been born with my whole being wired to hear Him. I'd understood when He'd promised to faithfully guide me. Plus, I knew I'd make it to Mount Jefferson because of my grandma's gift. She'd seen me there.

Again, I cleared my throat. "Sir—"

The ground tilted upwards to meet me, surprising me into silence. My flashlight's metallic clunk warned me I was passing out.

Another...obstacle.

The blue room dimmed. The deer eyes faded.

5

The footsteps were as stealthy as plunking hailstones.

I'd woken a while ago—back in my black burrow on the fur mat—and had spent my time in the dark praying for guidance...and for the world to stop rolling like a tumbleweed.

When the steps got closer, my fingers tightened around the flashlight. I felt for the "on" sensor.

I had a pretty good instinct about the footsteps. But I waited until the owner breathed over me to turn on my light. The beam blasted him full force in the chin.

"*Gawww!*" Micah staggered backwards with one hand shielding his eyes, the other holding his chest.

"Yeah. I'm awake." I smiled at the heart attack I'd given him. He deserved it for being creepy like that.

He crawled forward. "So, now you understand? You saw for yourself that my dad's—"

"Manic?" I clutched my spinning head and sat up.

He shook his. "Insane. No. Not *crazy* crazy...but...well, you saw. I've had to deal with him like that since...you know. Since my brother never came home. And my dad sort of cracked.

"The point is he's too far gone to understand I'm the one," his fist thudded his chest, "who's supposed to go to the Council. I feel like I've been...been...born to do this. I've got to stop hiding down here like a coward and do this for my family. For...you know...God. Don't you think He'd want me to? I mean, yes. He does. Plus, I'm stronger than a girl. Mel, that is. Sorry. No offense to you being a girl—"

"Don't apologize. I know I'm a girl."

He leaned in, locking his gaze with mine. "You and me, Dove. We leave now, and they can't stop us. And if you're still sick, I'll help you walk. Even if I can't carry you, we only need to be far enough away from here by morning so they can't find us. I put water in your bottle and packed food. You like mole jerky?" He tried to hand me my backpack but settled on leaning it against my unreaching arm.

My ears had pricked when Micah first started to speak. *Huh. Maybe God's called him.* But my thoughts had taken an accelerated 180-degree turn.

To sneak away...to hide from his parents...all to prove he wasn't a coward. And without any clue about what God wanted.

"Forget it, Micah." I flopped back down. "Pulling something like that on your dad and mom—for us to start a journey in deceit and lies—and against God's will, would be plain stupid. We wouldn't last a day. Well, you wouldn't."

"But...no. Dove. No! Are you so blind you can't see I'm right? Why can't you understand my dad knows I'm the best choice? Here's the thing..."

I yawned. He'd be here a while, trying to convince me I was wrong.

Good luck with that.

I rolled so my back faced him. He could stay all night if he wanted. As long as he left me alone enough to pray.

At some point, he gave up, and when I paused to grab my water bottle from my pack, it was silent. I shined my light around the empty burrow and let it go out. Good.

But a few moments later, more footsteps padded toward me. Melody's were lighter than her twin's. This time I turned on my flashlight before she reached me, directing it at the ceiling so the whole space shone bright except where our shadows stretched.

"Sorry."

"For what?" I unscrewed my water bottle. "I was awake. And it's killing me—I've got to know. Is it day or nighttime? It's impossible to tell in this skyless crypt."

"Oh. Uh, night I guess? Um..."

"Spit it out. Melody, isn't it? So I can get back to praying."

"Sure. Yes. Sorry. Oh, uh...I was wondering how you knew you were the one who was—is—supposed to go to the Council?"

"I've known for a long time. Over a year." I squinted at her, my lips at the container's opening. "But you want to know how? Uh, prayer? I ask. God answers. Plus, then there was my grandma's dream. Though it only reaffirmed what I knew—that I'd been chosen."

She scratched the dry grit of the floor with her finger. A row of squiggles, backward question marks. "Oh, yeah. Your grandma. Dad told us about her once. My big brother Zech could sort of do that too...well, before he, you know. Disappeared. You're lucky still having someone that receives dreams or visions or whatever. Easier for you, knowing."

Mmm. Lucky me, knowing—because of my

grandma's dream—the lives of my family, and most likely thousands of nameless others, depended on me getting to the Council. Knowing the violence and ugliness resulting if I didn't. Knowing I wasn't only another messenger, but *the* messenger for some reason God hadn't yet revealed. And because of His silence, I wasn't about to mention this to the Braes.

"Sure, Melody. Real easy."

She nodded, still doodling swift marks.

I flung up my hands. "It's not easy. And it has nothing to do with my gran. I'm going because God said, 'go.' And when God says, 'go,' I go."

"God says...so God speaks to you? As in, He talks to you like a real person? And you can hear Him?"

Before I could confirm, she unleashed her next round of questions. "So, what about me? Has He told you anything about me...like if I go, will I get home OK?" She studied me through spider-leg lashes, so different from the Strong family's invisible blonde ones.

"Yes, Melody. I can hear Him. And no. I don't know about you."

She went back to her question marks but then flung both arms around her knees, reeling them into her chest.

"I don't want to die like my brother. Or be lost forever. Or trapped...up there." Her lips pressed the ragged fur of her pants, so the only other words I understood were "I'd be dog food," and something about being hunted.

Her raw fear began to ooze into my thinking too. So, to try to block out her morbid mutterings, I wracked my gray cells for something to say. For anything to make her stop before she pulled me under too.

But comforting people's not my thing.

What should I do? Jab her in the shoulder and say, *Hey, you. No worries. You'll be back eating roasted mole around the fire with your family by Thanksgiving. So turn that frown upside down.*

I couldn't. Because I'm no liar.

I placed my hand on her shoulder. "You won't be alone, though."

I waited a few moments before I dropped my hand. Huh. She wasn't the least bit comforted we were in this together.

I jerked my thumb off the light's sensor and settled down on the matted pelt. *You don't know how fortunate you are to be partnered with me, wimpy mouse.*

But after staring at where the stars should be, I began to bite my thumbnail. Was she really better off with me than if she were to head out solo?

I was no Gilead. And I'd be more hunted than any other messenger in Oregon.

I'd scooted over on my mat so she wouldn't have to lie in the dirt, and after a while her irregular sniffing morphed into steadier breathing. It lulled me into a sense of security I'd never thought possible—not in this home that smelled like nature's decay. A home where a loose piece of bedrock could snuff me out. But since I'd never in my life slept where I couldn't hear others, I was glad not to start tonight. Back home, my hammock hung sandwiched between my cousins'.

My thoughts drifted to them. To Trinity. If only Trinity instead of Melody could come with me...or even Jovie who was seven...or was she eight now? Either way, she had loads more guts than this Brae mouse who was what? Sixteen?

Her, God? I'm assuming You know she's weak, gutless, and, if possible, more clueless than I am about what's out there. She'll be such a...a burden.

You truly want me to help her get to the Council, though, huh? You think I can handle this? Because I feel like I've got more than enough to handle. You know, what with staying alive...and making it to Mount Jefferson, which, for whatever reason, will keep my brother and family from dying—and all those other Christians. At least that's what Gran said. And You haven't said anything otherwise.

I feel like I'm drowning here again. Could You help me not mess up too much while I try to do what You've asked? I love You. You know that. I want to make You proud. To the end. Help me stay strong even if the end hurts. Even if it hurts a lot.

My skin tingled, and the little hairs on my cheeks and neck lifted.

He was here—had never left. A surge of joy that contradicted every circumstance in my life coursed through me. I surrendered to it and closed my eyes, able to relax. I drifted.

You are mine.

He sounded so fierce and protective. Though I was half asleep, my heart ached in response.

I love you more than you can ever understand.

6

I thought I'd fallen asleep in a black hole that stunk like a grave. But I opened my eyes to home. Home, where the air was bark and pine needles and the morning sun warmed my face.

Glancing down, my toes skimmed the tops of familiar maples. The fragile parts where birds perch a second before taking off. Not branches I'd ever climb.

I shrugged and peered through the leafy gaps at my home below. I needed to find my family I'd thought I'd already said goodbye to.

Our hammocks on the sleeping porches hung limp, the woven folds swaying in the breeze.

So, they were awake too.

I widened my search, hunting out my grandma's willow chair.

It rocked lonely, without its usual occupant. And the high platform where my grandpa acted as sentinel twenty-four seven was empty too.

My gaze skimmed on to the kitchen. The eating decks. The garden. The beehives. The row of catapults. The junk piles. The zip lines...all the way out to the Joyner's platforms. And still not a single mother, brother, grandparent, cousin, or neighbor in sight.

Impossible. Because my family had nowhere else to go.

I blinked. Where else would they be? *Where else?*

The forest's usual summertime mix of bright deciduous leaves, evergreen needles, and brown bark blurred under my scrutiny. Then, with my next blink, the forest changed.

The brown won, as it did during a scorcher summer season that burned every living green to a faded sienna. Only, the scorch took just seconds this time.

The sienna grew warmer, brightening to a rust color, then to red, in the end deciding on a deep, glossy maroon. Each leaf and needle was so heavy with the richness, it began to drip.

Plop. Plip plop. Patter, patter.

Below, the ground dewed up red too. I gagged on the gust carrying the metallic tang of blood into my nostrils.

Pinching them, I rose higher to escape the dripping twigs.

I stopped when a solar flare shot down from the heavens. The beam spotlighted a corner of my home's roof, illuminating a speck of pure white in the sea of dark red.

I held my breath and moved closer.

The white formed a bird. A pigeon? No. A dove. I must have startled it, because as soon as I named it, the dove extended its wings and took off to the west.

Red flowed behind in the dove's wake, so the blood no longer contaminated only my family's land. It extended to every horizon. It engulfed a mountain range. Fifty ranges.

Particular tree canopies dripped black with maroon. And certain isolated areas of land formed deep burgundy pools.

"Where the other Christian tree and earth dwellers

live," I whispered against the hand clasping my mouth. How did I know that?

My fingers reached after the dove, and I made my vow. I would catch it. Contain it. And make it take back what it'd done to my home and family.

I hurled myself after, gluing my eyes to the dazzling tail feathers.

For days I followed. Long days full of blistering sun. The night's moon gave me frostbite. Still, I wasn't able to touch that mocking white.

The dove landed on Mount Washington—a craggy peak I'd never seen but knew as well as my own name. But it only rested a moment, ruffling its wings over the oozy red before taking off again and slipping through my fingers. This time it flew north.

Again I followed, closer now. But I was exhausted. Ready to go home and search for my missing family.

Yet I gained. An inch. Two inches.

I was on top of the creature when at last it settled on Mount Jefferson's snowy peak. I lunged forward before the color spilled here too, but I stopped short.

With a gasp I stared down.

My hands and fingers had disappeared, and in their place were feathers. Long, snowy feathers. The blood...the red...everywhere was gone. And the dove I'd been reaching for—vanished.

~*~

I awoke next to the Brae girl, my body stretched out on the bare ground. Fumbling, I aimed the flashlight's beam at my hand, examining each tanned finger.

Had this been a dream from Heaven? Or my muggy intellect piecing together what I knew from my grandma and filling in the cracks?

I couldn't stay here any longer. Or go home.

I was God's dove and would stop that red by getting to Mount Jefferson before it was too late.

I was ready to fly.

7

This is what Hell will be like.

I eyed the snaking, claustrophobic, two-foot diameter tunnel I needed to plunge into. It was pitch black inside. I wouldn't be able to sit up or even raise my arms much.

But the Braes agreed this was the only way out of their home since someone from the enemy's side had guessed at the Brae family's existence. That was the reason their front entrance had become a poisonous-water deathtrap.

Quit it! I demanded of my heart-turned-woodpecker. Mr. Brae continued his run-down on the tunnel procedure. It was all about how I'd need to hold my body on the skateboard—an object I recognized since we'd had a few show up in the trash heaps— and pull myself through using the tunnel's side ropes. As if tunnel travel was no big deal.

Yeah. This was a big deal. For a girl who'd only known open sky and spent almost zero time under a roof, rolling through tunnels on my belly while deep in the earth placed me one hundred percent outside my comfort zone. But I picked away at a hangnail because the Braes watched me. They were probably curious to see if the neighbor girl who'd drowned and poisoned herself on arrival would do any better on exit.

Of course, they were also gathered to say

goodbye—everyone but Micah. He was probably off sulking somewhere.

One thing sparked real hope. This mouse called Melody didn't act as if this tunnel traveling was dangerous. Of course, she was used to it since this was her home and all. But it was more than that.

Apparently, Melody had a "special gift" of being able to predict danger and evil. At least, Mr. Brae told me so this morning between weird jokes. I didn't listen to them because I'd been too amped to get going.

Melody had a gift? Sure. It *could* be. Since life had gotten tougher for us Christians these last few decades, it seemed like God handed out spiritual gifts with more of an open hand. Or, it could be we believers were more in tune with noticing them.

Either way, it came down to more recognized gifts. Things like my own clear connection with the Spirit. And Gran with her dreams. And Gilead with his fierceness and natural ability to conquer anything physical. Even my fifteen-year-old cousin Trinity had one, although it wasn't so useful.

But Mr. Brae could be wrong about his daughter. Most likely, Melody feared everything—her dad, strangers, dogs, decision making—to list a few I had already witnessed. And since life stayed iffy at best for us believers, she was bound to be right sometimes when she cried out "danger."

Mr. Brae finished his farewell song about a clock that kept popping up to say "cuckoo," and Melody flattened herself on her own skateboard. No, that wasn't right. Her ginormous pack flattened her. Crushed her. Like an ant trying to lug a potato.

White knuckles gripped the side ropes at the tunnel's mouth while she craned to see her mom.

Their tears made me shuffle my foot back and forth. I couldn't pretend not to see them much longer. I stepped forward. "Fine. OK. I'll go first—"

She kicked off, propelling herself into the tunnel.

I lowered myself onto the other wheeled board—black with faded crossbones on it. *Perfect.* My own pack rested lightly against my spine, worth the offense I'd given Mr. Brae by refusing the basic provisions he insisted I take.

I copied Melody, bending my leg in an unnatural angle and grabbing the ropes. My eyes squeezed shut.

Lord, protect and guide—

"Well, Dovie Bird. You and my Melody are going to make a fine team up there!"

I wrenched my gaze upwards to discover white teeth grimacing through a black beard.

"Yes, a fine team you'll make. Although..." he cupped his hand around his mouth, his shoulders shaking, "never trust a fifteen-year-old with your secrets. My Melody told me what you revealed about yourself and your gift. So! It's perfect. She'll recognize the threat, and then you can talk to God...about it."

The last part fell flat. He obviously would have loved to have cried "and you can defeat it!" or at least "escape it."

I muttered, "Yes, sir. Shalom," to his toes and rolled headfirst into the yawning tunnel.

A few wheel revolutions later, darkness blinded me. By feel, I took small grabs at the ropes and walked my toes against the ground. My kneecaps jammed against loose pebbles. Any grooves that might've existed were too shallow to guide my wheels. I inched forward. My arm and leg muscles twitched to propel me upright so I could pummel the walls with my fists until I reached daylight.

Four times I couldn't stand it and picked up the pace.

Four times I ended up smacking into the tunnel's wall, which felt like smacking face first into a boulder. My heart would knock, and I'd have to pause and take deep breaths.

I was feeling my nose again for breaks when Melody's voice echoed, "Dove? Dove? Are you back there?"

No doubt Melody had made it to the end, miles ahead. She called down the tunnel once more but then stopped. My wheels bumping and my hyper breathing marked the minutes.

Keep moving forward. There's enough oxygen. Yeah, sure there is. Keep moving forward.

With my next grab and pull, my fingers stood out pale against the charcoal walls. I was so close to the end. I yanked both ropes, planning to free myself of the tunnel in one last victorious pull. Sluggishly, I bumped forward. And stopped.

I squinted at the ropes—slack lines in my clenched fists. Again I gave another hard jerk. That was a mistake.

A faint, scratchy noise grew as the ropes dislodged from the walls. Then a hiss started from the packed soil coming loose and slithering down. *Chrisssstian. Chrissssssssssssssstian.*

My shout went nowhere, swallowed up like the rest of me. I craned my neck to stay above the growing rubble while a total eclipse slammed down.

Inhaling what oxygen I could find in the dirt cloud, I tucked my head and squeezed my lips and eyes shut.

As I tried to burrow through the avalanche, my heartbeat thundered in my clogged ears. I couldn't breathe. My arms were trapped straight out in front of me.

Yet somehow, my body scraped forward, the soil sliding backwards against my stomach and over my neck.

8

I came gasping into the light. Bright light. Natural light. The kind I love. White hands locked around my wrists, still hauling me forward.

I shook them off and collapsed on my back, panting. Snatches of blue filtered through the elaborate root system making up the roof a couple feet above. I tasted sunshine through the grit.

"That's twice now. Twice I've saved your life just in time."

I ripped my stare away from a blue patch and found Micah. He was squatting next to me, still touching my sleeve. Worry lines pulled down his heavy brows. Behind him, Melody crouched with her knuckle in her mouth.

"Man, Satan's got it in for you." He swiped his face on his sleeve, smearing dust. "Those cables have never come loose before. Right, Mel? Dove, think what would've happened if I hadn't pulled you out in time. Whoa...too close."

He grasped the tree root ceiling as if for support and exhaled. His brown eyes peeped at me.

I wasn't dumb. He probably hoped this scare had changed my mind. That I'd declare I wouldn't travel unless he came with me for protection.

I jerked up, losing his hand. "Amazing how God provided you at the perfect moment. A mysterious disaster with a real miracle. Not something a person could ever stage."

"Yeah...yeah, that's right." The correct response. Too bad he couldn't hold my gaze.

"Yeah. God provides. Like He'll provide later if—OK, when—we run into more trouble. Micah, you'd better figure out a way back to your parents. You know better than I do whether they'll have sensed the cave-in and be worried. Shalom."

I knocked the silt and pebbles off my pack while Melody laid her forehead against her brother's frozen shoulder.

"Keep it quick." I crawled until stopped by the vertical wall of crumbling clay. Again I focused on the sky, poking my fingers up into sunshine pockets.

"Sorry, Micah. You tried. Love you. Maybe pray for me? It might help. She seems to think—"

"Whatever. Sure. Just go."

A grunt and scrape of a board through clay clumps faded while I ran my fingers over the network of entwined roots. Shafts of light broke through the hundreds of cracks between the smooth ribbons. Just like winter back home, gazing up at the crisscrossed, leafless branches that covered the sky.

Melody reached up so the sun poured through the spaces between her fingers like mine. "I wish he could go as messenger. Don't you?"

I turned my hands over, letting the light warm the backs.

She flipped hers over too. "You should've seen this sky room before it got all small. I still come here, even if it isn't so safe now. I don't know why, but it's easier to feel like God's close when I can see the sky."

I nodded. At last she'd said something I could

relate to.

But having a traveling partner with a common interest in the sky wouldn't keep me alive. I needed trust. And to know without a doubt she had my back. No secrets.

I studied her half-shadowed face. "Did he do it? Micah? Did he make the ropes come loose so I'd need his help?"

"Yeah."

I waited to hear her excuses for her brother. For her to say he loved her and wanted to spare her the dangerous journey. But she didn't. I liked her more for it.

"Well. Yay, Melody."

Her eyes went all baby deer again. The white patches between shadow lines on her cheeks flushed— probably with the realization of what she'd let slip.

I shrugged. "You know, the devil wasn't trying to kill me back there—only your brother. Much better. Now you lead the way out of this place. Can't be much worse out there."

9

I smashed against the boulder's baking contour. Sun-blinded, my eyes darted back and forth uselessly as I attempted to see any hunters. At Melody's nudge, I shifted to the boulder's edge and dangled my feet off while she inched the heavy-sounding shard back into its place to conceal her family's secret exit.

"From now on, we're always on our guard, Melody. Every step. Every sound you make. It may be the reason you live or die. Until you get the hang of being above ground, follow my lead. Do exactly what I do."

I wiggled off the boulder. The drop lasted longer than expected, and the landing jarred me, heel to spine.

Stunned, I blinked around at the unexpected mammoth pit I'd landed in. Then I leaped to my feet and flung myself against the pit's crumbly side.

Using an exposed tree root, I was able to haul myself over the lip in time to see Melody's descent. She went off a different side of the boulder and avoided the pit. But she landed sprawled like an upended turtle on its shell.

After struggling up, she joined me at the edge of the man-made pit. We panted, hands on our thighs, next to a hole at least forty-feet long and almost as wide. Its depth was jagged and varied. The place where I'd landed reached only a couple of yards down.

I pointed at a neck-breaking drop in the middle. "This was part of your home once."

Now it made sense—her explanation about coming here to watch the sky...even if it wasn't safe.

I followed her gaze to where the enthusiastic hunters had started digging for the underground Christian home at the heap of broken pine trees. Ripped-up stumps with mud-caked roots were scattered about. Another giant boulder—half the size of the cracked one we'd exited—rested at the pit's bottom nearest us, the exact point where they'd given up. And all around, bulldozer tracks etched deep in the baked mud.

How had my family missed the racket of trees going down? And of the machines roaring around out here? The tunnel must have taken us further than I'd guessed.

Yeah. There were no familiar tree-filled slopes in any direction, out to the horizons. The always visible, mammoth rock column, Steins Pillar, was missing. But I caught sight of a paw print next to Melody's boots.

I touched it and straightened.

Dog.

We were leaving our scent like crazy here. And scent was the most likely reason people with dogs and a bulldozer had hit on this isolated spot in the first place.

"Keep up." I sprinted around the pit with Melody at my heels. By the time we made it to the pines we'd lagged to a jog, and I held my side.

I'd been suspicious of it at the time, but now it was confirmed. All those brutal, muscle-building exercises of Gilead's had been a big, fat waste of time. I wasn't even a shadow of the ferocious athlete-warrior hybrid he'd tried to remake me into.

Given Melody's condition, I could be worse.

We dragged in air while plowing through juniper and bitterbrush. Because I was listening for it, I identified the sound of another body moving through the bushes not far away.

Human? Or animal?

"Get down. Freeze. And hold your breath." I dropped into a crouch and scanned the terrain.

She obeyed. Together our chests heaved like silent bullfrog throats.

It sounded like a human. Moving nearer. From the east, from the side of the slope where we'd been.

Time to test Mr. Brae's miraculous claims about his daughter. "Dangerous, Melody? Or no?"

Her eyes squeezed to slits. "No?"

I nodded. Still, we weren't going to be able to outrun whoever this was for long. We had to get up higher. It wasn't that I didn't trust Melody's supernatural radar for evil, but I didn't.

None of the trees here could conceal us all the way. But if we could get above eye level and stay still, we'd have a fair chance the approaching creature would move past and miss us. Unless it could smell us.

I gestured to our best bet—a sturdy aspen—and formed a sling with my arms. "Step up."

She backed away.

I had no time to talk her out of her fear of climbing trees. Or heights. Or whatever phobia this was.

I grabbed her hips and boosted her toward the lowest branch. In our mute struggle, her wind-milling legs connected with my ear.

Change of plan. I chucked her straight up at the branch and stepped aside in case she didn't catch hold.

Then I jumped and seized a limb next to where she clung. Using it, I swung myself up to the next set above.

On the branch below, Melody squirreled around making a ton of noise. Why did she twist foliage around her torso?

"Enough. Shh!" I massaged my sore ear.

Seconds later, Micah crested the slope.

I eased down until my mouth reached Melody's ear. "Don't you dare, sister. Hold your cover."

He'd slowed to a hunched-over creep. Ready to bolt if a chipmunk sneezed.

He stopped and held his breath to listen.

Melody wanted to call to him, but I shook my head. I had to end this tracking-us business. Now.

Something white snagged my attention.

The mass of gauzy web hung in the crook of the branch above me. Its center writhed with black bodies. I ripped a wide hole in the sticky fibers, and a couple adult-sized tent caterpillars spilled into my palm.

The first one I released landed on Micah's crow-like hair. And stuck. The next few bounced off, but at least one caterpillar went down his shirt because he shuddered and rotated a shoulder blade.

I squinted at my empty fingers. I remembered the feel of the ropes going slack, the panic exploding through my body. And the itchy dirt that still riddled my clothes.

I wanted more caterpillars.

I wanted them all.

The nest connected to one branch, but I made too much noise separating the limb from the trunk.

"What the—"

At least a hundred caterpillars rained down on his

upturned face.

He shouted and ripped at his shirt as if they were stinging insects. As he zigzagged back over the hill, slapping at his juvenile beard, Melody called, "I've got this, Micah, OK? You know I love you, but I got this. Go home." Her voice dropped. "I can do this."

I sat, legs dangling, and flicked a caterpillar off her sleeve. "It's not too late, you know. You can follow him home. Now's better than later for tapping out."

She squinted at a blue jay on the ground. "Am I screaming? Worms don't scare me."

I blinked. "Oh."

Her face broke into a wide grin, with a tooth missing like a six-year-old's. "Did you see the fat one by his nostril? On his lip? And it hung there?"

In the heat of the windless afternoon, the leaves of our aspen tree began to quiver, creating a cloud of flashing, rattling silver. It was as though God chuckled, enjoying the joke too. His sense of humor beat everyone's. Anyway, who'd provided the caterpillars? And Micah? And since I was going there, Melody?

Oh, OK, Lord. Sticking with Melody hasn't been terrible. So far.

With another snort, Melody shrugged off her bag and rummaged inside. She came out with two carrots—warm and super rubbery. I held one in my palm.

She reached over and bounced hers off mine—a carrot victory bump—then took a bite.

No. Not too terrible.

10

An engine hummed somewhere up ahead. From long habit, I scanned for a place of safety—the pine able to bear my weight. But I stumbled past refuge and into a clearing dotted with sagebrush.

I faced another road. Another reminder to stay on our guard. The devil's workers were nearby again. This was their territory, their road.

It'd been three days since we'd left the Braes' tunnels. Three days of avoiding a million roads and farmhouses.

A bunch of times, we'd hiked miles out of our way because she'd deemed farmland in our path dangerous. These detours had zapped whatever strength we'd had when we started, which hadn't been much in Melody's case.

Would I have to scale the black volcanic sides of Mount Jefferson with her dangling off my back?

At least I'd gotten her to ditch the hairy blanket, cooking pot, and cloak. We'd piled them in the aspen near the remains of the caterpillar nest, figuring Micah would find them someday. And now we'd entered the hot, high desert country.

Well, I was hot. Melody risked heat stroke wearing her head-to-toe fur. Her hair dripped as if she'd been out in a rainstorm, and her face glowed a brilliant shade of pink that wasn't all sunburn.

Thank you, Lord, for better clothing—long sleeves and pants woven from breathable plant fibers. My parents had drilled modesty into us Strong kids since birth. But they'd also pushed common sense. Never fur in August.

We crouched in the stingy shade of a sagebrush near the road to decide when to cross. Since we'd had so much practice at this, we didn't speak the words anymore. The engine faded away into the distance. A lone cicada's clicking started up.

I looked at Melody. *Danger?*

Her eyelids closed. *No danger*, her slight headshake replied.

I didn't feel the Spirit telling me otherwise. So I stood and forced myself to lead onto the pavement.

No matter how many roads we crossed, I'd never walk across them without shuddering. Never. The smell of burning tar. The sticky smooth feel of it under my feet. The artificial, too-bright yellow and white lines creeped me out more than the flattened jackrabbits that sprawled across them...

Melody got across quicker, but I caught up on the far side since she only stood there, staring down at an undercut ten-foot drop-off to the desert below.

In the distance, an engine whined.

Should we jump down this thing? Risk an ankle?

My pulse sprinted as if racing the engine that grew louder.

Help, Lord! Which way?

My eyes zeroed in on a spot about a minute's run ahead, where the drop-off from the road seemed a more gradual slope of scree.

I pointed to it, but my question pertained to the vehicle ten seconds from reaching us. "Danger?"

"N-no?"

"Your call—quick!"

"No."

Out of time. I stood my ground. But I turned in case Melody's spiritual hazard radar was off. I'd rather take a hit to the back than the front any day. But I wouldn't watch. I closed my eyes.

In the seconds it took for the car to rush past, my knee joints loosened and started to wobble. I peeked at Melody—an exact copy of my own braced-but-flinching stance—and then at the squashed-egg shape moving toward the horizon. I couldn't even see a driver, only a puff of white the same shade as my grandma's hair.

"C'mon." I began to jog down the white line. Melody's boot soles slapped behind.

"Danger."

I trusted her enough. I did a quick check. I heard only our own footsteps and breathing. The bare blacktop shimmered in the extreme noon heat. Otherwise, nothing in sight but a squashed goose.

I turned my eyes to the spot where we could get off the road.

"Danger."

Melody's voice sounded higher and farther away this time. I spun around. She'd stopped a few yards back. Paralyzed. Gasping for air double time.

"No, Melody!" I raced back. "Don't panic! You can't! You can't!" I shook her. I let go and took a deep breath.

With forced calm, I locked her red cheeks between my unsteady palms. Although her dilated pupils focused on mine, she clearly didn't see me. Shaking her hadn't helped, so slapping probably wouldn't either.

"Melody Brae. Spit it out. What threat?"

I tried again. "Melody. I know you can hear me, and you can't do this now. God's got you. He's got you; you're OK. You're with me. Now move your stupid feet and *run!*"

I dragged her with me, stumbling. Our feet tangled. What were we running from? I had no clue. But I could only think of getting off this road.

Danger. "Danger!" Ripping free of my grip, she breezed past and plunged into the thickest part of the bushes a few yards shy of where I'd aimed.

Good enough.

When I skidded to the bottom of the broken-rock slope, my palms stung and the foliage needled me. I threw myself onto my belly on the jagged stones next to Melody, who'd buried her head between her knees.

Fifty thudding heartbeats later, a soft whizzing-whooshing noise passed on the pavement above. Such a deceptively gentle sound. But one I've had nightmares about.

The sound of bicycle tires.

I despised cars and trucks—loud, bullying machines used by the criminals who visited our land to dump and vandalize—half weapon, half getaway machine. But I hated bikes more. Bikes were wicked and linked forever in my mind with Dead Nights.

On Dead Nights, nothing running on electric power worked. Not even our own flashlights—or my grandpa's spotlight that played a huge part in keeping our enemies at bay. The night sky became a menacing black without the city of Prineville's glow on the horizon, and the devil's workers were restless. And stealthier.

They'd creep onto our property on their

whispering bicycles. Sometimes to illegally dump trash. But usually with more hateful purposes.

My dad died on a Dead Night. He was shot while confronting a man who circled our home's trees on his bicycle with a container of gasoline.

I glared up through the jumble of briars at the man above, straddling his bike at the spot where we'd left the road. A strap ran across his sunburned chest, and the skinny barrel of his weapon peeked over his shoulder.

His hat's shade hid his face as he scanned the terrain. Had he seen us on the road from afar? Or was he so filled with his master's power that he could sense us?

Either way, he knew we were here somewhere. We Christians.

I tensed when he bent low and scooped up something from the ground. Before I could tell what, he'd launched it into the air. In a fluid motion, he reached over his shoulder and whipped his gun into a ready position, while the pebbles rained down onto bushes and stones.

One ricocheted off my cheek and stung. But I wouldn't be flushed into movement. Only my fingers twitched, curling around a splinter of rock.

Oh, Gilead.

My brother would only need this single shard to cripple the hunter who looked so much like our dad's murderer.

If my grandpa had been there, he would have corrected in his low drawl, "Stand down, son. You believe in the war? Then save it for then."

He said that a lot. "Save it for the war." Each time my brother had a clean shot at a trespassing vandal.

Gilead took my grandpa's words to heart. He devoted his life to being prepared for that fictitious future battle.

But Gilead and Grandpa weren't here.

OK, Lord. It's all You now.

I waited for the burning sulfur to rain on the pavement above. Or for the fiery tornado to touch down, ridding the world of one more bicycle-riding pagan.

I lay on my belly, camouflaged in the scree and bushes, praying for skull-crushing hailstones. He pushed off and then glanced back three times.

My body sagged. He'd gotten away.

As soon as his back tire disappeared over the horizon, Melody opened her lids she'd kept shut since she'd fallen. "We're good."

She announced it with that burst of confidence that cropped up every so often and always surprised me—though I never let on. She ruffled through her bag. Her family's folded prayer result spilled out. She tossed it back in.

"So, that there's the peak we're headed to, huh?" Her water pouch sloshed at the horizon of snowy peaks. There were a lot of them, so I didn't know which she meant. But my mind ran along the Cascade line, role calling the names long drilled into me.

Broken Jaw. North Sister. Middle Sister. South Sister. Mount Washington.

My gaze steadied on this last one farthest away. Smaller and dwarfed behind a rolling hill.

"Yeah." I dug out my plastic water bottle. "Yeah, that's the first mountain we're heading for. Our next one's more north, over that way. We can't see it yet."

I kept drinking despite the ultra-dramatic intake of

breath next to me.

"Wait...*first* mountain, Dove?"

"Of course. That's not Mount Jefferson—where the Council meets. Ahead is Mount Washington. Did you think we'd reach the Council in less than a week?" I snorted.

"First mountain? Why aren't we heading north, then?" She groaned and buried her face in her hands. "We're lost, aren't we? We're going to die out here—"

"Enough, Brae. We're not lost. We're going to Mount Washington first because someone is waiting there. For us. Someone who'll join us for the rest of our trip."

She dropped her hands, but her eyes narrowed. "Who? Who's joining us? How do you know this? Oh, wait. This is from one of your God conversations. Isn't it?"

"Ha. Wrong. My grandma told me about it before I left. She thinks a warrior will be joining us there...something God revealed to her, and He hasn't told me otherwise. I don't know anything more. So don't ask."

"A warrior?"

"I repeat, don't ask."

She did anyway. Enunciating each syllable. "A war-ri-or? A war-ri-or. Yes, yes, yes!" Her arms rotated in a tight circle. "Why didn't you say something about the warrior before? Think how good it'll be having someone with muscle on our side for a change!"

I busied myself with my warm, plastic-tasting water so I wouldn't be expected to cheer.

I didn't want a warrior—or any other person—joining us. Melody was enough. Plus, I thought it likely something super evil was coming at us. Why else would we need a warrior? It didn't bode well. Not at all.

But I kept my thoughts to myself and let Melody do her happy dance. No need to panic her yet. Her panic would only slow me down.

"So, you still coming then? Because it's not too late for you to go home. You could backtrack OK from here."

"Dove?"

"Yeah?"

"Let's go get us our warrior."

11

Melody's excitement about our soon-to-be traveling partner kept us moving at a decent pace until the late afternoon. Shadows lengthened as we passed from the high desert scrubland and into the trees again. Then, I was able to shake off the creepy feeling of spying eyes.

A thick haze had gathered above. It blunted the sun's heat and made the air heavy, tinged with the fragrance flowers release before rain. The patches of wooly sunflowers in parched crevices lifted their yellow heads skywards in anticipation. I imagined the drops on my face and tongue. Delicious.

I interrupted Melody's detailed description of her mom's ambrosia potato recipe...or ambrosia turnips. Some root vegetable. "Got any water left?"

"Huh? Oh, sorry, not a drop."

"Me neither. We'll keep going until we get to some. Then I'll find somewhere to hang our tent so we can crash for a few."

My steps seemed lighter. We could use my tree tent again. It was a woven structure I'd brought along that hung between three trees—a triangular hammock with a woven canopy. The last couple of nights had been toe numbing. We'd slept on the desert ground for lack of trees, which allowed the morning chill to creep into our bones.

"Oh good. I'm glad you know where water is, Dove. How far?"

I widened my stride, increasing the distance between us.

Of course I didn't know where or how far from us water was. Just because I'd never lived in a hole in the ground—like she had—didn't mean I was the expert on all things above ground. Which she constantly assumed.

I'd navigated us by the sun. And now that I could see it, by range. The obvious animal droppings told me water flowed nearby somewhere. Probably.

Lord Jesus, Son of Man, You know how it felt to be so thirsty. Remember how Your tongue stuck to the roof of Your mouth? How Your head ached? How Your legs got weak and trembly? Well, that's me right now. Oh, Jesus, I'm dying here. Please, can I have a drink? Enough so I can keep doing Your will?

Suddenly, the trees opened up to a small lake. Dead stumps and broken trunks jutted out from the far end, but most importantly, I saw no tire marks on its banks. No litter. No signs that humans ever came here.

The steady chatter of birds was reassurance enough. We staggered straight for the water's edge.

I'd gorge myself on water until I was sick. My skin tingled in anticipation. The coolness would rinse away the sweat, the layers of grime, the poison—

"Hey. You!"

I skidded to a stop and almost fell forward into the shallows, when Melody knocked into me.

It'd happened. We'd been seen. Talked to. It was too late to hide.

A tiny figure of a girl waved at us from the middle of the lake. "Hey."

She must've popped onto that stump from nowhere. I would've spotted those glowing pink strips of fabric she wore on her otherwise naked body from a mile away.

But my pulse slowed, and my fists unclenched.

We could outrun this...I was guessing five or six-year-old? Even if she tried chasing us, by the time she made it to shore we'd be long gone.

I eased my hand back and felt for my water bottle. I'd fill it and split.

A dark head bobbed out of the water in front of the pagan girl's stump.

My heart began to slam at the sight of the boy...or was it a man? Didn't matter. Either way he was bigger than me—I could tell by the size of his tanned shoulders that shone with the water I needed.

He swiped his plastered, black hair back. He apparently noticed us and raised a hand. "Oh. Hey!"

A low voice, not a child's. The laughter in it seemed like a trick to throw me off, so I'd let my guard down.

He mimed tugging at an invisible shirt. "Uh. Is it winter over where you're standing? Because that's a lot of fur you got on for a—"

The girl in pink catapulted from the stump onto his shoulders. They disappeared together in a splash that set the whole pond moving in a frenzy of chasing, choppy waves.

I ran.

Each step pushed my muscles until sharp pains tore at the tops of my thighs. I didn't slow.

Giggling started up from behind as I blew past the first tree. I heard deeper chortling too, the sputtered word "brat." Then...

"Wha—Why are you running—*hold up! Wait!*" His voice lowered but still carried over the water. "Cut it out, Jezzy. Get off me. I need to see...those might be radicals! No, let go. And stay here. You follow, and I swear..."

I wove around trees, searching for a decent one. But spindly cedars and pines with missing lower branches made up the whole dumb grove.

Melody's stumbling footsteps and ragged breaths grew fainter. She couldn't keep up. But the splashes at the pond had ended—he'd made it to land. I pushed myself harder.

Just one good tree.

Melody screamed. The high-pitched note hung in the air, ending with a muffled thud. A shout. And the crunch of sticks.

I kept running, my odds of escape much better. I'd reach the Council.

A much more necessary quest than joining in a losing battle to free the Brae girl and getting myself killed in the process. I wasn't saving my own life. I was saving my family's. Melody's family's. A whole nation of believers. I ran for their lives. I was the dove. God's messenger. I was important.

Right, God?

I smacked full force into something as solid as a tree trunk and bounced backwards, stunned, onto the brown needles.

My eyes snapped open but my lungs still couldn't function. Finally, I drew a deep breath of air and sat up. Nothing blocked my escape route. The closest tree grew over ten feet away in the diffuse sunlight.

I scrambled to my feet and shuffled gingerly forward, my arms outstretched. I waved my hands around.

Still nothing. No barrier—invisible or otherwise.

I crept forward, away from Melody's disturbing silence. Away from the excited voice. I couldn't allow myself to focus on that.

Something touched me again. Softer this time.

I froze. And stared down at my right hand where fingers—fingers I could only feel and not see—wound through mine. Once intertwined, I felt a tug. A pull in the direction of the people I'd outrun.

I waited expectantly but felt nothing else. The unseen hand slipped away. My own hand trembled, found my damp cheek, and I knew that the choice— either to run to the mountain or to go back—was mine.

I dragged myself back to where Melody went down, each step as though slogging through waist-deep mud.

"Are. You. Radicals?"

I slipped behind a trunk that did a rotten job of concealing me.

Melody's stomach hugged the ground while the Heathen boy, a teenager, straddled her pack, his knees on either side. Caging her in. He held her wrists behind her.

"Are you? C'mon tell me. Are you radicals? Fanatics?" He twisted her unresisting arms further, and she shifted her head to the side.

Tears smeared her cheeks.

I turned my face away. What...*what* was I supposed to do? Rescue her?

"Yay! You got one Woof."

I whipped around and took in the short, black hair plastered against the scrawny neck and round face, the pink outfit exposing too much tanned flesh. A pale pink scar ripped a line down her sternum.

"Jezebel." The boy spoke through clenched teeth. "I told you—"

"Yeah, yeah. I know. But you forgot there's only one of you. You need me. So that one," the girl aimed a stubby finger at my chest, "I've got."

She skip-hopped over Melody's legs and galloped straight at me. The boy's eyes overtook her path. They locked with mine.

"No! Jezebel!" He lunged after her.

The moment he moved off, Melody got to her feet. This time I let her lead, but his long arm stretched past me. It snagged Melody's bag and yanked her to the ground. He slammed into me from behind, his weight knocking me to the ground.

I rolled out from under him and crawled out of his reach. Free. But helpless to save Melody who was pinned again. Unless I fought.

Gilead, Gilead, how do I win this? What do I do?

He'd said it a million times.

A ruthless offense is the best defense, Dove. Use what you've got and deliver it fast and hard. An immediate, unrestrained attack—that's key.

Right. Attack. OK. But attack with *what*? What did I have? I clenched my skinny fingers into hopeless fists.

Then...*oh!*

I ripped off my pack, dumped out its contents, and, fumbling, snatched up the three-inch hollow tube. I jammed it to my lips and blew. An unearthly droning sound filled the air.

"Hey! You! Stop...stop it! Don't be calling for help." Melody's captor made a futile swipe in my direction.

I backed away, still calling the bees to come to my

aid. To rescue Melody.

C'mon, bees. C'mon. Bees had to live around here. Had to.

I blinked. My fingers and lips were empty. Silent.

I glimpsed my call wrapped in the girl's fist before she thrust it behind her back and skittered away. "I got the whistle, Woof."

The boy she'd called Woof threatened me. "Leave her alone or see what happens. And who were you calling? Who else is out here?"

"No one." I brushed off the pine needles stuck to my sweaty palms and began shoving things back into my bag. "There's no one else."

What was *wrong* with me? We'd been captured. I shouldn't be so OK with being captured. But my heart continued to beat at its regular pace, and my breathing didn't spike.

"Huh." He tightened his hold on Melody. "And don't lie to me. I know you're radicals."

"No. We're Christians. True believers."

He snorted. "Yeah, OK, whatever. Same difference. Fanatics."

"The warrior, Dove!" My partner cried out in Amhebran from the dirt. "Go! Find him. He can rescue me—I know he can. It's my only chance. I'm sorry I can't help you anymore. Hurry, please hurry—"

Woof shook her arm. "Hey, radical. Knock off the Christian...voodoo...or whatever you're doing. Use real words if you've got something to say. On second thought, shut up while I figure out what to do."

He grimaced. "Two? This is crazy. One radical I could handle. But two?"

As if preoccupied with his dilemma, he shifted off of Melody and allowed her to sit up. He whistled under his breath, although his fingers remained locked around her sleeve.

The kid, Jezebel, began to chatter. I supposed she asked me questions, since her gaze never left me and her lips moved a million miles a minute. But I didn't hear. My own shattering realization overwhelmed me.

Not a foe. I was certain that's what the Spirit had whispered. But...*what?*

That was crazy. Like saying Gilead was a gentle boy. Or my grandma a serious national threat.

Not a foe? Who? That pagan who'd attacked us? The one still acting like he might rip off Melody's arm?

Yet, that powerful sense of peace stole through me, even though a small part of my consciousness shrieked at me to snap out of it. That I couldn't be OK with something so, so *wrong*.

I couldn't shake the peace.

So, what then? Was I choosing *not* to escape from a nonbeliever if we had the chance?

I shouldered my belongings and approached Melody, flashing my enemy—who maybe was *not* my enemy?—my empty hands. *See? No weapons.*

I tensed when I squatted, in case he might grab my arm too.

But I was bigger than Melody. Plus, now he knew I wouldn't ditch her. He kept his hands off.

"Danger or not?" I murmured in Amhebran.

"What?" She tugged against Woof's hold to show how obvious the answer was.

"Stop. And think a moment." I shook my head. "No, forget that. Don't think. Feel. In your heart, what do you feel there? Are they a threat? Or not a threat?"

I got no response.

"Because I say 'not,' Melody. I feel like the Spirit

wants us to go with them. For now. And we should—"

A sharp sting near my eyebrow stole my breath.

The girl balanced on a log, towering over us with the bee call, hand on her hip. Her right hand clutched another pinecone in a threat. "Stop it, you. My brother said no voodoo."

I swiped my fingertips across my freckles, checking for blood. I spoke in English to her brother who thought his sister's pinecone attack hilarious. "Sweet kid."

"Warned you," he managed to choke out.

"Huh. So, Woof. Let's say you've caught us. What now?"

"I did catch you." He flexed his free arm so the thin line of muscles showed.

I waited. What? Was I supposed to swoon or something? I've grown up with Gilead. Muscles are as common as pine needles where I'm from.

He kept flexing another second and ended up being an idiot again.

At last, he stopped. "And quit calling me Woof. It's Wolfegang—or better, *Wolfe*. And I have no idea 'what now.' I've never gotten radicals before. Never even seen any of you. So what's the standard protocol? Ever been captured?"

I shook my head.

He sighed. "Well, unless I'm going to finish this and bury your fanatical remains in the woods here, I guess you'd better come home with me while I decide what to do. You people are more loyal than I'd expected. But not as tough. Unless you're packing— hang on. I'd better hold onto these."

He confiscated our bags, throwing them over his shoulder. "OK, Jezzy. You lead. And you two don't try nothing...or pinecones will fly."

Melody watched me through the ragged curtain of hair that'd escaped its coil. *Run for it? Now? Waiting for your lead.*

When I gestured for her to follow the girl, she gawked at Wolfe. Her head moved upward as if her gaze roamed from his bare toes to the triangular nose. She caught my eye. Looked at his uncovered chest. And then back at me.

"Sorry, Dove," she murmured in our language. She heaved herself up and limped after Jezebel. "You're sure it's the *Spirit* that's urging you to go with him?"

I didn't get what she meant. Until Wolfe put his fingers between my shoulder blades and shoved, propelling me after the others.

My face throbbed with heat. *As if* I'd ever mistake something like *lust* for the prompting of the Holy Spirit. And besides, how could she think I'd choose a godless, obscenely dressed guy? Never. Never ever.

Not that I was choosing anyone. If my family asked me to marry someday, then I'm sure I'd end up with...well, I didn't know too many people. Micah?

My head rotated back and forth, rejecting the idea—no doubt making the pagan behind me think I was nuts. I'd refuse to be forced, that's all. No need to ever get married. Not everyone did. At least I didn't think so.

I trudged after Melody.

How dumb was I? Thinking about my future marital status when being led to a Heathen's home in the heart of Enemy territory. One that had to be crawling with his minions.

Stay alert, Dove. Be ready. Pay attention to the Spirit.

And don't be distracted by anything—especially loser boys.

But that turned out to be impossible since the one behind me began to whistle, sounding like a sparrow. Sounding like my mother.

12

"So. You're here because?"

In the last ten minutes Wolfe had asked this one twice. And we'd not answered, twice.

Take a hint. There's a pattern.

"C'mon. It can't be such a secret. Are you passing through or what? Where were you going? Why are you here?"

He whistled some more. "Fine. How about this. *Don't* say anything if it was you who set fire to the dumpster behind the town's liquor store. Or painted over the women's clinic sign. Clearly radicals. You gave yourselves away by what you graffitied."

I focused on the slouched, defeated shoulders in front of me while we picked our way through the undergrowth.

"Yeah. I knew it."

I whipped around to tell him off for being so smug and confident that Christians would go around destroying others' property.

We'd done nothing to deserve this accusation. *I* wasn't the one who'd tackled Melody or stolen a bee call and two packs.

I glared into his widened eyes. His lips pursed to whistle and stayed puckered in surprise. I swung back around and marched on.

Waste of time. Waste of breath.

Satan was the Father of Lies. And this was his territory. And these were his people. Of course he brainwashed them into thinking we were as violent and destructive as *they* were.

"Whoa." He jogged to catch up. "All right. I see you're a bit hot and bothered about discussing your criminal past. So how's this? I promise not to bring it up again if you tell me your names?

"Oh, come on." He invaded my personal space while walking backwards to face me. "Don't you think it's unfair that you know ours, but we don't know yours? Of course, I can always give you nicknames. But do you think your predicament is going to get much worse by me knowing—"

"Dove."

He stumbled and fell out of my line of vision. "Dove? That's your—I mean...yes. Of course it is. Lovely name. Super common. Dove."

Jerk.

"What about her? The bite-sized screamer?"

"Melody."

Ahead, my traveling partner flinched.

Then Jezebel led us into a shallow clearing of unnaturally clipped, dead grass. She stopped skipping and readopted the role of stoic guard—the one she'd abandoned for balancing on downed trunks and chucking stuff at birds.

Yet it wasn't her but the manmade, brown structure edged in white at the far end of the grass that had me squaring my shoulders. It was a copy of the farmland shelters Melody and I'd killed ourselves to avoid.

And I saw two more that were identical.

Gilead's voice shouted at me as I approached this

first solid, boxlike structure. It roared when I stepped through its opening where Wolfe had slid a large sheet of glass out of the way.

No one jumped on me when I entered, which was the only good thing about the place. Looming walls blocked out the natural light.

My eyes lit on a few things I recognized. Things I knew from the junk piles back home—a chair with small wheels. Bunches of cardboard boxes on a table, one bright yellow with a picture of food on it. Things with snaky wires. Pictures. But so many I couldn't name. What were their purposes?

I rubbed at the rush of goose bumps beneath my sleeves. December air. I glanced at Melody for her reaction to this unnatural, cluttered home.

Her dark orbs lost focus, her skin bloodless under its sunburn. Before I could move, she hit the fuzzy ground in what sounded like a painful flop.

"Oh no." Jezebel rounded on her brother with a smack to his middle. "You killed her."

Smack. Smack. Her hands rained against his skin. He dodged the next set and knelt next to Melody's body.

I got in his way. "Don't touch her."

His outstretched hands whipped back. "What...I didn't..."

"Get water."

"Right." He leaped to his feet. Then swung around. "To drink? Or dump on her?"

His sister flew to a nearby wall the color of tree sap and threw open a door. "In the shower! Put her in the shower!"

She disappeared into the space beyond, and a blast of light sprang from its rectangular opening. "I've seen this before on TV. Trust me. This is what you do."

The sound of rain pounded down from inside the house. Indoor rain showers? Suspicious. But what was I supposed to do with this Brae girl if she died on me?

I dragged her dead weight forward...and almost dropped her.

What *was* this place?

A humongous, solid basin dominated the floor. Water drops poured into it from high up in the wall. Vapor clouds rose from the basin.

I shuddered. Everything in this room radiated the whiteness of new baby teeth. Creepy.

"Here." Wolfe held out a clear jar of water.

I couldn't hold Melody while pouring water into her mouth, so I lowered her to the floor. Her head lolled against the white wall.

Most of the liquid ran down her chin and neck, but a little must've made it into her mouth. She choked. Then coughed. Swallowed. And cracked open her eyes.

I shoved the empty jar at Wolfe.

"Rain?" Melody tried to focus on me.

"See? She wants to go in the shower."

I shook my head at Jezebel.

"It's raining." Melody fingered the wet fur of her collar.

"No way." I stayed firm. "You don't want the indoor shower."

I watched her mouth tug up at the corners.

"Yes. Please? No danger."

~*~

This must be a dream. Because it couldn't be real.

I sat on the fuzzy, sand-colored floor of a pagan home. An indoor shower pounded behind the door at my back. And the Brae girl, who panicked over everything, voluntarily bathed in it.

I rubbed my hands together, creating doughy rolls of grime. I bet it felt good, though. All that water.

"Popsicle time."

Jezebel was bored—now that the excitement of capturing prisoners and Melody dying had ended. I shared a sleeping porch back home with an eight-year-old. I knew how little-kid thinking works.

She skittered off somewhere. Thumps and a slam echoed from a different area of the home.

"They're no good. Power was out for too long again last night."

She sauntered back, holding something red on a stick. She stuck it in front of Wolfe's nose and then slurped its bright juice.

"All right, all right." He shoved her head away, his shoulders shaking.

She waved the frozen liquid at me. "You like popsicles?"

I swallowed hard, shook my head, and screwed my face into a grossed-out expression. As it disappeared outside with the girl, I wondered if it tasted as much like wild strawberries as the red promised.

The water falling at my back cut off.

"You know I'm going to figure you out, Bird."

I plucked up a long string from a crack between floor and wall—a perfect strand—and began unraveling its woven threads.

"Even if you don't tell me voluntarily, there are ways I can find out."

A thread snapped between my fingers.

"Oh—no. No. I don't mean...I'm not going to *make* you tell me or nothing. I'll find it electronically. Everyone's info is out there, including yours, waiting to be discovered, at least if the electricity will hold out for another while." He grimaced at the strip of lights above his head.

Since Melody had pleaded for the shower, I hadn't spoken. And on principle, I refused to ask for a favor. But for five years I'd been obsessed with Dead Nights. The sudden darkness. The reason lights and cars didn't work. The pure evilness of it all.

I waged a war in my head. The obsessed part won.

"And the electricity goes out because?" I retied the frayed ends of my string.

Wolfe leaned forward, grinning. "Nice try. But I'm willing to trade. An answer for an answer. Mine first since I asked first. What were you doing in Sisters?"

My retort was automatic. "Following God's plan with faith and obedience."

He waited with raised eyebrows, which soon lowered into a low, solid line. "That's it? Following God's...It doesn't tell me anything—"

"It's a true response and all you're going to get. Now my turn."

"Ok, Miss Charisma. You want to know about our town's freaky power outages? Which, to be honest, makes me suspicious that you care, but I'm not going to bother asking why you want to know or how you're going use this information 'cause you won't tell me, correct?"

I nodded.

"Ha!"

I cringed.

"Now I know the outages reach you since you're asking about them. You don't live too far from here. Right? I'm right. Right?"

I held up my string—now quadruple its original length—and squinted at it.

He sighed. "Fine. Well, in Sisters, when the lights go out it's a good bet some kid has let off a mini EMP. Although I know a few adults who've let off some, but they're happy to let us take the blame. And even when the power comes back afterwards, it's unstable for a few days."

He gestured at the strip overhead, which had dimmed and brightened twice since I'd slid to the floor.

I dropped the thread and squinted at him. Confused.

He noticed. "EMPs? Never heard of mini EMPs? They're, you know, those handheld devices made for soldiers to carry to interrupt the flow of electricity. Electromagnetic pulses. Their way to stop the enemy's communication, high tech weapons, vehicles...things that use electrical currents. Get it?

"So, when I was ten or eleven, we had this ex-SEAL military guy who lived in town and stockpiled a ton of them. Illegally, of course. Then he went PTSD." He laughed at my furrowed brow. "He went cr-a-zy. He handed them out to us kids on Halloween. Best trick-or-treating ever. The guy's still locked up, I think, getting his brainwaves checked. And the military officially ordered us to give up all EMPs, but I've still got a couple tucked away in my sock drawer. Like most people my age around here."

"But...*why?* Why do you want them?"

He thought for a moment. "Having the power go

off is annoying...but you feel like a god or something when you're the one doing it. Plus, it's hilarious. And it gets us out of school sometimes."

I shook my head in wonder. It's *kids* causing Dead Nights. For kicks.

"It's not that big of a deal, though." He came over and leaned his back against the wall. My wall. "It's not like the cops are going to arrest a kid for causing a short blackout."

I found my feet and stepped away with my arms crossed tight. "Just like they can't arrest me for being a Christian. Loving God isn't illegal either."

At least, I didn't think so.

He closed the gap. His arms copying, a dumb smirk on his face. "True, but hurting others who are more open-minded about what's out there is. Say what you like, but it's *wrong* for you people to say your religion is the only right one and condemn everyone else to Hell. All while you creep around, blowing up junk and setting fires to prove you're better than the rest of us."

The door swung open behind him. A blast of muggy air tinged with summer's flowers wafted out, carrying Melody with it. Dampish but fully-dressed in boots and pelts, she chattered in Amhebran.

"Dove, Dove! The water can be warm *or* cold. And it doesn't end. Ever. At least I don't think. I'm serious—as much hot water as you want. You don't believe me. Here. Go try it." She tugged at my arm, attempting to pull me inside the white room, but then she bumped against Wolfe. She stopped trying to pull me.

"Oh. Um. I'll...I'll watch the door for you." She gulped.

I decided to go for it. If I passed up this opportunity for water, I'd most likely shrivel up here on this fuzzy floor. After the hateful accusations he'd hurled at me, I'd rather die than ask *him* for a cup.

His body reclined against the rectangular opening I'd passed through. "Well, we'll see—about your arrest, Bird."

I shut the door in his face, but that didn't stop his words. "That's right. Go relax. Enjoy your shower. I'll be out here, checking out the FBI's Most Wanted page for who you really are. Let's hope there's at least a decent reward."

I brushed a metallic spot in the wall, and a waterfall-like burst drowned out the rest of his incomprehensible taunt. The water's warmth, taste, sound, the sting of it against my sunburned skin, nothing else mattered.

Melody hadn't lied.

It was so different from the frigid water bathing experiences back home. There, unless you hiked all the way to the stream, every drop was precious and never quite enough.

Dingy brown rivers collected around my toes, escaping down the fir-needle-shaped holes.

I watched the flow. Did it end up in a pond under their home? Or did it water a garden outside I hadn't noticed?

Goodbye grit. Sweat. Last dregs of poison.

What if enough poison came off me to kill their vegetables? With a smile, I unrolled my hair and scrubbed my scalp. My other hand clutched the long piece of white material that acted, I assumed, as a privacy curtain. And, of course, I still wore my undergarments—a cord-strapped shirt and fitted shorts that reached my upper legs. Their water-resistant material would be dry in an hour.

Opening my mouth baby-bird style, I took one last, long drink. Then I turned off the water, wrung it from my hair, and fast-coiled it back up.

The next few minutes I spent lacing the small plastic bag with the two prayer results I'd set on the slippery ledge back onto my undershorts. Finished, I peeked around the curtain and grabbed for the damp towel Melody must have used. My eyes skimmed this alien, winter-white room.

With a gasp, I leaped over to the spot next to my shoes—the place I'd left my clothes. On all fours, I patted around on the hard—now puddled—white squares. As if my missing tunic shirt and pants had somehow become camouflaged.

I whirled around, searching. I pried open a small door next to my legs and stuck my head into its dark, cluttered depths.

Slowly, I shut it, rolled back onto my heels, and hid my face.

My clothes—they were gone. Completely. Utterly. Gone.

I crouched there for about five seconds.

Then I got mad.

It took me another few frustrated moments to figure out how to wear the one towel in the room that wasn't maple leaf sized. No matter how I tried, it wouldn't cover all the skin it needed to. I wrapped the towel under my armpits and around my wet underclothes, which left my shoulders, arms, and the lower half of my legs still showing.

I yanked open the door, expecting to trip over Melody.

I didn't.

She'd vanished.

Not my biggest problem right then.

"Where are my clothes?" My hands death-gripped the towel while I stormed at Wolfe. He sprawled on a cushioned bench, holding up a skinny, rectangle electronic. Then he dropped it. The whistling died.

"*Where* are my *clothes*?" I was ultra-conscious of my gangly, fish-belly white legs and arms. A startling contrast to the deep tan of my face and hands.

He stared.

Rage boiled up, staining the room red. A snarl started deep inside. I began to shake. "Where are my clothes?"

He eased upwards and backed away. "Whoa, bird girl. Relax." His hands went up. "It was just a...a...I'm washing them—they're in the machine. Hang on."

In two strides, he left the room. His head reappeared. "By the way, seriously nice tattoos. Uh, right."

A minute later he returned holding a dripping wad of brown material. He handed it to me with a cough. "They're a bit damp still. Should I throw them in the dryer?"

My anger drained away. Leaving me with a hole in my chest.

I shook out my tunic shirt—a hand-woven, goodbye gift from my mom, aunt, and grandma. The fibers were created from special plants grown on our property. The Breastplate of Righteousness design stitched on the front tilted lopsided. Pathetic.

My traveling outfit hadn't only been a surprise but a tribute to the Armor of God from the Bible. The one my family knew I loved. And the only tangible

73

reminder of my family I'd brought with me.

"They were all stiff and brown. And I—"

"They're supposed to be that way."

"See, they're still good." He snatched the crumpled pants and flattened them. "They're not ripped or nothing."

Under his hands, the symbolic belt around the waist frayed and twisted like old corn silk on a compost heap.

I took them back and lurched toward the white room to put them on.

I will not cry over pants. I will not.

"That," he spoke from closer than I'd expected, "is the most wicked sword tattoo I've seen in my life."

I slapped my left hand over my right arm, hiding part of the ornate Sword of the Spirit that ran from shoulder to elbow.

He leaned over me. "What's that on your other arm? Oh, it's a shield—nice, the way it wraps around. I wouldn't have taken you for the inked type. Hey, I can see part of one above the towel. Something gray?"

I yanked the damp cloth up to hide the Breastplate of Righteousness no one was supposed to see.

But the moisture at my eyeballs dried. I still had Trinity's more permanent reminder of herself and home.

God gifted my cousin with the ability to create beauty out of anything. Out of nothing.

She told me once that when she met an object, her mind automatically saw its potential. To her, a body was a blank canvas. She'd been adding artwork to her own body for years—something her mom was OK with. My mom wasn't so supportive of tattoos.

Of course, that hadn't stopped me from accepting

Trinity's offer a few months ago. I couldn't pass up a permanent reminder of my spiritual protection and weapon. All guaranteed by my Lord's mighty power.

"Your ma and pop OK with so many?"

"Where's Melody?"

"Ha! I didn't think so. My grandma didn't do the conga either when I got mine. Did you see it? I've only got one. On my back. Not as cool as yours but...OK, OK. Don't go all postal on me again. Bite-sized screamers right outside. See? Through the glass there? Those are her boots behind the woodpile. She's staring at the clouds or something."

I nodded, not bothering to check. That girl was obsessed with sun sets. Every night, she'd watched the blue horizon melt into oranges and pinks while I'd set up camp. But tonight's sky was way too thick with gray clouds for color.

"It took her roughly, oh, one millisecond to bail on you when she realized it was only her and me." He flashed a hangdog expression, which I didn't buy. "I don't think she likes me."

"Try not tackling her so much."

He was still cracking up when Melody screamed.

I beat him to the glass door. But since all I could do was fumble the useless latch up and down, I had to step aside. So I was only second to reach Melody, who balanced on a pyramid of chopped wood. No, not even that. Third. A dog with droopy ears stood on skinny hind legs and sniffed her boot.

Melody's eyes were huge. They stared into the distance while her teeth clenched her knuckle.

The hound wasn't snarling and didn't look particularly vicious. So why did she act like her danger radar registered immediate death?

I scanned the area for blood, any sign of attack. My eyes hit on the nearest corner of the home, and I bit my lip.

Not the hound she's freaked out about.

Six teenagers came striding around it with Jezebel in the lead. She pointed at me. "See? Told you we catched us some radicals. I hit the tall one with a pinecone when she started talking her voodoo. It was so weird. The short one fell down and—"

"*No.*" Wolfe dropped the dog's collar.

Then *I* almost dropped my towel. Because his one word—'no.' And the way he'd said it. It was like expecting a bee sting and receiving a handful of honey.

He'd hinted at turning us over to some authority real soon. So, why act all concerned now about some other godless teens finding out about us?

I am with you.

A girl brushed past Jezebel to face Wolfe. "Hey, cuz."

She was as tiny as Melody, but my instinct registered the threat.

Her air of tough confidence, the way she stood— shoulders back, arms taut and ready—identified her as someone I'd never overlook or intentionally mess with.

The skin around her unnatural violet eyes gleamed black and green in the low light. "Well, well. Jez said you got us some radicals. I see she wasn't pretending this time."

Wolfe's frame slumped as if relieved. Without checking, I knew he smiled.

Myself, I was paralyzed, couldn't even jerk away when he draped his long arm around my tense shoulders.

"Jezzy!" He sounded mad—except for the note of

laughter that contradicted and confused me so much I gave up trying to figure him out. "You little liar. I'm going to whoop you if you don't cut it out."

His sister started to argue, but he snatched her up with his free arm and flung her over his shoulder. Out of the way of his conversation with the girl with shrewd eyes.

"Nah, Diamond. They're just some friends, my grandma's friend's nieces, who're staying with us. From Alaska. Colder up north there, you know—wear animal skins and all that. That's what must've given Jezebel the idea about—Quit it!"

Jezebel continued to kick him.

"So," he grunted between blows. "We were...were planning a bonfire. A welcome-to-Sisters sort of thing for tonight. You guys in?"

"A bonfire. Tonight. In the storm."

"Oh. Uh...yeah? Sure?" Then, "Umph!" as his sister's toes smashed his ribs.

"Let me down, let me down, lemmedown, lemmedown..."

The other two half-naked females sniggered at Melody in her lumpy, patched mole outfit, still crouched on the woodpile with her mouth open in a silent yell.

Diamond kept her suspicious purple slits on me. "What's your deal? Where're your clothes? Why the towel?"

Wolfe's arm dragged me to his warm side. I could feel Jezebel struggling against him. "Party planning."

I glanced up in time to catch his wink.

Thunder rumbled in the west.

"Nice, bro." The guy with shoulders sloped like snow-laden evergreen branches extended his fist for a bump Wolfe couldn't manage.

I peered through the pre-storm twilight at the expressions on these strangers' pagan faces. Excluding Diamond's, I read zero suspicion. Wolfe's arm glued me to the godless teenagers as an accepted addition.

Party planning? What was that?

I might not know, but I wasn't so clueless I'd missed the insinuation that went with it.

Bile churned, and I struggled to get out from under the stubborn, unreleasing arm. In the end, Jezebel's kicks worked in my favor.

Now free, I peered into the violet eyes. "He's a liar. I'm not his friend. And we haven't done what he says we've done."

In the breathless pause, Jezebel stopped twisting. Even the dog halted mid-snuffle.

"Don't," someone whispered. "Don't say it." Or it could've been a breath of wind. Or my own last whimper of self-preservation.

"I am a Christian."

My statement rang loud in the charged air until it was swallowed by more thunder.

"You...Chrissstian."

Radical! Killer! Spy! Jesus freak! Extremist! They spat the words at me from all sides until I was disoriented and dizzy. They surrounded and ringed me in. No arm hid me.

But I no longer felt like throwing up.

I gripped my Lord's promises, while wrapping my arm around my waist.

He loves me. He'll protect me. And no one here has a power that can touch His.

I am untouchable.

My heart found its normal rhythm. I opened my

eyes.

The females made the first move to grab me—although they seemed unsure whether or not I'd fight back. The Spirit warned me not to sneer at their fear. But scared of *me*? I didn't even have my bee call.

Their fumbling hands revealed something else: their exhilaration—the kind that fear feeds. Like gasoline on a flame.

Kaboom.

The males shot straight for Melody. They raced to scale the woodpile. Still balanced at its peak, Melody's lips moved. Unmistakably, they formed Amhebran words. Oh, God. Help me.

A second later, a wild cat's scream pierced the twilight.

The tiny hairs on the back of my neck pricked. I staggered from my quick release and whipped around, peering through the gloom at the line of nearby trees.

A sharp grunt broke the quiet. A boy hanging off the woodpile had fallen onto his back in the grass. Diamond, and a female with tufty hair nearest the tree line, sidestepped behind the tallest girl. A silent fight began. No one wanted to be closest to the woods.

The tufty-haired one lost. She cowered where she'd landed, flinching from the uneven bumps of forest. The dog whimpered.

Diamond glared into the shadows one last time before refocusing on me. She stepped closer, her hands balled into fists so I could almost feel them, hard against my skin.

"Well. Let's hurry then. And get this thing started. And finished."

With the cat's next crazed yowl, Diamond reacted, scuttling for the solid home where I glimpsed Wolfe

Erin Lorence

still holding Jezebel. She clung to him.

And now, I smiled. Only I had noticed Melody's trembling lips open and her throat move, synchronized with the chilling animal noise.

So this was God's provision to Melody's plea for help. He'd locked away her panic, but allowed her to use this miraculous gift to confuse our attackers.

Melody's foot inched to the edge of the roof, level with the woodpile.

Run for it?

Meet you on the other side. I chin flicked toward the boxy home.

As soon as Melody threw her last bloodcurdling cry, I bolted.

My bare feet pounded over the sharp grass. Two strides, four strides, six, eight...Shouts sounded behind me—they hadn't expected us to make a break for it right then.

I curved around the square structure and headed for the opposite side. Above me, Melody's silhouette hesitated at the edge.

My stomach plummeted. I faltered a step.

She wasn't going to jump. Of course not. This was Melody mouse...and it'd be a ten-foot drop at best.

Can't go without her, huh, Lord?

I flung my arms up midstride. Fine. I'd catch her.

The crippling blow hit me from the wrong direction—in the small of my back. I smacked the ground, knocked my chin, and lost my oxygen.

Paralyzed lungs...can't breathe...clawing panic.

Then I could breathe again, and the dog clawed my side and back, squirming to escape from under Melody, who, a millisecond later had slammed down on us both.

Extra weight pounded me into the hard clay. Another body joining our heap.

Diamond hauled me to my knees. Wolfe hadn't tackled us this time. The slope-shouldered guy pummeled the grass while rolling onto his feet. "Yeahr!"

After that, everything got confusing and jumbled together. And painful.

Faces, words, feet, and fists. None had distinct owners anymore. I closed my eyes and didn't try to keep tabs on who took a shot at me.

So what if Diamond's punches landed without mercy? She wasn't only clueless but an idiot if she thought she did this of her own power. She was a puppet, and Satan pulled the strings. The Puppet Master.

At my feet, Melody became a tight lump of fur. In the whirlwind of evil and pain, I clung to one sustaining thought: the Lord kept His promise. I didn't cry or show weakness. He'd done what I'd asked—he would keep me strong to the end.

No, this couldn't be the end.

Words rolled through my brain. Repeating. Endless. A chant between blows.

Not the end. Save my family. Please, no. Not the end...I'm the dove. Please, no. Not the end.

13

Peals of thunder boomed louder now. But it was the scattered raindrops that brought me back from a fuzzy, more comfortable reality where I'd drifted. When another set of footsteps crunched over the grass to where I sprawled, I played dead. The footsteps faded, and I let myself breathe. I cracked open my sore lids. Melody.

She huddled on her side a few feet away, her knees level with my throbbing chin.

I doubted she was as unconscious as she seemed. Either playing opossum like me, or too sore to move. Also like me.

Satan's teens had gone ahead with Wolfe's idea of the bonfire, despite the rain. Its heat and light didn't touch me where I lay, although its smoke did. It bullied away the fresh scent of rain meeting baked earth. Flames popped and crackled, weaving between excited voices.

Different kinds of crackling reached me too. Familiar from the junk pile back home. Plastic food wrappers.

My thoughts flitted to memories of clearing trash from our land, working with my cousins, and sorting out plastics. My grandpa perched in the tree canopy, his eagle eyes missing nothing, protecting us.

Glass shattered, interrupting my peaceful escape,

followed by something so horrible I almost struggled to my feet.

Another attack. The laughter, the yells of encouragement—they were all familiar.

Too familiar, I realized a second later, recognizing Melody's muffled "warrior" in Amhebran. I pressed back into the stiff blades.

Some sort of electronic device must be repeating the violence they'd committed. What was the probability they'd captured another Christian tonight?

I'd guessed right. For the second time, I heard the woman drive up. This time she approached from next to the fire instead of from the road farther away.

"What in the world are you up to, Diamond Collins? Does your mama know you're out here doing...what *are* you doing?"

"Hi, Mrs. Lee." Diamond sounded little-girl soft.

But then, someone called, "Wait! Let me, let me."

Forcing Diamond to speak normally. "You didn't hear? Radicals attacked in our woods today. Right here in Sisters! Terrifying, but we've contained them now."

"No! Where? Is that them? Well...I'm not sure you all should be the ones to take care of this. But, I guess with the way police let anyone go nowadays..." Her voice melted into sing-song. "Oh, hi, Bobo. You make sure to keep away from them nasty radicals. They eat doggies like you for dinner, yes they do."

The sing-song vanished. "By the way, Diamond. Bo got into our trash again last night. Papers and garbage everywhere."

There were some tut-tutting noises.

"It wasn't Bo. I never let him out after dark. Bet you it was these two. Stealing identities keeps them off the grid, so not to make you freak out, but I'd keep an eye on your accounts if I was you."

The woman gave a strangled cry, demanding to know if we'd been searched. Her goodbye was swallowed up by tires hissing over wet ground. Then the terrible background noises took over.

Three times they forced me to listen to the nightmare. Until every hateful word, every laugh, every noise from Melody was etched in my brain forever. I couldn't even cover my ears without giving away that I wasn't only alive, but conscious.

The shouts and bursts of laughter continued. Two silhouettes backed by flames pretended to throw punches and wrestle.

The rain steadied. It beat down the flames in the metal barrel, leaving a vague glow and a bunch of smoke. A couple of times, I caught the word "fanatics," but the rest of the sentences were swallowed up in the rising wind.

After an eternity, the talking dropped off—although someone's giggling continued, died down, and grew again. The ground trembled from thunder. Glass thunked against metal. Plastic wrappers crinkled. Someone began to whistle.

Then silence, except for the pattering rain and an occasional distant car.

My conviction grew with the silence. I'd been wrong earlier—back in the woods. Somehow, I'd heard wrong. I shouldn't have trusted the godless. We *should* have run for it. But we weren't dead yet—we still had a chance.

I eased my foot over. But before I could toe-nudge Melody, footsteps skittered over and stopped next to my head. The grassy rustle told me someone was settling there. I held my breath, listening to a bunch of ominous little tearing, ripping sounds.

Something solid—fingertips, it felt like—poked my leg, my arm, my other arm, my forehead. Each time they zeroed in on my sorest spots in some new form of torture.

I didn't flinch. Any movement would trigger another full-blown attack.

The fingers jabbed a painful area on my chin when I heard Melody flop.

"Micah."

No, no, no. Keep still. But I couldn't warn her.

As soon as she called for her twin again, another set of feet crunched over. In the strained stillness, I sensed the Heathen's scrutiny.

"This isn't good."

"Shut it."

"I liked this one, Woof." Jezebel's whine rose. "You should've stopped them—"

"I said. Shut. Up."

Melody's unexpected voice croaked, "She's not breathing! See?"

Someone grabbed my wrists, but I focused on being dead. Limp. I'd be as unresponsive as a blade of grass to whatever they did to me. That way it might end quicker.

My head lolled and bounced when they rolled me onto my back. I braced for pain...seconds away. I wouldn't flinch.

"Uh..."

"Do it. Now," his sister's voice demanded. "I said now!"

Something smashed my nose and mouth. Air billowed into my lungs. Uncomfortable and unnatural but...

Ahh. God's breath of life. Huh. I must've been worse off than I thought. But God wouldn't let me die. Not all the way. Now He was saving me, breathing me to life again.

More air gushed down my windpipe. I tried not to fight it.

Wrong! Wrong! Wrong! This air was tainted and bad. I felt it now, burning my throat—as if I'd swallowed gasoline vapors.

My lids snapped open, and I shot up so fast, black dots danced. I spat while scooting backward, away from Wolfe who scrubbed his mouth on his arm.

"How dare you?" My body shook with a suppressed cough. I clamped both palms across my mouth, peering through the rain.

The motionless figures slumped around the barrel a few yards away. They didn't react. I tensed anyway, waiting for the attackers to come.

Five long seconds passed. Then ten. Wolfe handed me my damp, balled-up clothes and shoes. "Yeah. They'll be out for a while. So you can cough, talk, scream at me, whatever."

Melody's nose raised in the smoky air as if to sniff out the level of our danger. Even in the weak light, she looked way better than I felt.

Huh. Wearing fur had defensive advantages I hadn't considered.

"Shut your eyes, pervert." Jezebel released a clump of plucked grass at her brother's face and yanked my shirt down over my head and undershirt before I was ready. My arms were peppered with three-inch rectangles of some sort of thin, neon plastic.

I ripped one off, which stung since it stole some arm hair.

"No." Jezebel confiscated the pink strip and tried to reapply it. "Don't you even know how Band-Aids work, dummy? See this?" Both her thumbs jabbed at the long scar I'd avoided seeing. "This means I'm an expert. Do what I say, and you'll be OK. Keep 'em on."

I tore my eyes away from the pale line. I focused on the few sprawled figures while pulling my pants on with unnecessary help.

Even moving this small amount made me ultra-aware of each bruise and the rawness of my elbow.

I tugged on a shoe. "Looks like some of your friends ditched you, Wolfe. And how stupid of the rest of them to all fall asleep at the same time. Oh. Wait. You're awake. So, that's it, huh? It's you. You're our guard dog. Let me guess your plan—tie us up, take us to jail. Oh, and for sure keep attacking us every time we move since you and your friends are so good at it."

He threw my backpack at me with such force I grunted. Then, he handed Melody hers, helping her put her arms through the straps. She shrank away. He tried again, and once more she recoiled. The process took time.

He sighed. "Where's the thanks?"

"Huh?" Jezebel's disbelief mirrored my own. "Are you delusional? This is all your fault."

He scowled at her. "Hardly. What I meant, brat, was why do you think everyone's sleeping so hard?"

He mimed pouring something down his throat.

"Drunk?" I whipped around, astonished.

"Like...like with wine? Like Noah?" Melody's neck craned to see the intoxicated teens. I could tell our experiences with drunkenness were the same. Only what we'd heard from the Bible.

Wolfe scratched his cheek. "Noah's wine? No, no

wine—nothing that nice. I only kept flowing the supply of what Tin's mom had on hand. And speaking of—I'd better get you both something to drink. A soda, I mean. And something to eat. You must be hungry since you've had a, you know, a long night."

A long night? I raised my eyebrows at the lamebrain inadequacy of this, but he missed it. His eyes surveyed the grass, his fingers, his sister...

She stopped picking the bottom of her big toe, sprang up, and shook my arms. Every bruise from armpits to wrists moaned.

She gave another brutal shake. "Me, me! I'll be right back with the most delectable thing you've ever tasted in your life. I can't tell you what it is, though. It's a sur-*prise*."

She flung her arms around my damp tunic. I was so unprepared for a hug that I allowed it. "It's cool you're not dead. I didn't get dead once either. That makes us the same, you and me—not being dead. We must be made the same. Tough. I bet we're sisters. Only our mom gave you away first because—"

"Jezzy. Enough. Go if you're getting them food."

"You're not Grandma, Woof. You can't tell me." But she sprinted for her boxy home.

I trailed her with my gaze. "You gave us back our stuff you stole. You're letting us go."

"Yeah."

"So you're fine turning Judas on your friends. Betraying them. All to help us escape, your enemies— who you're convinced do terrible crimes against the world."

He flinched. "Whoa. You skipped over 'thank you' and 'you're a great guy' and decided on that?" At last, he looked at me. "I don't get you. You *want* to be prisoners? And go to jail or to where they send delinquent kids?"

"Don't be a lamebrain. But I'm right."

"Well then, what do you want me to say? How about this. Promise not to go around blowing things up. And tell me where you're headed and why. And if it sounds decent, I'll let you go on your merry, fanatical way. And I'll deal with this lot in the morning. Actually, they'll probably think it's hilarious you got away." His grin reappeared. "You called me 'Lamebrain?'"

Melody shook her head at me in warning.

I rolled my eyes. How could she believe I'd tell this pagan anything important about our commission?

The rain trickled down my scalp. I shivered. His hair was drenched and the drops shone on his skin—the same as when I first spotted him. Yet now, I no longer saw him as a killer or a threat. Only an ignorant Heathen with messed up morals and too many questions.

"I won't murder anyone. Or blow anything up. Or hurt anyone. And that's something that no one here but her," I motioned at Melody who again gave me the let's-go signal, "and I, can say without lying."

I leaned forward. "And how deaf are you? I am not going to tell you, and will never tell you, where we're going. Got that? I can't have more obstacles when you run your mouth off to everyone. Lots of lives depend on us getting to where we're headed. So unless you're prepared to tackle us again, goodbye."

"Whoa!" Wolfe sidestepped to block my path. "If people are going to die—as in *die*—if you don't get to wherever you're going, then I think I *should* go with you. As a kind of guide. Or at least as a guard since you're a lamebrain at knowing who to avoid." He gestured at himself. A bad joke. "Plus, then I can make sure you keep your promises about not hurting people."

"*Dove.*"

Twin red dots glowed from under the chair frame by the barrel. The hound that'd been asleep now watched us.

Danger.

"Forget it." I brushed past. "And I always keep my promises. So, shalom."

Something hooked my pack.

"Pretty harsh of you to leave the kid this way. No goodbyes or nothing." He released me, so I slipped forward on the wet grass. "Abandoning her when she's doing something nice for you."

I straightened my straps with a jerk. "A second ago you offered to do the same, leave with us. Which is way, way worse since you're her brother."

"I wasn't going to up and leave this second without...argh! You're so...*so*..." He raised his fists, then dropped them and exhaled in a gush. "Fine. Only tell me one thing first. How'd you do it?"

"Do?"

"How'd you sit there and take it? When they hurt you? I could tell Melody didn't feel much through her animal skins and the way she was all curled up on herself—the smart thing to do, by the way. But you. You had to have..."

He swallowed. "You had to have felt it. Bad. And you sat there. You never made a sound. You even had this lofty *whatever* look on your face the entire time. That's what made them so crazy, you know?

"Why didn't you cover your head. Or defend

yourself? I saw you angry about your clothes earlier, and you didn't look like that at all this time. I don't get it. Why do you do that? React wrong, so different from normal people?"

Different? Not normal? Wrong?

I hashed this over half a millisecond.

No, I decided. *He* was wrong and had it backwards. I'd done it right—accepting what the puppets dished out—but not because I was so tough or anything. Gilead didn't honey coat his words. I'd believed him when he called me "a day-old cottontail."

I'd acted the way I had because that's what my Lord wanted me to do. He'd allowed the attack tonight, and He'd kept me strong enough to bear it. Without fighting back.

I'd done it His way because my thoughts, my movements, my heartbeats—they were all for Him. My *life* was for *Him*.

Even now, at this moment, unexplained energy and an urgency commanded me to keep going. Now, when I should be dropping from exhaustion, hunger, and pain.

That was because of Him.

How could I explain to this godless creature blocking my path what God meant to me—and what He'd *done* for me?

Could I find words for His extreme love—the reason He'd sent His only Son to suffer on earth to teach me? Or His passion to keep me forever, though it meant allowing His Son Jesus—both human and God—to die a painful death on the cross? And that His Son's life and love was so perfect that He'd conquered death while making way for the Spirit—the Holy Spirit who protected and never abandoned me or led me astray.

Lightning flashed overhead. The electric sky illuminated Wolfe's eager stance and the curiosity plastered across his beardless, drenched face. How could I say any of that?

I pictured his white teeth flashing when he threw his head back and laughed. When he told his friends tomorrow about what that Jesus-freak, radical girl had said. I heard their shrieks.

"Wolfegang?"

"Yeah?"

"Tie up the dog."

Whether he did or not, I didn't know. Because I never glanced back.

Melody and I took off around the corner of his home, escaping back into the woods we'd been led through as captives.

The moment the home's lights faded behind the trees, hail fell through the thin branch canopy that did nothing to protect us. Icy pellets slammed down with enough violence to wake up anybody out in it—no matter what they'd drunk.

Lightning flashed simultaneous with thunder. I pounded the ball of my hand against my ear, clearing my hearing in time to catch the sound of a tree splintering. Jagged wood slammed into the bushes in front of us, forcing us to change direction.

I hadn't much noticed the wind gusts before, but now they whipped around me—driving the rain and hail straight into my eyes and mouth, gathering around my ears with an eerie scream that rose and fell.

I heard the rage—Satan's howls of frustration that we holy messengers had slipped from his grasp. Melody's face lit up in the next flash, and I read the terror of the threat. I'd have had to be in a coma not to feel it myself.

Satan wasn't giving us up.

We ran blind through the storm that blocked the moonlight. So when the attack came, I couldn't see it. But I sensed movement that wasn't Melody or me or the wind or the hail.

She went down with a yelp, and at the same moment I landed hard on my outstretched hands. Something had grabbed my ankle.

Under my palms, the rough, solid tree roots sank back into the ice-covered ground where they belonged.

I shouted. And next to me, Melody screamed.

~*~

We didn't run. We were forced to feel out each step. Twice I stumbled but didn't fall again. But Melody did.

As I waited for her again, an odd shiver ran under my soles. Short, dragging sounds rustled from nearby—from all around—almost masked by the storm. Something poked through my pant leg.

I swatted wildly. My hand knocked against bare sticks of half-dead bushes. With sudden, tremendous pressure, the sticks jabbed harder against my shins and calves, boxing me in. They climbed up to my thighs.

The groundcover—plants and bushes I'd crushed under my soles moments ago—was attacking.

I yanked Melody to her feet before it closed over her head and ripped my leg out of the clinging foliage. "Not even any thorns. Only weak, brittle stuff. I'll break a path through. Stay close."

Darkness. Rain. Wind. Mud. Roots. Branches.

These were our enemies now.

Then, I heard the dog.

At the first bark, I lifted my knees higher, breaking into a bouncing jog. My feet smashed down the tangled bracken without hesitation, rising up for the next step before I'd fully touched down.

Faint barking. But the dog could be closer, its pursuit masked by the wind, rain, and my own crashing progress through the bushes. Had Wolfe forgotten to tie it up? Or had he changed his mind?

Or the others. Had they woken in the hailstorm and put it on our trail?

Or this could be a different dog.

Maybe this canine *wasn't* chasing us. Maybe it was only a coincidence.

Right. A coincidence.

My foot crunched down on a bush. Too late I identified its false position. A trick. Nothing solid existed below its scraggly branches. Only air.

14

As I plummeted the first few feet, I glimpsed the boggy ledge I'd stepped off. Then my hip slammed onto what felt like ice-covered mud.

I lost Melody's hand as I hurtled down the slippery slope. The black outlines of trees shot past, always out of reach. Within seconds they opened up to a flat sea of black.

Blacktop. My hate for this stuff hit an all-time high when it peeled the last layer of skin off my palms.

Melody fastened her fingers around me before I scraped to a stop. I struggled out of her chokehold, rubbing my smarting hands against the backside of my drenched pants.

"What is this place?" I took a few steps further out into the gigantic clearing of wet concrete. I whipped around, trying to see everywhere at once. On super high alert.

Whose authority had driven us down here? God's or Satan's? I guessed the latter's...although the fact that Melody wasn't catatonic with fear kept me from trying to fly up this steep wall of mud back into the trees.

I stumbled toward a lone pole stuck in the concrete—world's biggest lamppost I guessed—and wrapped my palms against the metal's coolness.

We stood in the dark, but at the far edge of the clearing a hundred yards away, an identical giant post burned orange at the top. Around it the pavement glittered with puddles. And farther away I made out the black, feathery curve of the woods, its slope way gentler than ours.

The glow also illuminated a couple of large shapes in the middle of the clearing, marring the flat emptiness of the space. Only silhouettes since the light came from behind them.

The largest reminded me of Wolfe's home, yet it was more massive. Near it, off to the side, a much smaller, roundish object reflected weirdly in the light.

I didn't realize I was transfixed on it until Melody interrupted. "You think that thing will help hide us from the dog? If it comes down here?"

"Nope." I missed seeing the puddle, stepped into it, and soaked everything up to my ankle. "We're getting out of here. Now. Head to the slope on the far side—over there where we can enter the woods without killing ourselves. We'll keep to the trees tonight—"

"No."

I tore my eyes away from the glimmering ball. She was standing hunched over. Her arms dangling. Defeated.

"What?"

"I'm done. I'm not going back into the woods. The trees, they're not helping us. They're fighting us. I can feel it. And I'm...I'm too...I can't fight back anymore. Not tonight. Sorry." The worthless apology died out in a whisper.

"One good, sturdy tree to hang our tent, Melody." I ignored the icy chill creeping up from my stomach. "I can make do with one. I promise after that we'll stop, and you can sleep as long as you want. I'll keep watch all night, and if anyone comes I'll—"

Through the heavy darkness I struggled to make out her slow, methodical head shake. I knew she hadn't heard any of my words after "tree."

I grew numb and tense. Watching her shrink farther into herself.

The dog bayed again, almost on top of us. The wind picked up too, screaming in triumph. Its rise and fall wound through the dog's frantic howling, an evil duet.

Your end is near. Your end is near.

I lifted my face to meet the storm. "Come on, God! You want me at the Council? Then fine! Get me there. And *her* too since I can't go without her!"

With a gasp, I cowered. I'd yelled at God.

The drops splatted against my bowed head and neck, the rain slower now. Heavier.

I shivered. This could almost be from my dream— it sounded like it. The red plopping onto the forest floor while I toiled on. Except for the darkness—that wasn't supposed to be part of it. Or the wind. Or dog.

I filled my lungs to shout again, then froze.

I breathed in another gust. I'd caught a whiff of something rotten—stomach turning. But at the same time, familiar.

Garbage. That single smell carried a thousand memories of home. Of Trinity made speechless by a piece of bent wire in the dump pile. The trill of my mom's voice, as pure as the birds' she commanded, while my cousins and I worked the organic material into our garden plot. And a recent one of Gilead, creating a hidey-hole bunker from pieces of a rusty, skunked-out camper.

The garbage smell wasn't only God's comfort. It

was His clue.

I abandoned Melody long enough to locate the huge metal bin in the inkiest corner of pavement. I cracked open the heavy plastic lid but didn't need light to know what waited inside.

The warm stench doubled me over, and I gagged. Worse than the skunked camper. Something for sure rotted in there.

I found my partner huddled where I'd left her. "OK. Good news. I got us shelter for the night."

Her eyes stayed shut. "I can't...sorry...not going up a tree."

"I heard you. We're not. And where I've found will even keep us out of the rain."

I didn't mention the smell. I didn't have to because in the few moments it took me to drag her to our shelter, smell was the most obvious part.

"What *is* this?" Her question came out muffled by the fur of her sleeve.

"I dunno. I'm guessing it's where someone keeps his trash pile. Here. Help me get this all the way open, and then I'll give you a boost over the side."

She didn't seem to understand, so I uncovered the bin myself. Then I reached over and squashed her hands against the top of the metal side. With a sigh, I gripped her around the legs and shoved up.

"Watch out for any sharp stuff."

With a crunch she came down hard on whatever was on the other side.

"Melody?"

"Ohhh nooo."

Oh good. She was fine.

I grasped the square, slippery edge and pulled myself up and over onto bulging bags.

Melody huddled against the wall with her shirt up over her nose, making little retching noises. But she'd find a way to let me know if she was hurt.

I hunted through the trash, avoiding anything sharp or squishy, rummaging for something durable and thin. I wanted wire to thread through the finger-width holes on the outside edge of the plastic top. That way I could keep it closed in case anyone tracking us decided to check inside here.

It was unlikely they'd get that far. In my experience, most humans tried to stay away from trash. Plus, if the dog got near, its owner would assume it had hit on the rotten food—not people—and call it off.

Yeah, we were as safe as we could be since normal people didn't like spending time in smelly places.

"Ah ha!"

I peeled the wide tape off large pieces of cardboard, tied and twisted them, and threaded them through the holes in the thick lid above. The tape cord spanned long enough to secure around the metal pole of a solid object at my feet—the leg of a chair I guessed. Last, I dragged the pieces of cardboard to the surface to sleep.

Melody ignored hers. I climbed onto mine and leaned against the rough wall, sticky and warm against my back.

The powerful smell made me lightheaded. But I wasn't hungry anymore—kind of nice for a change.

I leaned back and closed my eyes. The rain drummed steadily overhead.

Thank You, Lord, for hiding me from my hunters. For sheltering me from the evil. Thank You for freeing me from Satan's grasp. I thought he'd captured us back there, but

You are unfailing. Wonderful and mighty. I love You.

In my mind I saw Him. A massive lion, crouched over this garbage bin, furiously protective. At the same time, I felt wrapped in His protective arms that cradled me like a father would a small child. He'd never let me go. Love so iron strong didn't let go.

Joy unfurled in my stomach like moths excited to fly. The fluttery feeling spread until even my toenails and lashes warmed under the cloak of shimmering comfort. Without opening my eyes, I sensed that a golden, pulsating glow surrounded me. Its sparkling warmth drove away every terrifying memory. Every fear. Every ache.

I didn't notice Melody's crying until it got noisy.

"Well, don't sit there blubbering." I lifted my arm up in an invitation to come closer. "Come on. Scoot over here."

After a couple seconds she crunched from her garbage bag onto my cardboard. I draped my arm loosely around her, listening to the rhythmic plopping of the drops from the cracks overhead as they fell on the piles around us.

"Oh! I can feel...what is it?" Melody pulled away experimentally and leaned back in. "Feathers? No, it's heavier...and alive. Like a silent purr...but...wonderful. Are you doing that? Show me, Dove. I want it too."

"Shh." What if she ruined the comfort for both of us? But I relented. "It's not hard. Think of what God's done for you. Thank Him for it and mean it. That's it."

The steady tapping continued.

"Rain."

I couldn't believe it took her so long to think of a blessing. And such an obvious one. I let my arm drop. "You can say them in your head, you know. A secure place to rest tonight."

"A secure place, *not* in a tree."

I shook my head at that. "No broken bones."

"Escape from that Heathen boy, those wicked people, and the dog." I felt her shudder.

"Escape from the real Adversary."

"Our warrior. Waiting for us."

When she fell asleep mid-hum, I discovered my wet cheeks.

I reached up and felt around on the plastic roof for a leak. But I couldn't discover one.

Huh. I *don't* cry, avoiding thoughts and emotions that bring on tears the way I avoid defensive mama opossums.

So what was wrong with me? Exhaustion? A mental breakdown brought on by the pungent garbage fumes?

Then in a flash, I was lost in a memory from five years ago.

My mom whispered to me as I curled on my hammock. It was a Dead Night and my dad was in prison. I was scared and wanted him so badly I hurt like there was a bee sting in my gut.

"Now you listen to me good, Dove Strong. You've gone and forgot about hope. And hope always brings comfort. Always. It's hope's job. So stop dwelling on the what-ifs and have-nots and have faith—have *hope*."

Oh. That was what I had. Hope. Hope so potent I sagged with relief and was crying. For the first time since my call to deliver my family's result, I believed I might survive this journey and make it home.

Home.

The earliest I'd return to my house in the canopy would be mid fall—more realistically early winter. A foggy guess.

Both my family and the Braes weren't sure about the timing of this journey since our most up-to-date information was from fourteen years ago, when the Councils made their decision about the Rumor—aka the Reclaim—September fifteenth. So our agreed goal for Melody and me was to get to Mount Jefferson before that date. Before September fifteenth.

The hiccup was that since my uncle and Melody's brother didn't make it home seven years prior, we'd had no way of knowing for sure the dates hadn't changed.

I doubted they had. But if they had, that information would've been carried home by the last messengers. The missing messengers.

Quit it! I rejected the train of thought leading to the inevitable—why didn't my uncle return? Could my journey be for nothing?

With determination, I imagined the fuzzy white frost—or even snow—that would cover the bare branches and pines near Prineville. The frozen ground would shift and crunch under my shoes as I neared our property. But my grandpa would see me long before he heard me.

At his post in the crow's nest, he'd be watching for me with eyes sharper than a hawk's. Before I caught sight of a single familiar tree, the bell would ring—the one he used to alert the family of an emergency or a visitor—or in my case a granddaughter returning home.

Who would I see first?

Trinity or Gilead. They both spent their days in our ground-level garden and garbage plots, so they'd have a head start on the rest of the family when the bell started up.

But even if Trinity reached me first, she'd have two seconds to say, 'Cousin! What's the most amazing thing you saw?' Because Gilead would have tossed me over his shoulder, having appointed himself to deliver me to my grandma who couldn't make the climb down anymore.

I hugged my legs, hearing her worn voice alternatively shrieking out praises and scolding me to stop dawdling and what took me so long? Was I out becoming a worldly woman?

That's my grandma's harshest judgment. Calling someone a worldly man or woman.

Positioned at my back, Gilead wouldn't smile, but he'd hum. Like a cat purring, Gilead hummed when content. And not only because he loved me and was glad I was home—but because he'd be satisfied he'd done his part well. All that time spent drilling me on surviving in anti-Christian territory had paid off since I lived.

Well done, Gilead.

My mom would hover with her arms extended. Would her clear hazels be red rimmed? *Those* tears would be allowed, unlike the sad tears that weren't permitted at my departure—the ones that never happened.

After watching me a while, and touching me a thousand times to make sure I was really home, she'd slip out with my aunt. Together they'd prepare my most favorite meal in the universe: crow pie and honey roasted squash.

I gulped putrid air. My mom never had any problem catching crows. Or pigeons or doves. Even in the winter months they flocked to her as soon as she pursed her lips. A bird whisperer.

Then everyone, even my littlest cousins, would have to hush up for the next few hours. Because *then* I'd belong to my grandma.

She'd demand I regurgitate every detail of my journey for her, guided along by her abrupt, prompting questions. Some would pertain to the spiritual aspect—did I depend on the Lord for this and that? But a fair amount would be directed at filling her in on the world she missed and secretly mourned. I'd figured that out about her.

Drowsily, I shifted down on my cardboard. Would I tell her about the little girl in pink—her pinecone attack? And her weird sticky bandages?

Or about her brother? Would I say anything about his quick laughter? Or how he thought nothing of tackling someone, lying his head off, and whistling at his world's sin?

Funny. I didn't shrink from thinking about these two godless ones. The nightmarish feelings didn't crop up the way I'd have expected. There was no mental trauma in remembering.

But I wouldn't tell Gran about them.

15

I awoke to the excited clamor of magpies and crows—the same screeches and caws that had started my every morning since forever. But then I breathed through my nose. I wasn't home.

Sunlight filtered through cracks, illuminating Melody, slouched, upright, and unconscious against a broken bag.

I yawned, gagged, and touched the taut tape cord still wrapping the chair leg. I picked at the knot until it fell away, then reached up and pushed the lid. A bright shaft of light fell across Melody's dark brow.

"What's out there, Dove? What do you see?"

I squinted through the two-inch crack I'd created and let my eyes adjust to the brilliant morning. Evaporating puddles dotted dry concrete covered in white paint lines marching in parallels. Dense pine forest ran the perimeter of the flat clearing. The highest piece of land was the wall of exposed mud we'd slid down last night.

At the opposite end of the space were the two dark structures I'd noticed last night, although now in the morning light neither was dark.

The smaller one drew my attention first, for an obvious reason: it was supposed to. So shiny it reflected like a mini sun, burning my retinas.

A spherical, golden piece of...artwork?

I couldn't see details from here, but it had layers. The smallest, inner-most layer sparkled and tossed out rainbows the way broken glass does.

I forced my gaze to the left of it, to the massive walls of white and tan stones interrupted by vertically slit windows. A sturdy, orangey-red arch marked the building's entrance where masses of green vines scaled halfway up the sides.

"What *is* this place, Dove?"

I squinted at the scrolling, golden words. "The United Church of America. Spiritual Well Being Center."

The last half I gleaned from a smallish upright rectangle in front of the ivy. My lips continued to twitch, but no sounds came out.

A church. Here. In front of me.

I'd read about churches and had heard my grandparents describe them from their own childhoods. But the only church experiences I knew were the two-family gatherings in our tree home when the Joyners visited us on Sundays for worship and scriptures, before Mrs. Joyner swelled too pregnant to make the zip line journey over. Mr. William Joyner still flew over when he could.

But before me loomed a real church—a building big enough for hundreds of Christians to gather in.

Yet, how could it be so public? So open? Wasn't this anti-Christian territory?

Maybe this place was more hidden than I assumed. And only those led by God—like Melody and me—could find it.

But there couldn't be *that* many believers stumbling around these woods. A smaller structure camouflaged with the trees, and without all this pavement, would be way smarter.

My eyes scanned the woods before sliding back to the church, snagging on the glittery orb thing.

"What's your take on it, Melody? If it's safe, I'm going to check if any believer inside will give us food. And directions."

In our blind running last night, I had no idea where we'd ended up or which way to shoot. I saw no peak or horizon to help me. Only trees.

She shook her head, her nose scrunched. "I think it's OK, but...I don't know for sure. It's impossible to get a good read on the place. Garbage overload's messing me up. Sorry."

I pulled myself over the warm metal side. "Keep the top cracked open to see if it helps. And in case I need to hide fast."

Jogging around puddles, I glanced side to side. No one raced out to get me. The morning air was heavy with pine. I almost felt bad for Melody, knee deep in trash.

I moved in the wrong direction, not toward the church's glass doors like I'd planned, but I approached the golden spherical orb as if overpowered by its magnetic pull.

I stopped a few feet short. Up close, I recognized the orb. A mammoth statue of the world. At least twice as tall as me, the globe rested inside a bunch of complicated outer layers.

Don't stand in the open like this. Keep moving. Go!

I located the United States. In the world of bronzes, silvers, and coppers our country glittered green.

I couldn't tear myself away from the translucent green glass, so intense in the sunlight. My fingers skimmed the bumpy, strangely cool surface.

"*Emeralds*!" I clapped my hand over my lips and scanned the still empty clearing.

I'd never seen any stone more valuable than lava rock. But when I was five or six, I'd watched my Grandma Sarah dig out a green glass bottle from the junk pile. Her eyes had gone all shiny. "Your great grandma's wedding ring had a stone this color, Dove child."

I'd stopped sniggering.

"This, but greener. And more beautiful than maple leaves in June. An 'emerald,' she called it. If you ever meet clear green prettier than maple leaves, Dove child, you'll know it's an emerald."

My Grandma Sarah—my dad's mom—didn't live hidden in the trees when she was my age. Neither did my grandpa. So they knew a lot more about the world than the rest of us.

Back when they were kids, Satan hadn't dominated our nation yet. Christ's followers had been able to live—at odds, but for the most part OK— amongst nonbelievers.

That's how I knew about things like emeralds. And strange electronic devices you talked into so others could hear you far away. Phones. A couple broken ones had come through the dump piles. My grandpa had even driven something called a "bug" when he was Gilead's age, something I couldn't picture.

Would my grandparents know what this golden globe meant? Why did it have so many clenched arms? Why were they entwined in a loose, braided layer around its middle like the fat center of an unfurling daisy flower?

I inched my way around, forgetting the garbage bin at the end of the clearing.

Each arm's hand grasped another's. A gesture that symbolized two things—strength and unity. At regular intervals, a free hand stretched out as if offering a gift from its open palm.

I saw fancy star offerings, flowers, and complicated lines with squiggles that made no sense.

I leaned in closer and recognized one of these, taught to me long ago by my grandma so I wouldn't be ignorant—the symbol for Hinduism.

So each symbol represented...

My mouth went dry while I circled the sphere faster. Searching. Searching for the one I had to find.

The cross.

My hands clasped while my eyes devoured not only the cross, but also a tiny replica of Jesus Christ balancing in that palm. The representation of the love of my life.

I reached out trembling fingers.

Except...

I let them drop and leaned in. Nose-to-nose.

Instead of a gaunt, sacrificial Christ wearing a crown of thorns, this one was more than well fed. Unblemished and jolly. My stomach lurched.

Jesus lounged with the too-small cross in front of him, his arms draped around the symbol of torture as if they were old friends. As if his life and death was some big happy hoo-ha.

I backed away, stumbling over a stone in my hurry. *Unity in Diversity* curved across its rectangular surface. I caught an impression of a slot, some buttons, some words about payment.

I bolted. My feet thudded on the smashed

cardboard.

The hum of a vehicle's approach caught my attention.

"Where? Who's coming?" Melody released the lid over us with a bang.

The questions hung in the warm, putrid air around me. I wedged my shaking hands between my knees.

"But, Dove? It might *not* be someone wicked. Coming. I can't get a good read in here. So maybe you don't have to worry so bad?"

Who cared about a car? I didn't, not now.

That lie, that blasphemous image of a Jesus, made it clear—this place was wrong. Evil.

But yet...there *was* a Jesus here. And this *was* a church, according to the sign.

I gripped my hair. Would the Spirit whisper anything in my ear?

But I gave up fast.

And this car?

Even if I had a flea's chance that the occupant loved Christ and would help us, would I wimp out more than Melody-mouse and miss a possible blessing?

"Scoot over." I kneeled, letting her grip my cold fingers.

A road must run, hidden, on the far side of the church because the squashed egg vehicle rested by last night's working lantern. I squinted at the two women climbing out.

Christians?

None like any I've ever seen.

Their hair swung immodestly free in big swoops like curly willow leaves. And way too much arm and leg showed. The stick-heeled shoes weren't only impossible to climb in, but loud. They'd never slip past an enemy.

Melody breathed protest when my hand spasmed into a fist.

Click-clack. Click-clack.

They reached the arch I'd failed to get to, and the one with fiery hair tugged the handle on the frosted glass.

"No way." She yanked at the door again and then turned to her friend. The way the yellow-haired one threw her head back reminded me of Wolfe.

"I love it." She dabbed her huge eye. "With all you claim to give, and they're not even open. Talk about throwing your money away. And our time. Now what're you trying?"

"C'mon. You grab a mat too." The redhead reemerged from under the shadowed arch. "That's what they're here for."

The blonde backed away with her hands up. "Gross. I can smell the wet dog stink from here. Caroline. I'm not touching—let alone kneeling on that thing."

"It's *your* daughter's wedding. After that storm, I wouldn't leave your weather to chance. Come pray."

"Your prayers will be enough, I'm sure."

"Fine." The lady, Caroline, flopped her maroon mat down next to the *Unity in Diversity* rectangle at the globe. Gingerly she kneeled, and her hands came together, red-tipped nails skywards.

"You. Look. Ridiculous."

The air in front of the kneeler wavered until it solidified into an opaque bald head. "Greetings. And welcome to the United Church of America Spiritual

Well Being Center. Where unity is founded in diversity. And may you receive the peace you are searching for. Please listen to your options, make your selection, and follow the prompts for maximum fulfillment."

The sun inched higher in the sky while the disembodied head droned on, guiding the kneeling woman through a bunch of brainless activities.

Breathing. Visualization. Chanting.

I felt as relieved as the redhead looked when she at last blurted out her request for sunshine tomorrow.

There'd been a lot of giggling during the chanting. But the bald guy had kept unbreakable serenity when he'd reaffirmed the organization was spiritual and *not* religious. Although he'd almost broken his monotone when he'd declared the American Church's non-tolerance to those who were non-tolerant of others' beliefs.

In other words, this church was non-tolerant of me. Someone who believed in one way to Heaven and one Savior.

Bald Guy vanished and the birds sounded back up.

My nose wrinkled in disgust. Praying? These people deserved what was coming to them in the end. Fire and fury.

All of a sudden, a familiar girl's face wavered before me. Then her brother's. Both morphed back into the shimmering pavement.

I glanced toward the obscured road. Did those two ever come here? Since this wasn't some hidden, sacred refuge after all, did Wolfe and Jezebel ever come and kneel before this glittering globe and ask the bogus forces of the universe for electric power? And indoor showers?

What might life be like for someone like them? A pagan. Someone who didn't know the true God.

What was their point in getting up each morning? How'd they fall asleep at night without screaming in terror about their future?

But then, what were they supposed to do other than keep breathing and going through the motions of life? Give up and die? For them, death would be no better. It'd be much worse.

No way. I would not gnaw my nails over their eternity. Getting to my Council, preventing some unknown massive bloodshed, and keeping Melody alive. Those tasks were enough.

"Carol? What...where are you going?"

I jerked myself back to attention. I'd let it slide when the women reentered their smooth vehicle, but now Caroline poised on the pavement with a blank face, laughter gone. Under my stare, an ugly, focused expression solidified.

"To the dumpster over there..." She drifted off as if listening. "Hand me my purse. I want my self-defense knife/hairbrush Cain gave me. I need it."

I eased the lid down. In the gloom, Melody and I gaped at each other.

"What are you talking about, Carol? I don't see anything. Get back in the car."

"But—"

"If, no joking, you think a creep's hanging around over there, then get in and let's go. C'mon. Quick."

The engine started. I decided the woman who'd received a nudge from Satan had returned inside the vehicle. I took a breath. Melody copied.

Tires screeched, and a muffled voice cried, "Whoa,

whoa, whoa! Carol! Now where are you going?"

"Dumpster." Through the sides of the bin, Caroline's voice resonated low and angry. "Unlock my door and let me out—"

Her friend's laugh wavered, unsure. "And if you try for the window, I'm rolling it up." Her humor died. "Caroline? What's wrong with you? Put away your brush—I mean your knife. You're scaring me."

The engine revved. Over the sound of the tires rolling away, the redhead's reply was no longer angry but panicked and hysterical. "Stop, stop, stop! I've got to go. Let me out! I've got to. I've got to. I've got to."

The chant faded when the scream began. Caroline's scream.

16

The blood-curdling sound crippled me, reminded me of the day my dad had died while my mom watched from her platform—unable to get to him.

The high-pitched, vocal-chord-ripping noise of Caroline's agony grew.

I fell forward, away from Melody who curled over with her ears between her knees. Suffering and wickedness wrapped around my skull so tight I couldn't think. Evil surged through the air. Satan's anger. His punishment.

It pulsated and sparked around me like static, tugging at my skin, hungry.

I gripped my legs harder and tried to anchor myself to something substantial—anything—while swallowing the bile in my throat.

Hold on. Hold on. Hold on to His promises.

My lips mouthed the words.

They meant nothing.

Nothing existed. Nothing was real. Nothing except that never-ending scream of the Heathen being punished by her master for failing to stop me.

I've got you. Dwell on me. In me.

Yes. No...I can't.

I riffled through my crippled brain, trying to stumble on a promise I could cling to. One to keep me from falling apart and going crazy from the demonic energy that pressed down.

But the evil trapped me in a place where nothing good could exist.

In my mind's eye, I fell to the forest floor. Dogs descended. And Melody disappeared, lost. The pine needles back home welled up red while my mom cried—not for my dad. But for her son. For her parents. For me.

A million years later, the scream subsided, and the excited crackling in the air dissipated.

With a groan, I opened my eyes. Melody lay motionless. Unconscious, but breathing.

I rocked back and forth, clutching my head.

The sound of suffering had stopped. Had that lady obeyed her master? Escaped the car? Was she outside right now, standing on the other side of this wall, inches away, with her knife?

I dropped my hands and balled them up. Then I cracked open the lid a millimeter.

My breath came out in a gush.

The clearing was empty. No women and no car—as if I'd imagined everything. Only Melody's state affirmed it'd been real. And the unnatural silence. The birds, like me, seemed to sense something off about the air. A prickly heaviness about the place.

I sank back onto my cardboard.

I—Dove Strong—was a big, fat, stinking failure.

I thought I was strong in God. But I wasn't. How had I gotten so weak that Satan could overpower me? I'd cowered under his assault. Cracked.

And what had I done with the spiritual armor God equipped me with? My armor to withstand this type of attack?

Nothing, that's what. The Armor of God wasn't

something I could misplace. Stupidly, I'd forgotten to use it.

I nudged Melody with my shoe.

No response.

Slow and clumsy in the atmosphere of doom, I slid my fingers an inch past my sweat-drenched hairline to where the gold tattooed outline of the Helmet of Salvation hid. My helmet. The piece that protected my head from believing Satan's lies.

I clambered to my knees. My hands lifted skyward and plucked an invisible helmet, a reminder of God's gift.

Thank you.

After shoving it over my hair, my hands traveled down to my Breastplate of Righteousness. I yanked at the neckline of my shirt and located the rolling swoop of silver against my skin that marked its top edge.

"Lord, it is *Your* righteousness—Your perfection and not my own fumbling attempt at it that protects my heart from Satan's blows." I mimed, slipping the impenetrable—but invisible—breastplate over my head. Then, I smoothed it over my chest and stomach.

My hands paused in the area of my waist where my Belt of Truth was fastened. I began re-buckling the spiritual one, cinching it tighter around myself. Because I hadn't used it at all.

Truth! Ha! I'd let the father of lies fool me into thinking I was too weak to carry out my mission—that my failure was a done deal. But now I remembered the truth. It wasn't by *my* strength I'd carry this through, but by the Lord's supreme power.

My damp feet, encased in mud-caked cloth, were next. Under these layers, words etched in gold to form sandals spelled out *Shalom*—Amhebran for *peace.*

But I didn't need to readjust this piece of armor. Hadn't I traveled into unfriendly territory without lashing out against the godless? I stayed peaceful. As much as anyone could expect.

I brushed through to the next—my shield and sword. Had I attempted to protect myself with my Shield of Faith?

My cheeks burned. I'd doubted God's ability to protect me. I snatched another shield from above, this one wide and sturdy enough to withstand Satan's flaming darts. Never again would doubt sneak past and touch me.

And I wouldn't let my Sword of the Spirit grow rusty again, either. The last few days I hadn't kept His promises in the forefront of my mind, and during the assault I hadn't parried the blows.

Invisible sword in hand, I cut the air and sliced between garbage bags.

Melody, chin to knees, watched me.

"Just strengthening my armor." With a last grunt, I side-scooted and parried, denting the cardboard under my shins. "How's yours?"

Couldn't be in too great of shape. Since you passed out.

Still jabbing, I ducked to hide my grin.

Melody hissed.

I pivoted to face her. My sword and shield arms stayed out.

The hissing grew, accompanied by a rustling-rattle of plastic.

Her face and throat hadn't twitched. Either she was a genius at this animal sound business or...

I scanned the shadows behind her until I found it. A light brown coil with black markings. It stayed wedged in a crevice where the tower of stacked bags brushed the lid.

Venomous rattlesnake or non-venomous Oregon Bullsnake? I couldn't make the call without a head or tail in sight.

Another sinister sound came from under me. Faint rustling under the chair hinted it was still buried deep. A rustle...or a rattle?

Blood thundered in my ears, drowning out everything else.

Two snakes? Even more impossible we'd slept with them. But I didn't doubt the malevolent energy had woken them, riled them, and excited them to carry out their master's job.

A finger of movement made me look up. Another eased itself down through the largest crack over Melody's head.

Number three was a monster. As if on purpose, it kept itself crooked into the shadows so I couldn't see its head shape.

"Hey, Melody." My bored tone clashed with my adrenaline-surging body. "Shove over my way a little."

How brainless of me to hope she wouldn't have heard the snakes and registered the threat. In her complete, paralyzing, shutdown mode, her deer-eyes stared over my head.

Soon that monster would drop down on her.

I could grab her. If I moved slowly enough, I could pull her out of the way without precipitating an attack.

Unless she panicked. Or screamed.

So that plan was out.

She continued to stare at a spot above my head until a prickling raced over my scalp.

I tilted my head back. My gaze slid across the black, cracked plastic. They stopped at the silent viper whose triangular nose came a yard from my hair.

Slit eyes.

Not a bullsnake.

A rattler.

Melody's scream shook the bin.

I spared a glance her way—in time to see the monster free falling onto her arms.

Light flashed. A sonic boom shook me. The Brae girl was still upright and shrieking, but the snake had vanished.

I didn't question the miracle. The enraged rattling above my head told me my threat hadn't appreciated the noise and bright blast. I squirmed away with nowhere to go.

My eyes darted between the shivering cardboard and the strained crack above, where the muscular body glided deeper into the heart of the garbage bin.

A second miracle. Oh, Lord. Let there be a second miracle.

The creature above disappeared—but this time without a flash or bang or a vapor puff. The thing left the way it came. In a smooth, lightning-quick reverse.

I still gaped at the spot of the second miracle when sunshine blinded me.

Light flooded the garbage piles and rusty metal. Squinting, I made out black-rimmed fingernails on a scratch-scarred hand holding the bin's lid ajar.

I reached a hand toward the silhouette of a ragged, bearded face. "Help."

A long stick thrust straight at me drove me cringing to the side, dodging the forked end that seized the newly emerged rattler. The spear flicked up in a blur, flinging the long, writhing body away.

After the stick plucked another snake from behind

Melody, I escaped. Catapulting over the metallic side, I crashed onto hot blacktop.

The stranger tossed the lid open behind me with a reverberating bang.

Four snakes peppered the tar—a couple were smallish in size, but two were freaky giants. The flapping boot stepped down on the head of a live one, immobilized between the stick's prongs.

He bent to speak to it. "He will crush your head, and you will strike his heel." His boot twisted.

The rattling died.

I backed against hot metal. "They're dead, Melody." I attempted the same tone my aunt always used with little Jovie. "Come on out now. It's safe, from the rattlers. C'mon. Do you need help?"

I glanced inside. Eyes closed, her head rotated back and forth.

"Hey. No more of that." I snapped my fingers. "Get out. Now. If you don't, I'm leaving you in there."

While I waited for my threat to sink in, I kept tabs on the guy messing with the snakes.

I'd never met a filthier human. Even my six male relatives weaseling out of the once-a-week bathing couldn't compete. But I'd never before seen a beard so stained I couldn't guess its original color. The only way the shredded gray cloth covering his wiry limbs stayed together was because of the splotches of gunk coating it.

From under the shaggy brows I received unexpected eye contact. Intense gray. My dry throat spasmed in a swallow.

Maybe he wasn't Satan's agent since he'd helped us, but then who? Who was he?

Without blinking, he made another crunch sound

under his boot. His grip on that lethal stick turned his knuckles white under their tan and grime.

I needed Melody's help to make this safety call.

As I squirmed up, balancing my hips on the bin's edge, I felt a tickle way back in my subconscious. Of something I should know. Something I couldn't remember. A piece of information connected with this stranger.

Yet, I didn't know too many people. How could I have forgotten if we'd met? Had my grandma told me a story about a ragged stranger? Or had I seen his picture? Pictures plastered the walls of Wolfe's and Jezebel's home.

I dragged Melody up the bin's side with a couple new rib bruises that took my breath away. I let go too soon and her backside hit the asphalt while I held my side.

"Crush the serpent's head, and he will strike your heel."

Was this code? Him asking us to help him, or warning us to stay away? Whatever. I was keeping my distance from this snake genocide going on here.

I retreated a yard, dragging along the frozen Brae girl. "We should get going. And that was great, what you did. I'm..." I cleared my throat. "Uh, thanks—"

Melody shrieked and collapsed at those wrecked boots, trying to hug them while he retreated out of range. "Thank you, sir. Thank you, thank you..."

Her complete trust jarred me. But I shook with silent laughter. Because whatever fear the snakes hadn't been able to stir up in this stranger, this girl's sobbing gratitude did the job. Keeping his distance, he threw her a wary glance. Then went back to shuffling between snakes.

He threw back his head at the cloudless sky. Then he bent down and scooped up the two biggest rattlers—both headless. They dangled from his scarred fists as he neared, giving Melody extra space.

He thrust them at me. "If you offer your food to the hungry and satisfy the needs of the afflicted, then your light shall rise in the darkness and your gloom will be like the noonday."

My mouth opened in surprise. His words...that was pure Bible talk. He spoke in Bible verses.

Right then, I caught sight of the tattoo on his neck's sun-browned skin, half-covered by beard. It showed the true, sacrificial Lamb of God. Blood and thorns...and beautifully inked. The work of an artist. A genius.

Homesickness pierced my heart. *Oh, Trinity. I miss you.*

My stomach lurched in anticipation of the meat that'd soon fill it. No doubt this guy could use all the snake meat himself, but I was too starved to be a martyr today.

Stepping forward, I trod on another rattler's carcass as I grabbed the offered food. "Yeah. This will help keep us going a while longer on our way to—"

"Oh! You should come with us." Melody held out both hands to him. "Please, please come. Though, we're heading to Mount Washington first because, well, Dove here says someone's waiting for us there...a warrior, she thinks, but we're not sure which way to go to get there because we got turned around last night running from—"

I squeezed her wrist for quiet.

His lips moved, struggling to speak.

What if he was a prophet? This could be a message

from God.

My lips twitched too, impatient for his words.

"He waited another seven years and then released the dove again." He sighed as if he'd won a battle and then squinted at me. Expectantly.

I felt my face fall. He'd picked a random Scripture that included my name. Dove. He'd even messed up the words. It was supposed to be seven *days*, not years.

This guy was no prophet. Only a Christian who wandered around pagan territory because his brain couldn't figure out somewhere to hide like the rest of us. Even if he *could* kill snakes like that.

Melody patted his arm in pretend understanding. "Even so, that's good, fresh meat laying there on the ground. And we shouldn't leave it there to rot, right Mister, Mister, uh, what's your name?"

"Then Samuel said to all the people, 'This is the man the Lord has chosen as your king. No one—'"

"So, you'll grab them then, Mr. Samuel?" When he didn't respond, Melody motioned to me. "Or Dove can? You want Dove to? Oh, wait. Is it Sam? You want me to call you Sam? Is that it?"

I let my shoulders rise and fall in answer to his beseeching look. *What?*

"You!" The shout ripped across the clearing.

Melody and I whipped around. But Samuel—no way was he a Sam—didn't even glance at the church's glass doors where the bald man shook his fist at us.

I recognized the head. Although this time it wasn't semitransparent, and it had a body of snowy robes attached. They rippled behind him when he moved out of the arch's shade. The red dot in the center of his forehead glowed like an extra eye, while the gold symbols of his necklace shone mirror-like.

"Don't play deaf. I know you can hear me." His face morphed from red to violet. "I told you never to come back here, you bum! It's illegal to harass people who come to seek spiritual healing. And I don't want you digging in my dumpster either. The cops are on their way.

"Girls. Come away from him. He hasn't bothered you in any way, has he?" He recoiled a step, perceiving our earthy clothes. Our coiled hair. The bloody snake corpses dangling from my fists.

He stumbled backwards until half-hidden behind the arch. "Oh, ho ho! There's three of you now? Having a little *powwow*?" Sunlit white flecks shot out from the shadows. "A powwow in my parking lot? You all stay right there until the cops arrive."

Stay right here? How dumb. He was terrified and wasn't holding a weapon.

Samuel scooped up the snakes, shoving them inside his frayed shirt. He slipped between the nearest trees.

I followed him. Stepping onto the pine needles was a comfort to my rubbed soles.

Soon we couldn't hear the shouts. He led us through the increasingly dense groundcover until we passed between two huge lodge pole pines. More pavement sprawled ahead.

Melody and I hesitated at the road's outer white line, but Samuel strode forward until he straddled its blazing yellow one. He thrust his stick at the horizon—at Mount Washington's sharp peak. Dwarfed by a nearer hill, it loomed over the treetops in the distance. Dark, twisted, and larger than I'd ever seen it.

In all our blind running through Satan's obstacles last night, God had kept us perfectly on course.

The blacktop under my feet hummed the warning. We made it back into the protection of the trees before the silver pickup rounded the bend.

"Samuel!" Next to me Melody made a noise like a strangled cat.

We watched through the gaps of a berry bush, helpless to save Samuel still in the middle of the road.

The truck sliced past, blaring its horn. A white container flew out the window. Its contents—liquid pink—nailed him in the torso and thigh.

While the mess dripped down his body, he wandered down the yellow line, pointing.

I breathed again and darted into the road, catching hold of his arm. "Samuel. You can't stand in the open like that when cars come. You'll get hit. Killed. Get to cover next time."

He shook his walking stick at the horizon.

"Yeah. I see, I see. Mount Washington." I released his arm and scrubbed the pink stickiness onto my pant leg. "Now get off this road."

He followed me onto the coarse pebbles to Melody.

"Oh, Samuel. Please. Please come with Dove and me. There'll be people at Mount Jefferson— people like us, like you. Christians, you know? They'll help you. Give you food. Take care of you. Right, Dove?"

The smoky irises flickered to mine.

I shrugged. Then worked at some sap I'd discovered on my wrist. "Oh, uh, yeah. Sure. You could come."

Melody sighed. She sounded exasperated.

Although I appreciated what this guy had done with the snakes, if I talked him into tagging along, he'd likely lead us to the nearest group of Heathen, for the simple reason he didn't know any better.

In the distance, a police siren wailed. I forgot the sap and stepped for the bushes.

But Samuel traveled the road again, shaking his fist at the horizon. "Jesus replied, 'Now is not the right time for me to go, but you can go anytime.'"

Whew. Not coming.

Melody tossed up her hands. She strolled closer to the ditch where I'd seen some decent water.

I contorted my shoulder for my bottle. "Well if you change your mind and decide to get some help for yourself, Samuel, head for Jefferson." I finished checking for possible garbage sludge. "That's where we'll end up. Do you know..."

A frenzy of rustling to my left froze my tongue.

Melody emerged from the bushes, one palm cradling a few maroon-colored berries. She raised her other hand to her lips.

"Drop them, you idiot!" I reached her in four steps and knocked the small pile onto the ground. "They're baneberries—heart stoppers. Did you eat—"

"Hawk-a-bubbees."

"Out! Spit them out!"

She swallowed fast. "But...but...huckleberries? They're huckleberries. Not poisonous. I swear. We had a bush of them next to our pond entrance back home once. I promise."

"You'd better be right." I turned on my heel and marched back to the road.

Dumb Gilead and all his stupid warnings about everything. About lethal baneberries—whatever those were. He had me all paranoid.

I stumbled to a halt.

The road stretched empty. Both directions. I

scanned the still woods on either side of us. "Uh. Melody? Where'd he go?"

She paused in her hunt for scattered berries. "Samuel? *Samuel!*"

"Forget it. He's gone."

"What? But—"

"Yeah. How did you like that? Him leaving us right when you'd ingested poisonous fruit. Not hanging around to see if you died or not."

"Huckleberries, Dove."

"Whatever. My point—we're better off."

I scooped up ditch water too fast and ended up with silt. Then I marched back into the pines. We'd parallel the road, I decided, until the trees thinned enough to see the range. Or at least a horizon. No point in getting lost again.

"Super weird, though." She spoke through her mouthful, trailing me so closely she came down on the back of my shoe.

"Mmm?" I concentrated on the distant siren that had started up again but now faded.

"The way Sam *bam* appeared, then *whoa* disappeared. Hey!" She clutched my arm.

"Please quit touching me."

"But, Dove. Don't you see? He's an angel! Sent from heaven to help us. It totally makes sense if you stop and think about it."

For the rest of the day, I kept my eyes peeled for Samuel while we hiked through the wilderness paralleling the strip of road labeled Highway 20. But he never showed.

And no matter what I told her, Melody remained hung up on her crazy idea that we'd had a run-in with a heavenly being sent to help us.

I stopped arguing. But I didn't buy it. Something about Samuel convinced me he was as human as I was.

17

I wiggled my numb toes inside my shoes. In the predawn gray, I made out the motionless lump of Melody beside me, sleeping under the silvery, taped-together sheets I both loved and hated.

I loved the way they kept me from dying of hypothermia. Loved their weightlessness, and they took up zero room in my pack. I hated the way they made each of our sleep sounds—leg twitches, nose scratches—sound like prowlers stomping in dry leaves.

I bolted upright and pulled my own off with a crackle. I filled my lungs with the smoky air. It clawed at my throat.

I leaped to the ground and scrambled over to last night's miniscule campfire we'd used to cook our trout. The red mud and ash slop felt ice cold under my fingertips.

Five seconds later, I was back under our tent that dangled a-third of the way up a tree. Holding a broken tree limb, I nudged the sagging bottom section.

A frenzy of rustling above startled a passing chipmunk so much it ran over my shoe. Melody's deer eyes squinted down. "Whew. It's you."

I waved the branch. "Smoke."

She broke off mid-yawn. "Mmm? It's OK. Won't hurt us. At least, not meant to." Her head disappeared like a turtle retracting into its shell.

I headed toward the trickle of a stream. This time two trout waited for me in the shadowy spot.

While we ate, the sun emerged over the tree-covered slope that filled the eastern horizon and within minutes revealed every pine needle. But to the west, Mount Washington remained fuzzy and indistinct, veiled by the dingy cloud that clung to it. A solid plume of gray rose steadily from the peak's dark green base.

I gestured at it and added my remaining fish to Melody's. No longer hungry.

She shoveled it in with both hands and chewed mechanically, her eyes on the horizon. "I don't *like* it, but it doesn't feel like it's anything that's going to hurt us. Like, not from an attacker or nothing. You know?"

"Hurry and finish up, Melody."

Hugging myself against the morning chill and the dread that life was about to get more uncomfortable, I packed up my tent. By the time I erased every sign of our campout, Melody had sucked the fish juice off her fingers. And I was ready to shoulder my pack and face west—toward the mountain that continued to smolder.

~*~

We are taking way too long.

The constant thought nagged at me. It chipped away at my faith in a way nothing else in my life ever had.

Too long. Too long.

The warrior had given up on us by now. That is, if he'd even known we were coming to begin with, which had never been clear. Either way, he'd taken off for Mount Jefferson—and the Council—on his own. Without us.

Yet, because I couldn't force my cowardly self to say this to Melody, we plodded forward. Continuing on this now pointless detour to Mount Washington.

It didn't matter anymore that we'd passed the brilliant jade lake into the burned-out foothills where evidence of fires was everywhere—some decades-old fires, and others much more recent. We were going to miss the Council meeting. Or maybe we'd missed it yesterday, or were missing it right this second.

It had to be September by now. The destroyed trees told me nothing, but the chill of the thick air and the darkness that fell earlier each day, both promised early autumn.

For the thousandth time, my fingers smoothed the plastic-bagged prayer results against my leg. Again, I prayed my apology for failing.

My arms pulled my body up the slope using the chalky-white trunks whose branches would never sprout green again.

If only I'd left my home two weeks earlier. But how could I have known about the ravine with undercut sides we'd had to cross? Or that it would take us four days to figure out how?

Or the black bear. How could I have guessed he'd settle under our tree tent one morning before even the birds were awake. He hadn't moved until the next evening. Well, other than to rear up on his hind legs with those curved, brown claws against our trunk. The grunting noises he'd made at our feet, sniffing to make sure we hadn't escaped.

I'd heard Satan whooping *that* whole thirty-six hours.

Say it, Dove. Move your cowardly lips. "Melody, it's too late. The warrior's gone on without us. And we're never going to make it in time to deliver our families' results.

"Oh, and I sort of never told you this, but because I've failed, both our families are going to die in some freaky, bloody way that only God knows. And some others will die too. But don't worry about being an orphan because we'll never survive this forest fire we're heading into. Either that or we'll be eaten by the next demon bear Satan sends our way."

I heard a snarl. A clicking snap of teeth.

Bear! But I lurched away from a skinny boxer dog. Tethered to a downed log a few feet away, its threatening rumble escaped its bared teeth.

I hauled Melody upright and ran past the faded green tarp. The savage barking faded in the hazy twilight. Panting, we collapsed onto the warm ground.

"Sorry. My bad." Her ragged voice sounded used up.

"Then we have to stop for the night. Since you've proven you can't sense danger anymore." Everything—not only running into the dog without warning—had become her fault now. "You're giving up. Choosing to be weak and not using your gift. So stop it. It doesn't count that we're close. Close isn't good enough. Close means we lose. And if the warrior's still around here somewhere, we need to be focused on where he'll be waiting."

My "if" seemed to echo in the too-silent woods. And I wasn't ready for *that* conversation. "I mean, we can't stumble around this whole mountain blindly searching. C'mon. Think. Where?"

Where? Where?

I got no reply.

The heels of her hands screwed into her eye sockets. "It's this smoke. If it'd only clear out for one minute. It's leeching through my eyeballs into my cranium. Everything's all smudgy and unreal, you know?"

I swiped at my own streaming tears with my tunic. "Quit thinking about it. C'mon. Where'll he be waiting? Should we find a campground? Or a hiking trail?"

But I'd ruled out both options days ago. A Christian—no matter how capable—wouldn't hang out on the pagans' groomed turf.

I shook my head. "Forget it. It's dumb."

"So, then, we'll follow the smoke." She mumbled this into her fur collar—only half conscious, judging by her body's slump.

My gray cells struggled in my tainted oxygen supply, turning her words over. "Huh? What's that mean, 'follow the smoke?' Melody. Wake up."

"Mmm? What?" She jerked. Then she shrugged and resumed her slump. "It seems like... shouldn't we find where it's coming from? Forget it. Sorry."

"No. Wait a sec." I squeezed my eyes shut and listened for the small voice that guided me so well. At least, when I paid attention.

My lids snapped open. "You're right! It's the smoke. It *is* for us after all. But not something dangerous. It's for us to follow like a trail. Follow the smoke! He set the fire! And if it's still burning, even a little, he might still be there too."

Thank You, Jesus! Every step of the way, You provide. I love You!

More than you can fathom. The silent reply set goose bumps racing down my arms and legs.

"I'm coming, warrior," she sang into her cupped hands. "Hold tight. Don't give up on me." She released her message into the smoky air the way my mother does a bird. Flinging it up and on its way.

Even before I lumbered onto my feet, she'd shouldered her bag and was striding off through an impossible nettle patch that'd somehow avoided the last fire. "Let's do this."

~*~

A darkness of a Dead Night fell when we stumbled out from between the last of the ruined trees. The sooty blanket had eclipsed the quarter moon hours ago, leaving us blind.

Arms extended, fingers splayed, I patted and gripped the pieces of vertical rock in front of us—the true base of Mount Washington, I guessed. It was the first thing I'd felt in forever that wasn't charcoal or crumbled ash.

We have a smoker back home. The rabbit meat that comes out of it is brown, crusty, and shrunken. That was probably what my lungs looked like now. Twin slabs of smoked meat.

"Which way?" I tried to say the words, but I started to hack so hard my head drifted like the warm ash that resettled with each step.

Melody gripped my fingers. Still coughing, I floated after. My left hand trailed over the rough mountain next to me, never leaving it.

She must've chosen the right direction, though, because the air got thicker. And we followed the smoke to find the warrior.

I could breathe again. A hard slap of untainted breeze sailed down the mountainside and whisked away the smothering cloud.

While I pulled my collar down from my mouth and gulped in pure oxygen, I studied the orange flicker in the distance. A contained bonfire? We hadn't crossed paths with active wildfire in all our searching. Surely the out-of-control fire threat was out by *now*. Wasn't it?

Lord?

"Safe, Dove. Safe, safe, safe. That's him ahead. The warrior. I know it."

I removed my hand from her clutch. "Maybe."

Lord, is it? Is it him?

"Stealth mode, Melody. I'm not sure yet."

"But it is!"

"Maybe."

As we crept nearer the campfire's glow, I began to make out shapes. Two people sat. No, three. No. Two, because one of them was gigantic. Big enough for two.

A few steps closer...

Both strangers reclined against a fallen log or boulder, facing us. They didn't appear to see or hear us yet. Their beards tilted down while they relaxed their arms against kneecaps.

We inched forward. But the moment the edges of firelight illuminated the terrain under our feet, Melody did the most lamebrain thing ever.

She bolted. Straight at the strangers.

"Wait!" I grabbed at her and captured air.

She swung around—either because she'd heard me or to let me lead. It didn't matter why. Never in my life had I wished so hard I'd never met Melody Brae.

My foot caught one of hers planted in my path,

and I lunged forward. My stomach slammed down on the hard ground, missing the fire. "Oof!"

My line of vision was now level with two pairs of leather-clad feet, way larger than my own and smudged with black. I stared at those shoes.

Lifting my gaze, I discovered neither stranger had moved, except, of course, that they watched me now. Weirdly, neither seemed startled that I'd appeared out of nowhere sprawled at their feet—although the smaller one might have grinned. Not with his mouth— that stayed a noncommittal line in his thin beard. But with his eyes.

"Sorry." Melody's hand knocked against my hair when I glared up.

The firelight reflected off her deer eyes.

I followed her stare and then cringed against the ground, flattening myself like a cornered hare.

The giant had sprung to his feet so lightning quick and soundless I'd missed it. His bulk now towered over me. Giant—the word defined him. He made Gilead seem normal sized. Runty even.

I flinched away from the hand extended down to me.

"E-hem."

The fake cough came from the twiggy guy still reclining.

A millisecond later the giant resumed his place against the log. One hand divided and smoothed the dark blonde strands of his Adam's-apple length beard.

Gilead had developed that same childish habit the first few months his facial hair grew enough to fiddle with. A habit he'd long ago dropped.

My suspicious gaze roamed back to the cougher, who, like his larger companion, I discovered couldn't be much older than me.

Wide-set in his angular face, his blue eyes didn't laugh anymore. Under their façade of laziness, they scorched a path taking in my ash-flecked hair, sliding loose from its coil. The lopsided breastplate of my streaked shirt. The way I shoved myself back onto my feet with one arm.

"Ahh," he spoke in Amhebran, inclining his head at me. "*That's* why it took you so long."

18

I jerked myself out of Melody's excited grip and strode back into the darkness toward the smoke.

"Why's your elbow bandaged?"

I froze mid stomp and touched my long sleeve hiding the thin layer of moss wrapped around my healing elbow.

"And who did that to your face?"

I faced the fire, but that question wasn't for me. His gaze held Melody's while he mimicked his own tanned cheekbone.

Hers held the last stage of a bruise that'd never been impressive. By now it was the faintest yellow, impossible to see under the layer of patchy soot—a complete opposite of my own face, still a mess of scrapes and swollen areas that couldn't be hidden. I knew. I'd seen my damaged reflection clear enough on the lake's surface.

"I understand your reservation and caution. Both are essential to our survival as well. So don't worry, Song Bird." He nodded at Melody. "I won't take your silence personally. I get how worn out you are—you too, Dove of Peace. It's too bad you had to travel all the way to Mount Washington. It would've been much fairer for us to have met in the middle somewhere."

I crossed my arms. "How...do you know...who I am?"

He slung an arm over the log behind him. "I'm right, then. It's Dove of Peace, or, perhaps you go by Dove? Stone and I've been sitting here for a long time—which we'll assume isn't your fault, so don't storm off--trying to puzzle out other interpretations for the vision that kept us waiting."

"Vision?"

"Yes, Dove. A vision's like a dream. Something you see and by faith believe—"

I gritted my teeth. "What was your vision?"

"An image of two birds flying our way. A white one grasped an olive branch and trailed a smaller bird who sang the same beautiful trill over again."

I heard my partner's sharp intake. "A melody?"

He clutched his forehead. "Melody. How dense of me not to have pieced that one together. The 'melody' bird of my friend's dream also possessed the uncanny ability to locate and reroute around predator hawks. Long before the hawks could sight it."

I cleared my throat. "Before we break into applause that you know all about us, how about you tell us who you are? I was told to meet 'the warrior' at this spot. I heard nothing about two people. You called him 'Stone.'" The large hand twisting beard paused. "So who are you?"

"Reed." The skinny talker shrugged, intent on Melody, whose eyes were glued to giant Stone. The latter didn't raise his from his shoes.

"Ah! Yes." Reed clapped his companion's wide shoulder. "Behold. The perfect warrior specimen, wouldn't you say, Melody? He's tall enough for you?"

"Y-yes."

"And muscled enough? A warrior's got to be robust."

"Oh, um...yes?" Her voice sounded strange to me. Kind of breathless. Relieved? No. Happy. "Yes, yes of course."

"And let's see. What else do we like about our warrior? Ah. His quick reflexes! Don't you think, Melody, when he moves—"

"Cut it out!" I lurched in front of her with arms spread wide as if to block her from Reed's next question. "Melody, don't answer. He's playing you. Stone isn't the warrior. Reed is. So lay off her."

"You knew?"

I didn't answer Reed. I staggered from the intensity of my own reaction—the out-of-the-blue defensiveness that'd reared up inside. Like I couldn't stand for anyone to crush Melody. I'd had to shield her. *Had* to. And, well, shielding wasn't normal for me, unless it involved defending my Lord. And only because I loved Him so much.

Reed shifted against the log. "I meant to demonstrate the irony of God's workmanship. In other words, it was a joke. A bad one. Sorry, Melody. It's true, though. God made me the 'warrior' of the family. Even if he gave Stone the body for it."

"But not the smarts." Stone flashed a one-second smile. Then he ducked his head while his ears and forehead glowed pink in the firelight. "Observation. Intuition. Strategizing. Those are Reed's babies. I'm terrible at figuring things out."

"Well, my smarts are observing we're getting smoked out since the wind's changed. So..." Reed rose to his feet, causing Melody to clutch my arm and gasp. "Let's head to where we can breathe for the night."

"You've got..." For once in my life, I bit back the words that nearly flung themselves off my tongue.

You've got a deformed foot. And a short, twisted leg, warrior Reed. You, warrior, are lame, damaged, and weaker than I am.

And you've got a monster bobcat behind you.

Dumb to say since they'd been leaning against it. That log behind them—yeah, not a log—but the largest bobcat I'd ever seen. And I've seen more than a couple in my sixteen years.

"I've got what?" Reed turned to face me squarely. His lazy-lidded features had transformed to challenge, promising his readiness to tangle with anything—or anyone—who stood against him. To conquer or die trying.

I glanced at the cat that stretched and swiped a stubby paw over its black tufted ear. It settled at the warrior's side like I've seen dogs do with their pagan masters.

I pointed to the huge pile of pulsating red embers and blackened rubble. "You've got to extinguish that."

"Why? What else is going to burn around here?" Reed gestured at the charred surroundings in the limited light.

His eyes held mine a second too long and smirked. *I know what you were going to say. You chickened out—changed your direction midcourse. Experienced self-doubt.*

But his voice said, "It was a headache for Stone to find enough burnable wood to keep it going for you this long. I wouldn't worry."

"That's why mountains catch fire. Because of people like you. But that's not what I even meant about extinguishing it, Mr. Insight."

"Oh. Let them come." Reed shrugged, interpreting my meaning correctly this time. "The pagan workers who put out fires are long gone. And if any more of their kind decides to investigate such a small spark, then let them come. We'll be far enough away by then."

~*~

He wasn't joking about the distance we'd put between ourselves and their abandoned campfire tonight. They set a brutal pace—at least for Melody and me, who'd never imagined reaching the warrior only the first half of our day's quest. It must have been killer for Reed too, since his right leg stopped short and rotated inwards. Yet *he* led.

Then, I understood.

When Gilead halfway hacked off an appendage or electrocuted himself checking zip line defenses, he followed up the incident by working with a ferocity that dared anyone to even *think* he was injured or weak.

So, a disabled warrior-guy playing off his disability with a pace that gave everybody a stitch in their sides? I guess it made sense. In that macho-mentality sort of way that wasn't part of my own genetic makeup.

The air was breathable where we hiked—next to the vertical bluff. Sometimes we scrambled around fallen boulders, but even with this, my quivering leg muscles assured me we didn't gain elevation. We also didn't lose it. We hiked around Mount Washington's base without dropping into the foothills.

The filmy haze thinned enough for the moon's light to filter through, revealing that the forest to our right had escaped the most recent fires. I could also see that Melody and I had fallen behind.

I didn't holler "wait up" or anything. I preferred the extra distance between myself and that bobcat.

Never in my life have I trusted a cat. I wasn't about to start tonight.

"Hold it."

The group ahead halted. I could make out Reed's silhouette and the monster bobcat's. But I saw no trace of the giant's.

My gaze flickered to the feathery black shapes of trees down the slope and then to the angular warrior who crouched eye-to-eye with his bobcat, their foreheads touching. So frozen they seemed not to breathe.

The taut silence snapped. Creepy noises—a rusty groan, a fading siren, a rumble—emanated in a nightmarish duet from the human and wild animal. Then, Reed moved. Still kneeling, he thrust one arm out and pointed it at me. *Attack.*

Cold sweat drizzled between my shoulder blades. I uprooted and hauled Melody further into the shadows of a pillar crumbled from the side of the mountain.

"Easy." The pillar behind came to life and held me in place with steadying pressure on each shoulder. "Easy," Stone repeated. "Don't run off. You're OK. He's only sending Darcy back home to let our folks know you made it, and we're on our way to the Council now. It's our signal we'd agreed on, and this is the easiest access route to our home."

"Darcy?" I pretended my pulse wasn't hammering like a manic woodpecker against my skin while watching Darcy caress her forehead against Reed's beard. The cat leaped up the slope without a sound.

Then it melted into the boulders and night.

Stone guided us into a patch of moonlight. Walking next to him, I discovered his tread was as silent as Darcy's. And he'd somehow managed to shift Melody's and my packs to his own shoulder without me noticing. Tricky.

Melody trotted to catch up to Reed. She craned back her head as if trying to see their home at its inky peak. "Your home? Your home is up there?"

"Mmm." Reed ducked his head.

"How many of you live here together? What plants do you eat? I bet there's always enough. Is there? I don't see snow. Does it snow? Do you stay warm when it does?"

Melody's eager questions flowed nonstop while we wound our way around the mountain's base.

After overhearing yet another of Reed's vague responses that didn't reveal anything, I poked her. "Better drop it, Melody. He's not going to tell you much. He considers it probable we'll sell out his location to the devil and later return to pillage his family's food sources."

"No." Stone spoke for the first time since explaining Darcy. "That's not true. We don't think that. Tell 'em, brother."

Reed laughed. "I can't because she's right, at least partly. Melody, it's only habit—not that I mistrust you. Repeat your questions please. I'll try to be real this time."

~*~

By the time we stopped for the night, I knew *way*

too much about these brothers, Reed and Cornerstone Bender. Like their favorite food was turkey vulture. And the intricate, step-by-step process their mom used to turn deer hides into the leaf-thin leather clothing they wore. Melody had grilled them about that one hard. No one had objected when I demanded she stop with the questions.

I'd lagged behind during the grueling *Q* and *A* session. But now I caught up. Reed was explaining the setup of their community.

According to him—and unrefuted by Stone—their family lived with seven other Christian groups halfway up the craggy peak. They called their eight-family community the MTV—mountain top village.

Everybody in the MTV had a job, and the Bender brothers protected their village. They didn't live in the trees like my family. No surprise, since the upper part of Mount Washington looked pretty sparse on green. But the MTV didn't exist underground like Melody's either. The village divided its time between shelters in the open and a cave.

"Isn't everyone freaked out that the godless will get them if they're outside during the day?" Melody crunched in on herself as if to hide at the thought.

Reed frowned. "Of course not. They know I'd never let that happen."

She pulled upright. "Oh! Right."

I shook my head. "Except the major flaw with that line is you're going to be gone now, for weeks at least. Anything could happen to them. What if you get back home and everyone in your MTV is dead?"

For the first time Stone stumbled.

"*Dove.*"

"What, Melody?"

"No, it's OK, Mel." Reed's shoulders shook, which I didn't understand. "Wow. Have faith much, Dove of Peace? Plus, don't you think it likely I've prepared extra precautions in lieu of our absence?"

His brother fell back, shortening his stride to mine. "That's partly why he sent Darcy home instead of bringing her along. She can sense strangers' bad intentions. I guess sort of like her." He nodded at Melody. "Plus, you should see Darcy when she's feeling protective." He shuddered and gripped a shoulder strap, his knuckles blanching white. "It's...she's merciless...terrifying."

I eyed him. "You're no warrior, are you?"

He agreed with a shrug. "Boost up? This ancient deer blind's the best rest spot we got on this side of things."

I realized we'd stopped, and he gestured at a mammoth-sized, crooked rectangle of rotten boards halfway up three tight-growing pine trunks. "No ladder, but I can get you up there all right."

I backed away. After age four, tree dwellers don't accept boosts up or help down.

I held out my hand for my bag. "I'm out of water. I'll rehydrate before climbing up myself."

Reed stepped into Stone's braced hands. "You're in luck." He grasped the branch next to the crow's nest platform. "There's a stream not too far from here."

I turned my head in the direction of the whispering current. "Which is why I said I'm going to rehydrate. Melody? C'mon."

I knew she was out of water too, yet she hesitated.

"I could send Stone with you," Reed suggested from above.

I grabbed both our packs and steered her away. "I

thought you didn't like hanging out in trees. And," I threw over my shoulder "we made it this many weeks without a bodyguard. We'll survive another five minutes."

Reed's voice trailed after. "Don't drop too far down the slope. Or you'll end up in the smoked out area again."

Melody sighed. She sounded, what, *happy* again?

Sky alive! What'd happened to my traveling partner?

Then, it clicked.

I hoped her brain damage from smoke inhalation and high-elevation oxygen deprivation wouldn't be permanent. Her dad might not notice, but her mom was bound to. And that was one conversation on top of everything else I could live without.

~*~

I wiped the drips from my chin with my sleeve and capped my bottle. "You going to wash?"

"Nah. Too cold."

The high elevation and late night had woven themselves into an arctic result. Plus, the flowing water cut like February's ice. But thanks to Reed's self-proving pace, I dripped with sweat.

"Wait for me." I shoved my bottle into my bag. "I'll be quick."

"OK. Sure."

The stream flowed out in the open, its surface glistening in the scant moonlight. I remembered Reed's offer of Stone.

Surveying the smoggy darkness while rolling my

pant legs, I sighted no one but Melody, hugging herself and hopping up and down. I splashed downstream and rounded a curve that blocked her from view. Up ahead I saw what I wanted and beelined for the bushes that promised privacy.

Up close, the brambles overgrowing the stream's edge weren't as concealing as I'd thought. Their branches crumbled between my fingers to brittle splinters, and the smokehouse odor filled my nostrils, which meant I'd wandered too far downhill—at least, according to Reed.

I scanned the stillness of the woods once more before balancing my bag on the tallest section of bush. The moment I let go, my belongings splashed into the shallows at its roots.

With an irritated huff, I bent to fish it out. A small, manmade object on the pebbles caught my eye. I turned the thin rectangle over in my hands. Cool, smooth, but also warped on one side. As if its plastic had melted.

The thing reminded me of the electronic Wolfe had held in his home—the one he'd dropped when I'd demanded my stolen clothes back. This smaller electronic had undergone fire damage. The reason it'd been discarded here as junk.

A sharp edge sliced open my lingering fingertip. I inhaled and released the broken junk back onto the rocks.

Light blasted up. Brilliant light shone from beneath the cracked glass rectangle that faced the sky.

I crouched down in the shallows with my back against the charred bushes so I could study it. Yet I didn't dare touch the image of a man's upside-down face that'd appeared.

I gasped. The man wasn't a picture. The image *moved*. He panted for breath. Sweat trickled off his forehead, leaving lighter trails through patches of soot. An ominous orange glow waxed and waned around the edges surrounding him.

"This is Thomas J. Parker of Portland," the man rasped from next to my fast-numbing feet. "It's day five of our hunt to locate a clan of local fanatics living hidden—illegally—in this national park. Authorities said find proof. And that's what I've got now. Proof. Which is only another reason to get out of this godforsaken place.

"I'm the only one left. Two days ago my team disappeared. I think they're dead. They were, *we* were, further down where the fanatics set that first fire. Murdering fanatics. Maybe I'll be dead too, but—"

A deafening *whoosh* and *bang* drowned him out.

I bit my lip. I recognized that eerie sound. The unmistakable sound a surge of fire makes as it explodes from one treetop into the next.

The crackling roar died…and then I could make out the man's voice again.

But I wished I hadn't been able to. I wished I knew how to make it stop.

Because the man cursed God.

While he ground my Lord's name into the muck, something in my chest hardened. And I gazed into his panic-stricken eyes without gnawing my lip at all.

"Heard that? That's fire. Straight from Hades. Hotter than anything on this planet. Set by a pair of fanatic demons. Been trailing them, hoping they'd lead me to…but it was a trap. A set up. The whole thing. They got me where they wanted me, boxed me in with more hell fire. I'll keep to the water now. My last chance—"

A gigantic shoe eclipsed the image. With a *crack* it extinguished the light and silenced the desperate voice.

I staggered backward and, with a final splash, sat down in the stream.

My eyes located the human figure, pillar-like on the riverbank. "You killed him."

"Please." Stone motioned me forward. "Come on back with me. Forget what you—"

"What I saw? What I heard? Touch me, and I'll scream."

"No, no, you can't. If you do, and they hear, then they'll come. Please. Don't. Don't make more come."

I eased up from the stream but located no escape. He loomed in front of me, agile and fast. The frigid water pushed at my legs from behind and spilled out onto treacherous, slippery riverbanks that kept the forest at bay.

Trapped. I was as trapped as that dying Heathen in his last moments. Had he died where I stood? Not that I cared that the blasphemous man no longer existed. But Stone had killed—no, *murdered*—the man. In cold blood and not even in defense. In defense I could stomach, but not this. And he'd murdered a bunch of others too, if I believed the doomed man. I did.

All around me rushed the crimson of my dream. Bright rivers of warm red wound between the pebbles, dripped from the bushes, and soaked my shoes.

I blinked. The red transformed back to hazy charcoal. Nighttime. And only icy water stained my shoes dark.

"Did you do it with your bare hands?" I managed through my chattering teeth. "Or did you let your fire—the one you set—kill him, *them,* for you?"

"I…they came searching, and then it was bad, and Reed—I can't explain. He can."

"Will you hurt me?"

"No, of course not—"

"Melody!"

"Shh…don't make them come. Please. And she's too far away to hear. Back at the campsite. With Reed."

I knew now. Even if I could do the impossible and outrun Stone—I couldn't. Reed had Melody. A hostage situation.

I forced my rubbery legs to take steps forward, out of the numbing water, over the slick rocks, and past him. When my clumsy feet faltered, I shook off his hand. I sprinted for the pines with the platform.

~*~

I out-climbed Stone. Which gave me zero satisfaction.

Melody, Melody.

As soon as my eyes cleared the platform, I found her. I recoiled from the terrible picture before me—her reclining on her elbows, so close to the murderer next to her they almost touched. Worse, they shared a blanket. A blanket!

"Get up, Melody." Perched on a dead limb next to the uneven boards I extended a hand for her to grab. "We're leaving. Come on."

"She knows, bro!" The bigger brother landed with a muted thud opposite me.

"Melody!" I beckoned.

"Both of you. Watch your voices." Reed tucked the

bearskin's edge around Melody, who blinked at me as if waking. She continued to chew on something that made her cheek bulge.

"They're murderers." I watched her shrink from my words. "I'm getting out of here. And I can't leave you behind, so come on."

Over the blanket, Reed draped his hand over hers—a protective motion that made me want to knock it away. "Don't be a drama queen, Dove. Stone, what's going on?"

His brother held out the shattered electronic. It rested tiny in his palm and as innocent as a pinecone without its light and sound. "We missed this, bro. There were words on it from that last one. She listened to some of it before—"

Reed's eyes darted to me and back. "You didn't stay with her."

Stone's head fell into his hands. "She wanted to wash. Behind a bush. And I was giving her privacy."

"Melody?" I urged.

She'd swallowed and pulled up straighter, a good sign. Except her hand still rested under *his*. "I don't understand, Dove, but...I don't feel they're bad like you say. Wouldn't I know if they're bad? Murderers?" She shook her head. "You're wrong this time. You've got to be. You're the one who led us here. And now you say you made a mistake, and we're leaving without them? That makes no sense."

"Respect your friend's wisdom, Dove."

"Thou—shall not—murder!"

He shrugged. "Well, we didn't, so stop shouting or we are going to have real problems—right now. We're much nearer an enemy's camp than you know. Now come off that limb before you break your neck. And sit down. And shut up."

Stone sank obediently onto the boards and blew on his fingers, reminding me how hypothermic I'd become. Wet. Shivering. Worn.

I swung onto the platform and settled as far as I could from the others, with my back against a trunk. I pressed my chin against my knees, my arms to my stomach, and racked my brain for what to say for Melody to believe me. To get her to come away with me now.

I closed my eyes.

"Mel's right," Reed continued, oblivious to my need for silence. "You've depended on her God-gifted sense for recognizing evil for weeks. Why stop trusting her now? Plus, you're forgetting Gran's dream. Wasn't it *her* belief that God's plan is for you to join Stone and me for this leg of your journey?"

My mask of aloofness slipped because he pursued this point. Pounced on it—a bobcat on a wounded chipmunk. "Are you going to disobey the Lord you claim to love so much? Disappoint Him? Rely on your own wisdom instead of His?"

I glared at Melody, who ducked her head. There's only one way he'd know about my passion for God, or my gran's dream.

"I don't know what lies you've been fed." He wiggled the slim rectangle between his fingers. "But these are the words of a depraved man whose time on earth ran out the moment he set foot on this mountain. He was part of a team whose twisted obsession was to hunt down and terminate God's people.

"Stone and I were aware of this army the moment they entered our foothills. That first day we gave them clear warnings to leave. Warnings they chose to ignore.

We even separated them in hopes that on their own, each man's vile desire would weaken. But every heart was so possessed that each chose to chase our tracks into the heart of the inferno you've seen evidence of.

"They could've walked away and lived when they smelled smoke and felt the heat. Their hunger to catch and destroy me and Stone and our family overpowered their self-preservation. Now tell me. How does that make us murderers?"

"You set the fires." I ticked off on my fingers. "You created false trails for them to track. And you *knew* what would happen. That they'd die."

A sudden flash of insight dredged up Gilead's reminder. *A ruthless offense is the best defense.* The pieces began to fall into place.

"You had to get rid of them. You knew you had to kill *them* before you could leave with *us.* How else than by ensuring they died could you be confident in your family's safety when you're away? Your attack was premeditated. Premeditated murder."

"Not murder, but yes, yes. Of course. I plan out everything I do." Reed waved my accusation off like a mosquito. "But you're not understanding, Dove. I'm not the General in command. I'm only a foot soldier, a private—"

His brother sniffed.

Reed's teeth flashed. "OK, Stone. Fine. A lieutenant, then. I'm a lieutenant who receives the orders and carries them out. My point is, *I don't make the orders.*

"My connection to the Lord is similar to yours, Dove. You hear the Holy Spirit? Me too. You obey always, every time? So do I. We're the same. Only, my God-given gifts happen to be crafted for winning battles—in defensive strategy and offensive maneuvers to keep His people protected from Satan's attacks."

Wow, Melody, I grumbled. She must've spilled her guts if he knew about my unique ability to hear God.

"Now let's drop this for tonight, girls. Before Stone here starts to weep. You're hungry and tired." Reed tossed a brown pouch at my feet. "Deer jerky. Eat some. Not to point fingers, but you girls took so long getting here we'll have to start at dawn to get to the Council in time. So get some sleep."

Stone lifted the edge of another warm-looking pelt blanket in a mute offer.

His brother yawned. "Might as well get comfortable since no one's leaving this blind tonight."

Even Melody sat up straighter at this.

Reed switched to an apologetic tone. "You both know way too much about us. You get captured anywhere near this place and my family's as good as dead."

While the others settled down under their pelts, I pulled my metallic sheets from my belongings and tucked them around myself. With my wet shoe, I nudged Reed's leather satchel my way.

Once the others slept, I shoved a huge chunk of meat into my mouth. It was wonderful. Tough. Salty.

I leaned my head against the rough bark and chewed. Sleep was out of the question. The uneven boards purposely pressed upwards into my tired bones. I missed my hammock. Missed my spot next to Trinity under my maple branch.

A thunderstorm of loneliness descended and soaked me to my core. With a frenzy of rustling, I curled in on myself.

But I'm not alone. You're here. What do I do? Give me

wisdom, God. Was Reed's story true? Was it Your will that those men died? Were these Bender brothers carrying out Your vengeance? I know nothing about strategy and battles.

Oh, God. I feel sick. I've been captured again, except this feels worse than before with the Heathen. I never feared them. I knew You'd rescue me. But now I don't know. I don't want to be here.

I waited, feeling more alone than I had since I'd left home.

Lord? Where are You? Why are You so far away?

Still, I received nothing. But He hadn't left me. God didn't abandon. So why the silence?

He did everything for a purpose, I forced myself to remember. Fine. So what's the reason, then? Did He want me to draw closer to the other humans for comfort?

Sorry, God. Not tonight. Not even for You. Unless, OK. Here's the deal. I won't, unless You let me hear You say, 'Dove, you can trust them.' OK? Say that. Let me hear Your voice, and I'll believe You.

God doesn't allow people to bribe Him—or call the shots like that. I knew it. But I'm human. So I gave it a shot anyhow.

19

I must've slept. I opened my eyes to bright moonlight...and scratching. And...was that an animal's snuffling?

I'd fallen over. My cheek rested against the platform. Now I shifted my head to peer down through the wide cracks between the uneven boards.

Brown fur on a sleek body. Too small for a bear.

The animal moved, and a head flashed into view. I recognized the familiar square snout and the pointy ears. A frayed piece of rope trailed behind.

Go away, I pleaded with the boxer—the same dog we'd run into yesterday when it was still tied up. I swallowed hard as it reared up against the trunk.

The dog itself didn't scare me—not much. But where was its owner?

I strained to listen for footsteps over the clawing sounds. Now I understood why having a Darcy cat might come in handy. Every dog I'd ever met— including this one—would hightail it if it stumbled upon a bobcat's predator scent. And take its unwelcome owner far away with it.

I glared at Reed's dark, motionless form in the opposite corner between the others.

Would it have killed you to keep your dumb cat for one more night?

As if he'd heard me, Reed rose into a crouch. I

slammed my eyes shut and listened to him limp his way over to the platform's edge.

Then I peeked.

He still knelt, but his back faced me now, all bent over at an awkward angle. Even so, I still made out his outstretched arm. He leveled an object at the dog below.

I recognized the object—a weapon so forbidden back home even Gilead never asked for one.

I pressed my eyeball against the wide crack and braced myself for the gun's loud retort. Mentally, I cringed. The dog's body would crumple, fall, and life would drain away.

I heard a quiet hissing. Through the space, I saw the stream of water—a gossamer line— that ended in the hollow of the dog's up-pointed ear.

The boxer yelped in surprise, and the sleek body vanished from my line of vision. I closed my eyes. It was probably making its panicked exit down the wooded slope through the undergrowth and trees.

"I don't kill dogs for fun, Dove." I heard Reed limp back over and settle on the planks near my feet. "Quit pretending. I know you're awake."

I abandoned my fake slow breathing and crackled into a sitting position, clutching my blankets tight. The rough bark chilled my still-damp back. I shivered while he set down the water pistol and picked up his bag of deer meat where I'd left it.

He spoke around his mouthful. "I'm not a monster. Stone and I rarely kill God's creations. Ninety-nine percent of the time there's a more creative solution for a problem."

"A creative solution, like letting Darcy loose on the problem." I remembered the sick expression on Stone's face earlier and shivered again.

He nodded and swallowed. "Yes. Rare as well, but yes. Though I do think it's hypocritical of you to bring that up since you wished for my pet a few moments ago."

My breath stuck. I *had* wished for Darcy. Was that part of his warrior gift? The ability to read minds?

"Whatever you want to believe, Reed."

He offered me a piece of meat before upending the bag over his face. "It's only natural. My bobcat was still fresh in your mind. The boxer made an appearance. And from what Melody told me, the last few run-ins you've had with dogs was bound to make you feel a little over reactive."

"Well, I'm not hypocritical, so don't call me that." I eyed the water pistol. "*I* am not the pretender."

"Oh? And I am? How so?"

"When we met, you pretended to be, well, you should've told us what you did to the nonbelievers that died. That you were responsible."

"When? As you lay in the ashes at my feet? Is that when I should've said, 'Oh, hello there. I'm Reed. This is Stone. Sorry about all the smoke, but we just finished destroying four men with fire. No worries, though, because it's God's will. Enjoying your journey so far?'"

"Yes."

"Yeah, right. In any case, I didn't pretend. I have it straight from your mouth you knew I'd be a warrior. The word *warrior* in itself implies something."

"OK, but—"

"And—" Reed gave me a lazy-lidded smirk I already hated "—I think you're the one not being real. You're pretty judgey about me defending my home turf. But you're telling me you and your family do nothing—nothing at all—to protect yourselves when enemies show up? A tree dweller, right? You can't be hidden *that* well in the canopy. So, what do you do when unwanted trespassers visit?"

"We rely on God to protect us." Despite my truthful response, my fingers fiddled with a frayed edge of my belt.

"No physical force? Not ever?"

"Well, sometimes we'll use a bucket or two of water—but only to put out their fires."

He held up his pistol. "Water. Like I used now."

I released the belt's ragged strings and leaned forward. "I've no problem with how you dealt with the dog. My problem is with you creating an inferno to—"

"Distracted. You're getting distracted. What else do you do?"

I settled back against the trunk with my arms tight. "Fine. Light. My grandpa shines this huge spotlight rigged up in one of our maples on trespassers. They prefer the dark and take off when the light touches them." Except not on Dead Nights. No protective illuminating beam then. Only darkness. And fire.

Reed seemed to be waiting for more. I still wasn't sure if he was mind reading me—if that was even a thing—so I tried to be careful to *not* remember our other more dramatic defenses.

Like the huge fans twenty feet up in the trees closest to our home that could blow a climber right out. We'd never had to use the fans in my lifetime, but they're there. In case. And we'd never had to electrify the zip line cables for real, either. But Gilead always kept the device to charge them in place and in running order.

Another one I avoided thinking about was our bees.

This defense we *did* use. A lot. Mostly because using bees didn't depend on an intruder's specific location like some of our other defenses. Anyone showing skin on our property got stung. Day or night, anytime we summoned, the swarms came to our aid.

But the result was only *painful* for our enemies. Not lethal.

Similar to our bee defense, my mom and aunt could get the flocks of birds going at the right time of day. I'd seen men as old as my grandpa howl like toddlers and dive for their trucks while dodging the clouds of starlings that swooped around them. My mom and aunt orchestrated the whole thing with their whistled commands from a platform set high above the chaos.

As Reed's pupils bored into mine, I struggled *not* to think of Gilead. But failed, since my brother epitomized homeland defense.

When a threat entered our land, you'd find my brother lurking nearby. His face wearing that concentrated glower. His whole being fixated on his enemy target.

He could hit anything—moving or still. Whatever at-hand object became an effective weapon to stun or wound. But a glimpse of him in the shadows encouraged vandals to change their minds and take off.

I'd warned Gilead not to rely too much on this fear factor. God had gifted my dad, Jonah, with fierceness too. And Jonah Strong was dead.

"A bell."

"A...a bell?'

"Yeah. When my grandpa rings this giant metal bell on our roof, they assume we're calling for backup and take off super-fast." I snorted at their stupidity. As if we had backup.

Reed didn't blink.

My grin faded. "What?" I flung up my hands. "That's it."

"Hmm." He tucked the water pistol into his pants. "If you say so. Well, let's take those things—water, light, and...bell ringing. And we'll dismiss the water since, according to you, that's for putting out fires."

I nodded. Wary.

"Spectacular. That leaves us with light and noise—Old Testament stuff, right? Like from the Bible how God's people terrified their enemies in Jericho with lanterns and trumpets—which led to the collapse of the city and God's victory?"

I nodded again. Super wary.

"Stupendous. OK, Dove. Then I'll keep my points to the Old Testament. Think about King David, Jesus' own true-blood ancestor, defeating the 'tens of thousands' in battle. Even Abraham—God's chosen man in the beginning—rode out to save his nephew Lot. And killed quite a few enemies before returning home—"

"Yeah, Reed. That's Old Testament. All *before* Jesus. Jesus' life changed everything. Jesus revealed our new priorities. He didn't wipe out everyone who didn't obey God. He made it clear the adversary is Satan."

My lips and tongue continued to form words—unplanned sentences I'd never string together in a million years. I'd lost control. "And to win the 'battle' on earth is to bring as many people to God—to get as many people to believe in Him and love Him—"

I clamped a hand over my lips to check the flow.

Next to me, Reed became more excited, snatching at something I'd said and arguing with examples from the Bible to support his pro-violence ideas.

I didn't hear any of it. With my knees drawn, my brain worked so hard my cheeks smoldered despite the low-forties temp.

Had I said out loud that Jesus' purpose for believers was to bring others to Him? Why? I'd never believed that pertained to me. Or to my family. Or to any believer who lived nowadays. Because we were past all that now.

It was too late for persuasive conversions. The lines had been drawn. There was us—Jesus' followers. There was them—Satan's followers. And there were no crossing sides any more.

This wasn't my own opinion either. Sixty years ago, my grandparents, along with every other true believer in the nation, had gone off the grid in order to survive. Back then, every attempt to share the truth about Jesus with nonbelievers had ended badly. As in, homes destroyed. Land "repossessed" by the government. Jail time for the outspoken. Whole families attacked.

And the pay off? Not a single conversion as far as Gran and Grandpa had known of. The Councils— Christian leaders who'd banded together in each state to support persecuted believers—were newly formed back then but still respected. So when the Councils had unanimously decided Christ's followers needed to protect themselves, Gran, Grandpa, and the rest of America's believers had listened and faithfully disappeared out of Heathen society.

The time of harvesting souls for Christ had ended years before I was born.

And Grandma Sarah wrong? Even considering this notion made me feel as if the deer meat had sprouted maggots in my stomach.

My grandma had never—and *would* never—purposefully make a decision against God's will. Since babyhood I've been trying to copy her way of living for God one hundred ten percent, of recognizing His voice and obeying. Even when I didn't have a clue why He asked me to do something.

So could Gran have been wrong when she and my grandpa went into hiding?

Impossible.

Wolfe and Jezebel, a voice in my head bleated.

Quit it, I reprimanded. *Remembering them does you no good.*

What was wrong with me? Thinking about them so much...it was sick. And I was sick and tired of this ache I'd carried—the one I'd been trying to ignore since my run-in with these two.

I recognized my flaw—my weakness bordering on sin. I stayed hung up on these two who didn't belong to the Lord.

An epiphany struck—either that or a super-traitorous thought straight from the Enemy's quarters. *But what if my obsession with them wasn't a flaw? What if it wasn't a sin?*

Could it be a seed of something planted by the Holy Spirit? Something He wanted me to think, to feel?

I chewed on this idea, testing to see if it could be true.

Of course the rest of the world was lost, I knew. But was the Spirit telling me these two were special?

That they were able to...what? Believe? Cross enemy lines to our side?

Was it possible? Could this brother and sister come to God's side? Of course my Lord could make it happen, if He wanted to. But did He?

The thought of them becoming like me—becoming true believers—felt too huge. It left me breathless.

As I dragged in a ragged lungful, Reed was still babbling. "—so, you must prepare yourself, Dove. Because this time when the Councils declare open war to take back our country, it won't be water pistols and ringing bells. Blood's going to flow."

"Perhaps in seven years." I adopted the severity my grandma wore when she wouldn't be argued with. "Though I doubt it. But not now. God wants peace now."

He folded his arms. "You mean war."

"Pray harder next time, warrior."

In the moonlit stare-down, I burned with frustration at his wrongness.

I swatted at the air and the fluttering bat that clipped me. I curled my upper lip. "So I take it you're a devout believer in the take-back-our-land Rumor?"

"You mean the Reclaim? What's not to believe? How could you not know...oh wait. Dove of Peace." He slapped his leg.

"What?"

"I understand now. Why you got labeled with the symbol of peace in that vision. You still don't see it?"

"See. What?"

"This, Dove. If you have to believe in peace to feel secure, then you're unable to grasp the reality of an upcoming war. So arguing with you is pointless. Your mental processes can't handle the truth of a crusade.

You'll be in denial until it happens, and most likely even then. You're handicapped."

I gawked while he settled back and pulled his leather hood up over his face to sleep.

Handicapped? I hunted for a pinecone or twig, anything mobile to chuck at him.

"Truce, then?" He stuck out his hand for me to shake. And lowered it when I didn't. "Truce. And you'll travel with us—even if convinced we're murderers—until God tells you otherwise. After that, you can go your own way."

I gave up my futile search since even the empty meat bag had vanished. "God calls the shots. Not you. So the moment He says '*go*,' I'm out of here. *And* I'm taking Melody."

"Agreed. Take second watch since you're done sleeping. No one leaves this tree."

Of course, after he breathed slowly I decided what I should've told him about the Rumor. Why only idiots and ignorants believe in it.

The crux of my argument? My unshakable, undeniable, unarguable truth?

The Reclaim wasn't Biblical.

And if God didn't put it down in the Bible, I shouldn't buy into it. No one should.

All my family members—Gilead excluded—scoffed at this sketchy promise to take back our country. My grandma didn't even know from where it had originally cropped up.

Decades ago, during one of my grandpa's perilous treks to pay property taxes, he'd run into an old childhood friend. This true believer had whispered the Rumor into his ear while on his way to his own forest canopy home to scrounge up weapons.

The whisperings spread like pollen in high wind. By the time my dad and William Joyner met in prison, both families were praying about it. And the Braes had sent their own messenger seven years ago.

But no one I knew who prayed about the Rumor ever got confirmation. My grandma never received any directive from God about it other than *peace*. He didn't want us killing for land or power. She was sure. And so was I.

Stone spoke from the shadow of his hood, startling me. "Maybe the answer is more complicated than any of our puny human brains can understand. Don't tell Reed this, but I think maybe you're both right. Only God knows how."

"Your brother and me will shut up, Stone. Go back to sleep."

"Nah, he meant for me to keep watch. Not you. Anyhow, you need the sleep more since, you know, you're a girl. And with all that walking and climbing you've done. Do you know you out-climbed me tonight? That doesn't happen. So, yeah. I don't know too many girls, and never one like you. And, uh, it wouldn't be right for you to get all, you know, weak. And tired."

The heat radiating from his hidden face scorched me. I haven't met many people in my life either, so I could honestly say I'd never met anyone like him before. But how lame to say it.

I curled up in a ball and closed my eyes. "Word of advice. Stay low. The bats are out."

20

Stone flung himself into a juniper. "Get back!"

Crouching with the others behind the bushes, I studied the man in the khaki uniform and brimmed hat. He appeared to be examining the back of one of the two cars, their cocooning layer of ash promising they'd rested here more than a day.

"At least you girls are consistent."

I tensed at Reed's compliment. "How so?"

"Consistent, Dove. It took you eight hours today to accomplish a hike that should've taken three. That's comparable to your three-week journey to Mount Washington. I could've done it in a weekend."

"Cool it, bro." Stone hadn't taken his eyes off the cop-looking guy now leaning against the worn wooden sign. *Mount Washington Nature Park.*

"It's my fault. I'm the slowest—"

"No, no. It's fine, Mel." Reed patted her foot. "Only I'd hoped to be gone before *he* showed up. Now we're going to have to wait him out."

"Vehicle's here." The cop spoke into a black object pulled from his waist. "But no sign of missing persons."

He listened for a minute to what I thought was a type of radio. I'd heard of those. He responded in monosyllables before tucking the radio-thing back into his belt, next to another object that made me cold.

He ignored the weapon and crunched off the gravel, settling against a tree that faced the narrow road. He peeled a banana.

A tower of flexed muscle at my shoulder, Stone didn't miss a single bite or swallow. Loitering here made my muscles tight too.

My eyes roamed to the woods. "What are we doing here?"

Other than Melody's tight shrug, I got no response.

The man cop nudged his hat over his eyes. By the time the sun touched the western treetops, his snores rivaled my grandpa's—and my body ached from its taut, crouched stance.

Reed stood. "Come on."

I watched him limp into the clearing. I released the breath I hadn't known I'd held when he passed the man and veered for the road.

Feeling lighter that Reed's plan didn't include attacking this Heathen cop, I picked my way after the others. My feet copied Stone's, pressing down on dust patches in the gravel so they stayed soundless. When I dropped back into my crouch with the others near the tire of a vehicle, I couldn't see the cop man. But his snores didn't falter.

I raked my fingertips through the car's grime while waiting for Reed to reveal which direction we'd head in. I guessed north.

"Inside. Now."

Stone darted into the car door's opening. Through the filmy glass I saw him propel himself to the front area behind the curved wheel. Next to me, Melody's dilated pupils fixed themselves on my face.

Danger, right? I thought at her.

She swiveled. "I'm...I'm sorry, Reed."

Hey, Melody? Earth to Melody! Pay attention. Danger?

"But I've never...I won't be much help when it comes to pedaling or getting this thing to move—"

"What are you talking about?" A bead of sweat rolled into his ash brown beard, betraying his stress. "Can you sit? 'Cause that's all you've got to do. Sit. No pedaling. But Mel? Dove? Before you can sit, you've got to do what?"

"Get in." Her obedient response disappeared with her body inside the vehicle.

The rhythmic sleep sounds from the tree line droned on.

"This is beyond nuts. *You* have a car, Reed?"

"Do now."

"Huh?"

"Spoils of war. Now, ladies first."

"You mean this car belongs to the godless—"

"Belonged. Past tense. They don't need it anymore. We do. Get in."

"No. First I'm going to have to pray about this." I sank to the ground. "Because this seems like"—my pointed glare nicked him—"*stealing.*"

I heard a sigh. And a small click—like a snap. A half second later my knees left the gravel, and a callused hand smelling of soot pressed my nose and chin.

I opened my eyes in time to land next to Melody with a bounce. The door eased into place, trapping me. Stone's apologetic eyes wavered next to the murky glass, but a blink later, his wide shoulders settled inside the car in front of me, next to his brother's narrow ones.

I yanked at the door's plastic pieces. "Let me out! Let. Me. Out."

My demand—it rang familiar.

I remembered Jezebel. Enraged and helpless, stuck in her brother's stubborn arms.

The car awoke with a purr. "Easy. Easy."

Reed patted an expanse of the smooth, black interior. For a moment, I pushed aside my fury and leaned forward, like Melody, to watch the brothers move this thing.

Stone twisted the wheel a hard left. With a blow to my back, we shot forward in a tight arc and plowed over a lone sapling. The fir needles vanished beneath us when Reed leaned over and wrenched a lever. We skidded to a stop—all but my body, which continued moving forward until it connected with the back of Stone's chair. Our vehicle moved again, racing backwards in a high-speed zigzag.

Through the billowing dust, the cop-man's silhouette staggered up. His hand fumbled at waist level.

I ducked. But we bumped onto the road, hurtling forward. A flash of trees later, and we slid onto a wider road.

"I don't get why we're doing this!" I had to yell for Reed to hear me over Melody and four screaming tires.

"You want to walk all the way to Jefferson?"

I peeled my upper body off the closest glass. "Yes!"

"It's over fifty miles. We'd never make it in time. Now quiet, so I can help Stone!"

~*~

Two tiny lights pricked the darkening horizon. I sat up straighter. Within moments the dots became life-sized car headlights.

After a shuddering whoosh of brightness, the darkness returned. Our car lurched to a stop, separating Melody's death grip from my arm.

I picked myself off the floor again and perched back on the edge of the slippery car bench. In front, the two brothers must've come to a decision, because they flung open their doors and leaped out.

Seconds later, Reed slid behind the wheel. In front of me, the artificial glow of the car's interior lit up one of the giant's temples that gushed with sweat. He trembled as though he had a bad flu.

Warrior Reed was no better at this car thing than Stone.

Cars killed—I'd seen enough animals squashed on the road. I'd never realized before that living creatures *inside* a vehicle risked becoming smashed pulp as much as the ones standing in its path.

While my gaze stayed glued to Reed's hands—my body ready to react and brace when they moved—I prayed. But my queasiness blocked my ability to hear any heavenly instructions. Such as *rip open the door and jump for it.*

I clutched my stomach. "We're there. Tell me we're there."

"Close." Reed hung onto the wheel as we curved around another bend. *Thud.* To my left Melody hit her side window. "The trees have gotten thicker. A good sign. Greener around Mount Jefferson."

I pressed my face to the filmy glass until it bucked me off. I couldn't see any green—only the few yards of flat black in front of the car's headlights.

Then, I gasped. I saw the evergreens' black, swaying branches in detail, all the way to their feathered, triangular tops. And the misshapen clumps of moss lower down. And fern fronds filling in the gaps between leafy plants I'd never seen before. Ominous red and white flashes of light bounced off everything.

"Police," Stone pointed out.

The car's engine hummed up an octave. At the wheel, the warrior didn't slow us when cedar branches dragged against my glass. We jostled back onto pavement and veered for the opposite tree line. The siren filled the night with its nonstop wail.

"What happens to us? If they catch us?" Melody stayed on the floor where she hunched over her bag.

I remembered my dad's arrest—the iron circles stuck around his wrists when they'd led him away. The anxious year I'd had with him gone. And his joyful return, muddied by the fact that he yelled out in his sleep most nights...for reasons he refused to explain.

My jaw clenched in resolve. "We won't find out."

At my feet, she hugged her pack tighter. Then she looked down sharply, as if surprised it existed, and rummaged inside.

A loud bang drowned out the wail.

I ducked. "They're shooting at us!"

"Easy. Only a tire going out." Next to Stone's braced, sweating bulk, his brother cranked the wheel.

"Can't. Control. It." Reed's body rose in an effort to hold onto the wheel. "Some help?"

"Help. He needs...help him!" Melody struggled up, still gripping her bag. But Stone beat her there, his hands secure over his brother's.

I was focused on the action up front—and on

keeping myself on the slippery bench. So, I almost missed Melody, who ducked back down and whispered something. Something like *God, help me.*

My world became chaos. I couldn't react in time—couldn't fathom how fast things could go one-eighty in all directions.

The engine died and the siren cut off. Then everything went black. Deaf *and* blind.

Screaming shattered the quiet. Screaming tires. Screaming voices. No, only one voice screamed. Melody's. Gravity shoved me where I wasn't meant to go, and I grabbed at whatever my hands met.

Shouts punctuated the screams while my pupils fought to dilate, searching for anything they could grasp. Even the car's dim light vanished.

Out of my whirling blindness, a pole-like object carrying white flashed and flew at my head. I yelped as it smashed against the glass with a teeth-rattling crack.

My world stopped spinning. Melody's voice wafted from somewhere behind me. "I didn't...I didn't..."

My body was wedged between the brothers. My vision finished adjusting to the skimpy moonlight, enough to see my shoulder pressed against Stone's outstretched arm—the barrier between me and the shattered front glass.

Dazed, I dropped back onto my bench and gripped its edge. I stared dumbly down at Melody, still crouched and hugging her belongings.

I leaned over. Something was wrong with her face. No blood, but her expression—it showed more than shock or terror. It showed extreme guilt.

Nearby, her hand gripped a small object,

unfamiliar and high-techy looking.

I let go of the seat to see. Her thumb clamped the side of it, the same way mine does when I trigger a flashlight's 'on' sensor.

She spoke again in that same terrified whisper. "I didn't know it would do that. I promise I didn't. I didn't know. I—"

"An EMP." Reed groaned and reached over his chair back for the object. "That is a mini EMP. Where did you get it?"

She thrust the EMP thingy at him. "I don't know. In my bag. It was there, and I thought God had—I don't know what I thought. Take it. I'm sorry. So sorry."

God? No, God hadn't put the EMP in her bag.

Oh, Wolfe. Why? Why'd you give it to Melody? As a joke? Did you know it would destroy us when she found it? Did you know we'd be captured?

"No, it's OK, Mel." Reed sounded way too fine for someone blood-streaked eyebrow to beard. "Mel. Listen to me. All you've done is level the playing field for us. Yeah, our car's dead—but so is theirs...and so is their radio and the equipment they rely on. And we're nearly there. See that area of trees up there?"

Unable to speak, I followed the line his finger made to the blob of feathery blackness perched on a lumpy hill silhouette.

"If we can make it up that debris to those trees, we'll be safe to hike. So, crew? Now's the time to call out if your legs are broken. Anyone? On the count of three, we go for it."

On *three,* we discovered only two of the four doors opened. As my feet crunched down on gravel, a stranger's voice rang out. "Stop! Hands above your head. Get on your knees. On your knees! Now!"

I fell as if I'd been hit.

Reed hollered, "No! It's a bluff. Get up! Their car—it's trapped them. They can't get out. Run! Go to where I showed you! Stone, I need you over here."

I didn't pause to see what he needed help with. Or if he shouted the truth about the cops being stuck. I anchored Melody to me and scrambled out of the ditch and onto the gravelly slope. I glimpsed the black clump of trees crowning a smooth rock face. It was so vertical a spider couldn't scale it.

No boulders rested between me and the precipice. There was nothing to hide behind.

"Get up." I grabbed fur, dragging Melody off her stomach. We struggled up the steep incline. Sediment and pebbles dislodged from under my soles with each upwards push, slithering down in our wake. The air around me got thick fast. Each time I fell, I tasted its gritty soup.

"Up. Get up, Melody." I punched a spot under my ribs.

"Danger."

"That's why you're getting up, Brae. C'mon. Up."

She responded slower to my commands, hesitating a few extra seconds before pushing herself onto her boot soles. Giving up.

Then came the sound of someone scrambling on the loose stones below us, only a few yards behind.

"On your feet now or," my whisper rose to match the noisy rock fall, "or it's all over!"

Our climb had gone from too silent to a series of avalanches happening below that had nothing to do with my own feet or Melody's. Or Stone's, since he moved with the tread of a cat. *Where had the brothers gone? Ditched us?*

The slab of sheer rock reared up in front of me, forcing me to stop. Panting, I limped sideways to my left. A second later I fell to the ground, covering my head.

At the second gunshot, unexpected weight smashed me against the shards. When I opened my eyes, I couldn't see anything but the inside of Stone's tree trunk arm and Melody's black braid bun.

"Reed!"

"Shh, Melody. Easy. He's OK." Stone readjusted his torso so he covered us instead of crushing. "Hold still another second. He's OK. You'll see."

Hold still? I couldn't even move my arms an inch. This was like something Gilead would pull. But I couldn't stay mad when I heard the next shots.

The deafening metallic explosions rang inches away. In the pause, and through the high-pitched ringing in my ears, I heard a stranger's shout. "What are you doing? Stand down. That's an order. Stand. Down."

"Fanatics!"

I pictured the second stranger's bloodshot eyes squinting into the night, his weapon trained on me.

"I swear there're fanatics up there. Try to break my neck with rocks?"

Three more shots made me press my bruised cheek to the ground so hard my nose ran.

"Holster your weapon and stand down."

"But they're right, there, Captain. I swear. See that white square thingy up there?"

"I see nothing. Only a trigger-happy newbie who's about to be kicked off the force."

"No. Trust me, Cap. Trust me. I know. I've always

had a sixth sense when radicals are involved. Like I can smell 'em out. Up trees and down holes. We have to..."

"Fire again and it's your badge. Get your head on. What if you hit them? You gonna leave their bodies out here for the animals? We can't transport dead—or even alive—prisoners right now if the car and radio are as shot as I think they are. My phone doesn't even have a charge, and I'll bet yours is the same. They must have gotten ahold of one of those stupid contraptions those kids in Sisters set off that kills the power.

"Now, shut up and listen." He kept talking over the shooter, trying to interrupt. "I don't deny there are fanatics up there who deserve to be taken in. But think for a moment, man. Pick your moment. This isn't it."

"It's always the right moment to bring down radicals. Listen. We'll get promoted, even be on the news. I have a plan—get this. We lock their bodies in the cruiser and hike down the highway. Someone'll be by, and we'll call the station and—"

"No. We're not stinking up my car with a bunch of dead fanatics. Even a half a day in tomorrow's heat will create a stench we'll never get out. Now holster that thing and do something useful. Go see if you can get the emergency lanterns working while I check the cruiser's battery. Go. They're in the trunk."

Footsteps hurried through gravel. "Yeah, lanterns. I'll show him where those fanatics are. Flush 'em out. Then he'll see..."

The weight lifted. "You OK?" Stone tugged me to my feet so abruptly I teetered. "I didn't smoosh you too much? Melody? All right?"

Somewhere around us, Reed grunted. "No rush. Anytime. Serious though, Stone. This is heavy."

I hadn't been able to move my head enough to see

Reed. He kneeled six feet below. The shadow of a large rectangle engulfed him. He struggled to keep it upright as though it was a shield.

Stone leaped down to his brother, took the flat object from him, and held it one-handed as if it were a piece of cardboard. But it couldn't be. The warrior had called it heavy.

"Get them all, bro?"

"Think so." Reed clambered to his feet with a grimace. "Caught twelve. How many shots did you hear?"

"Twelve."

As they bumped knuckles, a tiny tongue of fire sprang to life below. I watched the golden circle grow, trying to grasp that Reed had performed *a miracle*.

He'd saved our lives. Saved us from bullets that—until they'd started exploding around me—I hadn't truly expected.

But Reed had.

He'd expected them and formulated a plan. He'd drawn the fire to himself with some crazy object he'd found. Then he'd used it as a shield to catch every bullet fired.

Which meant he'd told the truth last night about his God-given gift. He did have one. Because no mere human power blindly caught bullets like that—not without some serious heavenly guidance.

A faint metallic *thunk* dragged my gaze from the illuminated cop car at the ditch to Stone. He'd lain the warped metal rectangle—white marked with a large, black '55'—at his feet, the white thing we'd smashed at the road. A road sign minus its pole.

Reed gripped Stone's shoulder. "On it?"

"On it."

The giant picked up a rock fragment. Like Gilead would, he held it a second to learn its weight, then hurled it down the slope. Glass shattered. A curse echoed. And the flame died.

Reed faced me and Melody. "OK, crew. We've approximately two-and-a-half minutes until the next lantern's lit, assuming there's another. Let's assume. So, let's be in the woods before then."

Stone's arm locked across my back and guided me around the base of the precipice. Walking became effortless, as if my feet traveled a path on my property. No point fighting him and starting a landslide, I decided, letting him swing me up a slope.

He helped the others too—carrying Melody part of the way with his free arm and once offering a hand down to his brother behind us, who, far from stealth mode, breathed like one of those dogs with smashed faces. Panting like they do when they're done racing around on their useless, short legs.

The hissing clatter of the avalanche starting behind us mixed with Reed's irritated grunt that he'd triggered it. It dawned on me that, physically, the warrior wasn't any smoother or more capable than me. Except for in the moments when God allowed him to be—like when catching cops' bullets.

I limped to the first evergreen and collapsed behind it. The cartwheeling debris faded out and gave way to the stream of threats bouncing off the bluff.

I buried my head in my arms to muffle the stranger's voice…even though I recognized it. No. Not the voice as much as the evil energy of it. The energy that drove the sheath of hateful words and gale force of rage straight at me.

The same dark power had crippled me with the

scream in the garbage bin. And snatched at me during the storm the night we escaped the attacking teens.

I heard Satan. Gnashing his teeth, ripping his hair, and beating his fists because I, the Lord's messenger, had escaped. Again. On *his* terrain.

I sensed when Stone knelt. He patted my hair. "Don't be...you don't have to be scared."

"That's right." Reed breathed normally again, while his twiggy frame loomed over us—twice its normal size. "Because even if they make it up here to investigate, which is doubtful, we'll be far enough away. Let them come."

I slammed my lids down, trying to block out his ominous words—the same words from yesterday that had acted as a signal for us to become tireless machines, hiking on and on through the night.

Not again. Not tonight.

But...Reed was God's chosen. His warrior. Receiving messages, catching bullets, doing miracles.

I shoved myself to my feet and tugged on my traveling partner's hand, still clamped over her ear.

21

"You're wasting your energy. There's no point searching for a way up to the Council, because right now we're where God wants us. You've proved we're on the right mountain. That's all you can do. So, relax." I continued to recline on a fern bed and plucked an unfurling fiddlehead to nibble. "Wait for God's timing. Believe me. He's made it clear." I touched my ear. "He'll show us the way when it's time."

It was September eighth, according to the Benders. A mere week before the Council met to decide. I couldn't explain why I didn't bite my nails off with fear that I'd miss the vote and decision. It wasn't as if the addition to our group cleared up anything in the way of information.

No one from the Benders' MTV had ever traveled to Mount Jefferson before. I'd sort of assumed Reed knew more than I did about our mission's final stretch. But he didn't. So we were all guessing when it came to knowing exactly when. Or where. Or how to get to the where.

"Yeah, I don't do—waiting." Reed peered through a break in the wilderness at the snowcap above us. Despite killing ourselves to find a way up, it was still unreachable. "Not unless I have it straight from Him. Which I don't. Only from you."

A wisp of a cloud next to the peak's white

evaporated in the sunshine, so deceiving. My toes scrunched in my shoes to ward off the air's bite.

"I'm done sitting here." He shouldered his satchel. "A way to the Council exists and we've missed it. I'm going to find it."

"Suit yourself." I yawned to cover any outward sign of the knot in my gut. It doubled and tightened painfully when Melody heaved herself to her feet too.

She should stay here with me. *Because*, I told myself, staying would be way better for *her*.

She needed the break, the rest. Yesterday I'd noticed her face had become too sharp, despite the extra meat due to Stone's hunting abilities. Her eyes were always too big now. Even when she wasn't freaked out. And there hadn't been much to be physically scared of lately.

I ignored the sounds of departure and spoke out loud to myself—and to whomever wanted to listen. We'd wasted too much energy circling Jefferson, trying to discover a way up its impenetrable sides. And how did we even know the Council's camp was *up high*?

Sure, my grandparents alluded to it being "up." And up made the most sense. But we didn't have proof.

Proof. I grimaced at the unspoken word. After our first day's failure to find the Council, Melody decided we were on the wrong mountain. In one of her bizarre, self-assured moments she refused to believe either Reed or me. For the first time, Reed and I agreed on something. We hiked Mount Jefferson.

I'd pointed at the peak. "What do you expect, Brae? A lit-up path with people hanging off shouting 'Mountain Council up here! This way. Follow the arrows.'? The Council has to be impossible to find.

Otherwise Satan's workers would've destroyed it day one."

Reed had lowered his arm he'd pointed at the range on the horizon—geographic evidence that he wasn't guessing. "You're right, Mel. I respect what you're saying. If you have qualms about our location, we need to find you tangible proof."

"Proof? Sky alive, how are you going to find proof in this endless wilderness?" I'd seen no trace of humans since we'd left the highway days ago. It was the perfect place for a hidden Christian Council.

I'd gone along with the whole let-the-warrior-lead mindset and had trailed them back into the dense wilderness of the foothills—to meander.

At sunset the second day, Reed had found Melody's proof. He'd kneeled next to the sign— "Jefferson Park" etched crudely into ancient wood. He'd pretended to present it to her. Then, he'd winked. "No more doubting me. Right, lady?"

Her eyes had squinted happy in her pink face. No doubt the reason she disappeared through the trees now without a backwards glance at me.

"So you're staying, then. Not joking?" Stone paused between a mossy stump and a hemlock on his way after the others.

"Yep. Because there's zero point in going, and this is a good spot. I got water. I got food." I motioned at the huckleberry bushes we'd stripped this morning where clumps of spherical green already ripened purple in the afternoon sun.

His beard bobbed, but he didn't go. "You won't leave here while we're gone? People get lost, hurt in this thick growth sometimes."

"It's a no-brainer, then. Save your strength too.

You don't have to do everything *he* does, you know. You and Reed. You're two people. You should act like it."

It felt awesome to say this out loud. Maybe I should run after Melody and tell her too.

His sun-bleached brows drew together while he grabbed for a foot-long garter snake. He tossed it away from the berry bush. "Yeah, I do have to do what he does. He's the smarts. And I'm the body. And a warrior isn't whole without both. Apart, our gifts are wasted. Together, well, you know."

"Reed tell you that?"

"Sure. But it's true."

I raised my hand in farewell. And chalked up another victory for warrior Reed. Drawing people to himself and holding them there. It was like drone bees sticking to their queen.

I stood and hoisted myself into the hemlock. Drones don't have a choice, but Melody and Stone? I'm pretty sure they did.

~*~

I began the day alone foraging, washing, and then climbing into a tree with a decent seat. The remaining daylight hours I spent soaking in sunshine and praying. And listening.

God didn't reveal where the Council hid—but I also didn't ask. I trusted Him. I wished the others would trust too, but I didn't waste time moaning over it.

Of course, I wasn't safe. Satan prowled, and I camped by myself in cougar and bear territory.

I thought about my bee call. I'd have been nuts not to. A hive positioned a couple hundred yards off, a monster, buzzed with potential. But I'd accepted the fact it was gone forever when I'd checked my bag and found it missing.

Jezebel's doing, no doubt. Her face would be a solid purple from trying to get the whistle to make a high-pitched noise. All the while, she had to be running for her life from the swarm she couldn't lose.

When night fell, I became ultra-aware that I huddled in a strange green forest alone, a million miles from home. While curling up in my tree tent, demanding sleep to come—and pretending I didn't hear animals move—I began planning Jezebel's and Wolfe's conversion.

The idea kept my mind busy, even if it was all a fantasy. If I survived the trek home, I would never leave again. Ever. Unless God called me to be messenger again in another seven years.

The blankets over me rattled, so I refocused on Jezebel and how she'd believe the truths I'd tell her about my Savior. Kids latched onto whatever ideas sounded right to them.

But Wolfe...I clicked my tongue. He'd be a big problem, with so many years of falling for Satan's lies.

While winged creatures fluttered outside my tent walls and warm-blooded ones crept around below, I struggled until I pinpointed what doubts he'd probably have and figured out my arguments for each one.

Every time I became sure I couldn't lose the argument, I pictured him raising his eyebrows at me and whistling. And my confidence fumbled.

A person can't whistle and smile at the same time.

But *he* could. That is, when he didn't throw his head back and let the laughter burst.

That's the problem! I groaned. Humor. I couldn't argue with humor. And he thought everything—regardless of whether senseless or important—was a big hoo-ha. A joke.

I closed my eyes and went over our few conversations, examining them for the key to my victory—some weakness or chink in the armor of humor.

I flung up my hands in defeat. Sky alive, there was no way!

I heard Satan chuckle. Worse, behind my burning lids I saw him—dark and beautiful—towering like an old growth pine over the lake. He'd plucked sister and brother out of the water and gave them a satisfied pat while fiery ropes lashed their waists.

Jezebel and Wolfe fought their bonds with little-girl kicks and well-placed blows, but the Enemy tossed them into the air and pulled open a section of his black cloak. The cloak's pocket swallowed them. I couldn't hear them—couldn't even see the lump their bodies should have made beneath the midnight cloth. It was as if they'd been dropped into an abyss. A pocket abyss. Separating us forever.

The Enemy patted his pocket.

"No, Lord." The rough, woven fibers of the tent floor strained against my damp forehead. "That can't happen. Let their names be written in Your Book of Life. Let them know You and Your glorious name. Show me how, Lord. Show me."

~*~

I watched as Reed abandoned his mossy walking stick and collapsed next to the green pool. He began to throw handfuls of water onto his streaming face and spoke between splashes. "So, this is what we know. Where the wilderness stops, the rock faces start. And every stretch of terrain that leads somewhere promising is too steep to climb, an avalanche waiting to happen, or it's cut off by a deep crevice."

"Hmm. Shocker."

He ignored me. "Which means we've missed something. Which means we're going to have to take more risks. Because we didn't come all this way to sunbathe and get fat on berries."

Ooo...ouch. I shrugged. I'd endured worse insults.

"OK, Mel." He hunched a shoulder to wipe his dripping beard and took up his mossy stick. "Come water up so we can make it there before dark."

Make it there?

"Uh. We found a better spot to camp—better since it's higher up." Stone held out his drawstring bag for the few berries Melody finished collecting.

I added my pile of dandelion greens, unable to tell if he avoided eye contact because he was nervous I'd say "no way" and be left behind, or because he'd be forced to make me come. As in, carry me.

We both knew I wasn't a Melody mouse, so forcing me to go with him was bound to get messy. In the end, I'd lose.

I blinked and held it, listening for any insight about my relocating.

My fists unclenched. "Sure. I'll come. But we won't try anything dumb. And we wait on God. Agreed?"

I threw my pack over my shoulder—half-full of tent since I repacked each morning—and scrambled after the others. Reed was already out of sight. "Agreed? Hey! Right? You all agree?"

~*~

Venus shone star-like in the twilight when we spilled out from tight clustered firs into a semi-flat clearing. Ferns and low ground cover blanketed the shallow hollow in a jumbled mess.

"Here."

At Reed's decision, Melody plopped down snow-angel style in the ferns and studied the darkening pastels overhead. The brothers, who'd spent the trek obsessively stuffing useless nature into their sacks, discussed the warmest shelter for night. As the warrior nodded at a hollowed-out log, his hands twisted vines from his bag into a rope, and his brother bent to readjust the downed trunk. I was the only one who spotted movement between the trees.

Before I could yell, a stranger peering backward tripped over Melody. By the time they both found their feet, four other strangers had trespassed into our campsite.

For three thudding heartbeats, we stayed rooted.

"Melody!"

"Oh!" At Reed's growl, she remembered her gift. "Um. Um. Not a threat." The shock ebbed from her face and she pointed. "See? They're like us. Aren't you? Aren't you Christians?"

I didn't exhale or sigh because they dressed in too-bright clothing. Not "off-the-land" enough. I backed up until a maple pressed my shoulder blade.

The tallest stranger—a dark-skinned girl in blue—stepped forward.

"Yes. You guessed right." She unstuck a lock of bushy hair from her damp face. "Though it's brave of you to reveal yourselves as believers so fast. Not many of us will do that nowadays. But, I assume you're not afraid because of the strength of your group?" She nodded first at Reed and then at Stone.

She turned to me next. Her lips pulled up higher on one side, and her brown eyes thawed my gray ones a little. "And you spotted us first. Every group needs a good lookout to avoid trouble and stay on the right paths. Speaking of right paths, anyone know which way to the Council?"

Two newcomers whispered, and one forced a laugh. But I stayed focused.

There was something about her sincere voice and relaxed movements. *Trust me. I'm on your side. A friend.*

I believed her.

I threw off the irrational feeling and interrupted Reed's theory on the Council's location. "Don't pay attention to him. We've no idea."

Someone guffawed, and the tension broke. The clearing became a sudden hive of activity. Watching it, I realized no one from this new group was much older than me or the Benders.

I tailed the girl in blue to where others threw backpacks, walking sticks, and themselves down on the green tufts. I touched the strange, thin material of her sleeve. "It's weird. You know, that I'm not that old. And neither are you. And that kid over there's about ten. God's so surprising, calling who He does. He's amazing, though. Don't you think?"

After glancing at the boy—the one with messy curls and a dust-streaked face—the girl in blue wiped the confusion off her face. She replied with that same tilted smile. "Unfathomable. Amazing. And awesome."

"Rebecca." The dusty boy tapped two twigs of his armful together to get her attention. "Quit schmoozing. You're fire queen, so get it going with that dry pile while we gather more wood. And don't talk your way out of it this time."

"Hold on. We don't do fire." My hands formed an X, nixing the idea. Since that first night on Washington, we'd avoided bonfires.

"Here." Reed tossed some dried grass twists from his sack onto the pile of kindling. "We definitely do fire from now on. Good strategy to draw any others seeking the Council. The bigger our numbers, the better."

"Oh." I hadn't considered other Christians searching too.

Rebecca patted my shoulder. "That's what makes traveling together so worth it. All the different ideas—and talents and gifts. When we join together and share, we become—not only unshakable, but wiser and better. You know?"

I shrugged, seeing her point. But it was hard to get worked up over that kind of teamwork.

When the hovering trees darkened to match the sky, I sprawled between Stone and a fierce-browed girl who didn't speak. The bonfire toasted my face and hands as well as the rabbit meat skewered on my branch. I didn't even wince at the popping flames.

Melody sat across from me, beaming into the blaze. I nodded back and felt some of my burden slip.

OK, God. This was why You told us to not force our

own way to the Council.

The mute girl on my left crammed the last chunk of meat in her mouth. Then, after rubbing her fingers on the ten-year-old's hair, who rammed her for it, she pulled some junk from her bag—including two pieced-together bark and wood objects. The kid next to her grabbed one away and patted the grass clumps around him until he found twigs.

I bumped against Stone, removing myself from the swordfight zone. I have cousins—sticks plus kids equals weapons. But instead of fighting, both stick holders closed their eyes. Their hands began to move over the wood and bark pieces...and blur.

An underlying beat and clattering rhythm echoed off the trees, filling the night and killing the conversations around the fire.

The beat became a praise. Praises don't have to be words, and this was a drumming soul worship. It lifted me higher to Heaven.

But I slammed back down when the words started.

"Jesus, Jesus, warrior Lamb!

You will give us back our land,

No more hiding at Your call,

With Jesus we will conquer all!"

Chills ran to my fingertips at the revelation that everyone who gathered here believed these words—believed we were going to war. To fight in Jesus' name. To conquer.

Passion painted Reed's face. Next to him, Melody's lips moved with the rest, repeating the refrain.

But she didn't believe we'd conquer. She and I, at least, recognized God wanted peace.

I pulled my knees to my chest, cut off from the rest

by the battle chant. Despite the fire's drawing warmth, I wanted to slink off into the night.

God would protect and bring me to the Council. I rummaged through the tangled ferns for my pack. My hand slipped through its strap.

Not alone.

I released it and breathed deep.

Thank you. But what then, God? Do I stay to convince everyone here You want peace? And no matter what answers their families have mistakenly sent, they must deliver a message of peace? I can't do that! When I talk, no one ever listens to me—

"It's Dove, right?" Rebecca hovered over me, tossing wood, piece by piece, into the fire. "What? The dove bird doesn't sing?"

I stiffened. She bit her lip. She wasn't being judgy. Like Wolfe, she used humor.

I created a spot for her between me and Stone. "I do sing when I want. In my head. God understands." I leaned closer until I smelled the smoke clinging to her black strands. "I'm tone deaf."

She didn't laugh at my confession but motioned at the little kid creating the rhythm. "That's my brother. Josh. The most obsessive, music-addicted grub you'll ever meet. And I promise if we let him in on your secret, by sunup he'll have you playing something that doesn't involve tone or pitch like you've been born doing it."

She tossed her full water bottle at his tapping foot. "Twenty-four-seven he's either making music or trying to get everyone around him to. Pushy little guy."

The singing dropped, but the endless beat continued like waves of rain in a storm, gusting and pattering around us.

I watched her brother's hands. "That's not natural. No one's that good. That's his God-given gift, then? The gift of music—worship?"

She pulled my skewer around and slid off a piece of the blackened meat. When she burned her fingers and almost lost it to the ashes, she laughed. "You're observant, for sure. So, do you have a...?"

I lurched up, dropping our meal.

Melody. I needed to see Melody—to better read that deer-eyed stare.

Under my gaze, her torso pulled up like it wanted to spring away. It slumped, and she twisted her arms around her legs, trying to hide inside her own body.

Melody? Where's the threat?

"Dove, what's...?"

I thrust my hand at Rebecca and saw Reed notice. He followed my concern back to the girl at his side.

"People. Enough drumming." He shook Melody's elbow. "What? You feel something's wrong?"

When she didn't respond, he pulled her stiffly to her feet, repeating himself.

"Yes." Her breathed affirmation hid itself under the pop of the fire and the steady, gentle drum roll. "Or...someone?"

"Someone's coming."

She nodded and blinked. Their eyes locked.

"An enemy?"

She started to bob again but hesitated. "I don't know."

Reed held her upper arms. "OK. You're not sure now. But it's human—not an animal? It's one or more humans in alliance with Satan?"

I missed if she nodded because I'd closed my eyes to focus.

I didn't feel any approaching threat. None. Almost the opposite—I had a definite sense of anticipation. Goosebumps raced.

Reed's voice flowed like a current of strength across the uneasy, shifting circle. "Be prepared to run if you can't fight. Stone and I'll draw whatever this is to ourselves. There's an empty den with creepers ten minutes northeast of here—seven if you're running. Mel knows it, so keep with her. That's where we'll meet up."

I continued to listen for heavenly directions. Instead I heard a bird's warble.

"Ahhh. Fire, fire, fire. Waaarmth."

My stomach plummeted to my ankles. I opened my eyes in time to see Wolfe lurch from the blackness of the trees and into our circle of light.

22

The drum roll broke.

Jezebel's brother squinted, his wrong clothes and Heathen-style hair yelling *nonbeliever*. He rubbed his hands in front of him, warming them on the fire's brightness.

"Your smoke's been like a mirage so long I gave up thinking it was real. I was supposed to get here before it got so dark. And cold." His lids slid half-mast. "Fire, my friend. I love you, fire."

He spotted me. "Hey. Bird girl!"

I was numb. Speechless. Rooted as he moved my way.

His hands dug around in the pockets of his blue and green jacket, until one surfaced holding my bee call. "Jezzy still had this when you took off, and I figured it might be important."

The tiny, tubular call dislodged and arced across the firelight. In the same moment, he fell to his knees and bent over in an extreme bow with his arms cranked behind him. Stone stood over him, holding his arms. The giant's brother held a flint-like shard to the newcomer's jugular.

Wolfe resisted half a second. "Ow! What the—"

"You're trespassing on God's people and are not allowed to speak." Reed gestured Melody forward with his free hand. "This him?"

"Yes."

Wolfe peered up through his dark strands at her. "Yeah? What? What did I—"

"I said no talking."

I could've sworn Stone's muscles didn't twitch, but Wolfe grimaced. "Take it easy, big guy."

I glanced around at the frozen group, disgusted. Rebecca positioned herself defensively in front of her brother and leaned forward as if she might interfere.

I was finished watching.

"Dove." Reed thrust his palm out. Up this close I could see the razor edge of the rock he held against the brown skin.

I stopped in front of the trio. Then, before anyone could stop me, I knelt and slipped my fingertips under the weapon's edge. They stung as I pulled the rock away from the hairbreadth line on the captive's skin.

"Dove."

I ignored Reed and kept my hand in place, separating rock from throat. "What are you doing here, Wolfe?"

His answering smirk came slow and forced— unlike his speech that flew like hummingbird wings. "So I'm allowed to talk now? Because I was under the impression I'm supposed to shut up. You guys need to coordinate better. Because if *you* say it's talk time and *he* doesn't agree, guess who'll be breathing out of a different air hole? Me, that's who. Not you. Or him. So you all figure out this talking-or-no-talking dilemma and let me know."

"What—are—you—doing—here? Answer me, Wolfe."

He swallowed with a wince. "Like I said. I've got your whistle thing."

I shook my head. "Not good enough. The truth. You traced me a hundred miles and then hiked through this wilderness. Why?"

His Adam's apple bobbed. "I don't know! OK? Is that what you want to hear?"

Startled, my hand shifted, but I caught the rock's edge in time.

Wolfe sucked in a breath and went back to the laughing tone. "You know, it seemed like I should probably find, I mean, after a dream like that, what else could I do? Which goes to show I've become as delusional as the rest of you if I'm obeying dreams about—" He broke off with a grimace. "Hey, hey, hey! Joking, big guy. Ease up."

I stood. "Let him go. The Lord's guided him here. Even though he doesn't have a clue. Plus, he believes he's done me a favor. He's returning something taken from me, so you're wrong. He's not an enemy. He's a friend."

"A friend?" With a hard laugh, Reed yanked up my sleeve. I couldn't break his grasp and everyone ogled the scab marring a huge chunk of my sword tattoo.

He waved it in victory. "Friends don't do that."

"Errgh!" Wolfe craned his neck to see his massive keeper. "Will you quit that? I swear I never touched her. Did I, Dove? I never touched you. That wasn't me that did that. Tell them."

While I lowered my sleeve, I remembered his arm around me, pinning my shoulders while we faced Diamond. "He didn't hurt me. That was someone else."

Reed pulled Melody forward. "And her? Did you harm her?"

Wolfe hesitated. He *had* tackled her to the ground. Twice. "I...er...don't recall."

"Enough, Reed." Hands on hips, chin raised, I faced him. "Release him. We're still at peace with nonbelievers, so he's not a prisoner. Plus, he's done nothing wrong."

Reed spoke over me, as if I were a chirping cricket. "Get the coils of rope from my sack, Melody. Two of them."

As she obeyed, I realized how brainless I acted, wasting my energy on the wrong person. On the wrong brother.

Over Wolfe's bowed head, Stone met my gaze. I reached out my hand and found his—the one that secured both of Wolfe's wrists. Stone's skin warmed my chilled fingertips.

Then the miracle happened. The iron tendons and muscles relaxed under my touch, until I felt Wolfe jerk away. Wolfe hightailed it for the black wall of trees. I hoped he wouldn't slow until he touched pavement.

He stopped short. "Bunch of psychos!"

I dropped my hand and backed away until I stood in front of him at the clearing's edge. "This non-Christian won't hurt anyone. Can't you understand this is God's doing? How else could he have found us? He hasn't got the intelligence to do it on his own."

Reed stopped goggling at his brother. "You are so wrong, Dove. So. Dead. Wrong. All shed blood from this moment forward is on you. Every drop. Your fault. Remember that."

I blinked hard against the gory red his words conjured up, and shivered at the ice trickling down my spine. Then I straightened.

"I'm good with that."

23

After the warrior slipped away—saying something about setting snares to feed the thousands—I returned to the fire and watched the flames. It was easier than explaining my actions to the group who watched with raised eyebrows.

"You gone yet?" I threw over my shoulder. But I knew Wolfe wasn't. I heard him breathing from next to the giant mass of rhododendrons.

"Uh, I thought I'd wait until the sun comes up to go?"

"Then it's going to be a long night for you over there. Cold too. Don't be a scaredy squirrel. They won't touch you." I glared around at the others. *You'd better not.* I glared the longest at Stone. He inclined his head and pretended to skewer meat he'd secured earlier.

Wolfe grumbled something I didn't catch, something like, "As if every night hasn't been a long night since you." He released a lungful of air the way people do before acting out in faith.

He plopped down next to me, reaching toward the blaze. "Could it be any colder?"

The girl next to him shifted away, and Rebecca nudged her brother. The drumming revved up while two boys argued over which leaves make better beds, their eyes flickering to me.

I turned my back on them all. "Cold? Um. You're

on a mountain? Be grateful. If we'd camped any higher you'd be whining about the snow right now."

He shuddered. "Sure. Tomorrow morning I'll do my touchdown dance and celebrate that my fingers are still attached. Even though my toes lay in a black, frostbitten heap next to me."

Stone glared at the sizzling meat. Wolfe's gaze turned from him to Josh's drumming hands and Rebecca, slouched and appearing to watch them.

Wolfe turned toward Melody and the girl asleep next to him. "So. These are the ones you're saving, huh? Or did you do it already?"

Stone's and Rebecca's heads swiveled like weathervanes in high wind.

I ducked mine. "Shh. Don't talk about it. Since it's, uh, complicated. And I'm not sure. But speaking of other Christians, last I heard you thought they—*we*— were monsters. Makes you pretty brain dead to go to all that work finding me. Since all we do is attack people and set things on fire."

Wolfe threw his head back and let loose, stopping when I stood to leave. "Hey, was I wrong? In case you missed it, your boyfriend over there didn't hold my hands because of my soft skin. He about took my arms off. And his little compadre was pretty stab happy with his knife."

"Not a knife." I sat back down. "A rock. And he's not my boyfriend."

"So?"

Stone rose and slipped away between the same trees his brother had.

My teeth released my lower lip. "So. Why risk coming here? For real this time. You said something about a dream. Was that why you came? Because of your dream?"

"And like you said, let's not talk about it because it's complicated. I dream a lot, so I doubt this one's something to get worked up over. But if you want to talk dreams, there was this one I had when I was ten. They called me Ninja Wolfe."

I covered my ears. "Forget it. Instead tell me, how'd you know I'd be here on Jefferson? I for sure didn't tell you. And I'm willing to bet my life Melody didn't. You track us?"

He jerked up his jacket collar. *Caught*.

"That's it, then. But how did we not see you?" *Or sense you?* Melody's lids drooped as she stared into the fire. Was she slipping? Was her gift weakening?

"As soon as you all took off that night, I remembered your whistle. So I grabbed Bo and booked it after."

I chucked a maple seed pod at him. It fell short and helicoptered to the ground. "You! It was you with the dog that first night! You know you scared us off a cliff with all that barking?"

"Yeah? Sorry. I hadn't thought of that." He pulled an apologetic face that fell way short. "We gave up in the downpour and went home. Good thing, though, because I ran into Jezebel, on her way to join us. Totally lost but wouldn't admit it, of course."

He laughed. "Yeah, you should bite your nail. Just so you know, she considers you a big, fat traitor, abandoning her like that and running off. It seems you broke the sacred sister bond thing you two share. And the next morning—"

"You mean the next morning after your dream."

"Er, OK, after that I went back to where I'd lost your trail and wandered around and then out of nowhere this raggedy homeless guy showed up. And he, well, he reminded me a lot of you."

A raggedy homeless guy. In the woods the day after the rainstorm. Samuel, no doubt. With his black-rimmed nails, discolored beard, and filthy clothes.

"Flattered, Wolfe. Thanks."

"Well, if you took a shower more than once every—how old are you? Fifteen? Sixteen? If you took a shower more than once every sixteen years..." He broke off, shoulders shaking.

I turned away with a frown. Rebecca grinned too, although not in my direction. Her brother must've said something I hadn't heard. Something funny.

Wolfe elbowed me. "What I *meant* was the guy was fiercely peaceful. Yeah, I think that's right. His fierce peacefulness reminded me of you. So, I asked him if he'd seen you and which way you'd gone."

My forehead wrinkled in disbelief. "And he told you? You understood him?"

"Uh, sort of. He muttered something like, 'It is impossible for man, but God makes it not impossible.'"

I scrubbed at my face in anguish while he butchered God's perfect wording. "'With man this is impossible, but with God all things are possible.' And you deduced from this we were heading to Mount Jefferson?"

He grinned and pulled a thick square of folded paper out of his pocket. "Well, yeah. And it helped when he kept pointing at two peaks on the map that I sort of took from Melody's bag. Here."

I snatched the stolen paper and unfolded it until I held a battered map with rips at each fold. *Willamette National Forest* ran across its top.

I traced the red line we must've driven from

Mount Washington and the wide blank of high desert, empty of marked towns. I traced all the way back to the area near Prineville. My fingertip lingered. *Home*.

"She had a map." I peered across the fire, where Melody's forehead bumped onto her kneecaps and stayed there.

He let out a sigh of relief. "You're not mad? It was tucked into the bag's lining, and it's out of date. But, hey. I hope me having it didn't mess you up."

I help up a finger. "Hold up. You said Sam—er—the homeless guy, showed you two peaks. How'd you know which one? Did you...you didn't try Washington first did you?"

My heart accelerated. Darcy slinking between trees. Raging fires. Nonbelievers snuffed out like ants underfoot. And Wolfe wandering around searching for Christians.

"Nah. I took the 'impossible for man' part literally. From the two he showed me, I chose the one that's hardest to climb. Jefferson is a Class four and five. A person's got to be an expert climber to get up it."

"Oh. Huh. That was actually kind of smart of you, Wolfe."

He scooted backward in surprise. "Are you saying something kind? To me? Did Dove—what's your last name?"

"Strong."

"Did Dove Strong call me smart? That's the first thing you've said that doesn't shred me like broken glass."

To my right, someone snorted, and I whipped around. Rebecca again. Coughing.

I got to my feet and headed for the trees where Stone had vanished.

Wolfe's voice trailed after. "Wait, you're taking off now? Your conscience doesn't cry out at leaving me here, surrounded by radicals who I'm guessing want nothing more than to be rid of me? That's pretty cold, bird. Especially since you built my hopes up with that sweet compliment."

Biting my cheek, I strode out of the fire's glow to have it out with the Benders.

"She'll be back," Rebecca said. "In the meantime, how about handing over that branch you're holding like a spear? We'll get some rabbit on it and call a truce for the night."

24

I still smelled the campfire behind me when Reed's low murmur stopped me.

"...I can't believe it, she's not even that pretty, Stone."

I stood behind a tree and hid from view. *Huh?* What girl were they talking about? They'd only met Rebecca and the other girl hours ago, and I couldn't imagine Reed saying Melody was ugly.

I shifted uneasily, pressed my forehead to the bark, and hugged the oak. My foot tapped soundlessly against its roots.

Hurry up and agree, Stone. Let's end this discussion about me so I can come out.

"Well, I dunno, Reed. I know her hair's not brown, but it has whites and yellows. You ever notice how it kind of shimmers white in the sun? Like feathers of a real dove?"

The warrior made a disgusted noise, which covered my gasp. "We're not on some double-date campout right now. You understand that? Yeah? Because I'm not sure you do. I one hundred percent need to know you've got my back—every single moment. If it comes to a real battle, you and I have to be in sync—with one person calling the shots. You do agree I should call them?"

"Of course, Reed."

"Not you? Or her?"

"No."

"Good. Because hear me, brother. If I can't count on you—like I couldn't back there—you might as well head home and send Darcy."

"No. No! I've got your back, Reed."

"Sorry. I didn't quite hear?"

"I've. Got. Your. Back!" The roots under my soles vibrated with Stone's promise.

Footsteps approached—running, reckless footsteps. I'd traveled enough miles with Melody to recognize them. I held my breath and tried to become moss on the oak.

"Reed!" Melody shrieked. "You left. And it's coming. Big time. I can feel it so badly I can't breathe. I can't stand it. Oh please, let's go to that den to hide. It's so evil I can't remember...I can't remember how to..."

I leaned around the trunk but didn't catch the rest. I pictured her face crushed against the warrior's concave chest.

"Shh. Shh. It's OK. I've got you. That Wolfe guy still there?"

"Yes."

More soothing noises. "And Dove? She's there with the rest, right?"

Again, her words were muffled. "...not with you?"

Crashing feet stampeded past me on my left side. Racing for the clearing without bothering about stealth.

"Stone! Wait up, brother."

~*~

Blinking in the brightness, I located the warrior

flanked by his bigger brother. Both towered over Wolfe. The latter held a lump of cooked rabbit in his palm. His eyes darted between them and the charred stick two feet away.

"The name's Wolfe, and I've no clue where your girlfriend went. Maybe she didn't like the way you detach people's arms like building blocks and decided—"

"Enough." Reed shoved him with his foot. "Forget the girl. I give you one more chance. Tell us who you're with. And don't lie—we know your comrades are near. You no longer possess the element of surprise, so start talking. Fast."

Wolfe sprang to his feet and frowned down at the warrior. Even so, standing didn't give him any upper hand on Stone. "*I* don't know! If someone's coming, why ask only me? How about them?" He gestured around the circle. "They're pretty decent once they thaw out. Warm. Friendly. The type to have tons of friends who'd drop by for a..."

He faltered under the neighboring girl's thunderous glare.

The warrior held up his hand for silence. "You're Satan's only proven ally here. And whoever's coming yields Satan's power. I doubt a coincidence."

Wolfe shrugged. "Must be. No other explanation."

"I have one." Reed gestured at dropped-jaw Christians on the ground. "Melody? Is this fear familiar? Have you met this evil before—from specific people? You mentioned once that each threat has its own flavor. Have you tasted this threat before?"

She squeezed her arms tighter around her torso. "I thought so. At first. I can't tell for sure. It's so..."

She swayed. In a flash, Stone supported her with

his arm.

Reed paced among the group. "Brothers and sisters in Christ. A heavy satanic force descends. The time has come to defend not only ourselves, but our land and our Council. Our enemies dare to attack us on this land set aside by God for His people. So I charge you to be brave. Be bold. Be the first believers to fulfill the Reclaim to take back our land, starting with this mountain."

Josh scratched his curls with a drumstick. "I don't understand why—"

"Whoever is with me, stand. Stand up. And if you're with me, you'll agree that this enemy," Reed jabbed a finger at Wolfe, who reacted like a deer mesmerized by approaching car lights, "needs to be treated like one. Melody's gift of recognizing wickedness proves he's involved. She recognizes this coming threat. She's tasted it, met it before. It's *his* people."

The accused backed, with hands raised. "Whoa. Wait a minute. This is nuts. I don't know nothing. If you want me to go, I'll go."

I glanced around the clearing where no one else had stood. "Are you mental, Reed? You are trying to force us to sin? The Council hasn't decided on war. The decision isn't up to us. It's up to God—and the thousands of believers who've been praying. So for us to make this choice of violence ourselves would be a sin. There's no other word for it. Sin."

Reed flicked his chin at me. His brother released Melody and joined me. His face betrayed no relief that the girl with shimmering hair showed up, unharmed.

"Wait." I wrenched my head away from his reaching palm. "I thought of more words for your plan. Like *murder*. And *wickedness*."

Stone's hand found its mark, pressing against my lips.

Rebecca stood. "Hang on a sec. I appreciate your warnings and that you have a plan, Benders, but I think we all have a say in this. So get off Dove and let her have hers."

Reed nodded, and Stone released me.

Anger's heat licked at me. I shoved Stone.

"Well, Dove? Spit it out, then."

I ignored Reed, fingering my tunic—my Breastplate of Righteousness—until the last clinging hot tendrils evaporated in the chill air. "I will follow your lead, Benders, and stand with you. Not because I like you but because I know God created you with an ability to keep us safe. But leave Wolfe alone. And don't think of killing whoever is coming, or even really harming them. Otherwise I'm leaving. Right now."

Wolfe's glowering neighbor bounced up. "Me too."

"I'm with her," Rebecca said. "But I'm also with you too, Reed. As long as you accept Dove's stipulations. No killing."

"Fine, fine." He held up his hands. "We don't have time to argue details. But believe me, Heathen, I will personally stop you if you try to interfere."

Wolfe's attempt at whistling was a pathetic warble.

"Quick now. Everyone, what are your go-to defenses back home? Ones we can use here? Shout them out. Keep in mind our limited resources."

Joshua rubbed his curls into a messier frizz. "Defenses? But back home we don't—"

"Fire," Rebecca cut across her brother.

"I'm a decent throw. And shot." The guy I'd heard called Hunter kicked his way out of a pile of ferns. "And I've got an extra slingshot for whoever wants it."

Melody raised her hand. "Animal...you know...sounds."

"Stingers. That is, if I can have my call back." I hadn't missed Reed's subtle pocketing of it earlier on his way to set snares.

I met his eyes but saw no embarrassment. Only satisfaction. And a smirk. *So much for ringing bells and light.* "Easy victory. Everyone, prepare what supplies you'll need to fight—er defend—yourselves. I give you four minutes. Stone, count us down. Melody, stay beside me. I need to know when our opposition is steps away. Heathen, keep out of our way. And all of you remember, the Lord God is with us. No one can stand against."

A subdued drumroll began, keeping pace with Stone's countdown of the seconds.

I skittered into the warmth and knelt next to my pack, pulling out a plastic jar of bee repellant. My fingers fished out a golden blob—a mixture of liquid smoke, bee pheromone, and oils from the mint back home—and began to smear it over my face. It'd cover all skin not covered by clothes or hair.

A couple feet off, I felt Wolfe's scrutiny, his face scrunched up, as if watching something icky happening. Not mad at being falsely accused. Or scared sick at what was about to happen. But grossed out.

The skin of his arm was showing.

"Where's your jacket?" I slapped another glob onto the back of my neck and squished it towards my hairline. "Get it. Put it on."

He motioned at the fire where blue and green cloth stretched on a branch next to it. "It got soaked while trying to find you on a creepy mountain."

I worked the oily repellant into the spaces between my fingers.

"Why, you ask, was it soaked when it hasn't rained? Well, Dove, it's sort of embarrassing. I lost my cool and leaped in a pond. Yeah, I did. Actually, that'd be a good backup plan for whoever's coming—lure them to the water's edge. Sneak up behind and make a noise like a possessed frog. Then *voila!* They panic, fall in, and we sit back and watch them grow weak from hypothermia."

"Wear it. Even if it's wet."

He rubbed his arms and then stretched them at the dying blaze. "So. What's with you and skin? I've never met a girl so squeamish about a little bare epidermis. Or maybe this time it's *my* skin that's the problem?"

"Yeah, it's a problem." I handed off the repellant to Reed's outstretched hand. He passed it to Melody, who dipped a finger inside and sniffed. She set it down.

Wolfe's silent amusement grew.

"What?"

"So my skin's causing you a problem? Like what? Impure thoughts?"

The green and blue blur smacked Wolfe flush in the face.

"Ow!" He clapped his palm to his eyebrow. "Zipper."

I stood to help Melody. Stone stood on the far side of the fire with his back to us. His low voice ticked off the seconds. A couple feet away lay the jacketless limb.

"Trust me on this one, Wolfe. Cover yourself.

Unless you enjoy pain. Irritated bugs and bare skin don't mix."

25

Shield of Faith. *Check.* Helmet of Salvation. *Got it.* Belt, shoes, sword, breastplate. Yes. I wore my full armor. I was ready.

The crazed wildcat yowl drowned out my call's droning buzz as well as the small, shifting noises of the dying campfire at my feet.

I knocked Melody's arm. The hair-raising echo dissipated into the woods. "No more. If Reed's right—if it's the same nonbelievers that Wolfe knows—then they'll recognize your sound. And head right for it, for us."

"But Reed told me to, Dove."

I wasn't quite sure which bush at the clearing's edge hid him. I let my glare touch each.

Not only did Melody and I have to stay in plain view, waiting for the attacking force to show, but also Reed instructed Melody to purposefully bait them—to lure them in. *If* he was right about who this was.

I so hoped he was wrong and these were strangers drawing close—strangers who'd run away from a wild cat's cry, not towards it.

I worked my call again—blew until I had to stop. Too dizzy. Plus, I heard the swarms, and I didn't want them on us until necessary.

The length of Melody's arm pressed against my sleeve, her muscles taut through her fur.

I thought a moment. "I never did ask how you do that. And what other animals can you be?"

Her arm relaxed a fraction. "Four. I do four. Deer, cat, frog, and this one. Guess."

A melancholy wail of something almost human rose up next to me. I shuddered at whatever unnatural thing this was, pleading for help.

She giggled. "Peacock. Terrifying, right? Micah's best at creature calls, though. He can sound like every—"

"Melody!" Reed's whisper came from the bush behind us.

"Sorry."

I started to ask in a louder tone what type of deer call. But she was transfixed on the black blob of rhododendrons.

My mouth became the high desert at noon.

I sensed it now too. Danger.

I gripped her hand, positioned my bee call, and started buzzing with all the air in my lungs.

In the scant firelight, seven bundled figures climbed out from the bushes. No faces—only hoods, coats, bulging hiking bags, a couple of walking sticks.

Dizzily, I found my breath while a single bee zipped around the tattered sleeve grasping a forked stick.

"Samuel!" Melody lurched forward, but I hung on. Samuel slipped sideways into the trees and disappeared.

The largest newcomer made a move to go after.

"Nah—let him go. We don't need him no more. See? They're right there."

Melody's grip cut off the circulation to my fingertips at Diamond's voice.

The girl with violet eyes I couldn't yet see paced forwards. "You know why we're here, radicals? You must've known we were far from done with you when you decided to take off."

I struggled to throw off my shock at seeing Samuel, and the worse one that he'd led my enemies to me. "So? What's stopping you now? We're right here. Unless we Christians are too scary for you?"

I forced my lips into a smile and beckoned, taunted with one hand. My other still clung to Melody's. Her hand began to shake.

"Hey." The guy who'd lunged after Samuel circled the shadowed clearing. "I thought you promised Wolfe would be here, Diamond."

"Did I get here before you?" She thrust an arm at me. "Ask the fanatic chick."

I didn't reply, too busy inviting the swarm the rest of the way. A girl pointed at me with a giggle but then got distracted swiping an aggressive bug.

Diamond stepped towards me. "Stop it. I said stop it!"

If I was the anxious type, I'd have been worried. They only had to take the call away from me—like Jezebel had. I wasn't worried. Anyway, they'd run out of time.

The clearing darkened and began to vibrate.

"Wasps!" A boy fell.

Others flattened themselves to the ground too. Only Diamond, the biggest guy, and a tall figure with a humongous backpack made a dash for the trees.

They stopped short as a line of fire slashed the dark earth. It grew until an inescapable, flaming ring surrounded them all.

Melody and I poised motionless at its center. The

repellant did its job, but the bees still crawled over my hair, face, and clothes. Tiny clinging feet invited me to swipe them off, which was risky. Instead, I focused on watching Reed's two-part plan unfold:

Part one—we'd trapped them.

Part two, we weakened them.

The bees distracted the enemies away from me and Melody. Preoccupied, they flailed their arms, leaped to their feet, and crashed back down, yelling... They seemed more panicked about the number of insects than the stings. Pain screams are different. Worse.

I closed my eyes and wondered if Melody had remembered to bee repellant her lids and if the smoke from the fire ring protected the hidden Christians and one nonbeliever positioned around the perimeter.

The smoke-sedated bees calmed on this side. But the waist-high fire walls would soon burn themselves out. Would fire and stingers convince Diamond and her group that they'd lost? To back down and leave?

Chaos surged around me. Without moving my lips, I prayed Hunter, who held a sling weapon, shot straight. I couldn't dodge projectiles wearing bees like this.

Through cracked lids I saw the tallest girl dump her blanket bundle onto the trampled ferns and sprint. Trapped, she stumbled and cursed as she fell.

I forgot the bugs and opened my eyes wider. The bundle had sprouted a leg and an arm.

As the whole thing rolled over, the blanket fell off. Jezebel sat up, rubbing her eyes and blinking.

Her fist found her hip. With a huff, she jerked her bag's pink strap back onto her shoulder. Her fingers rubbed the line of her sternum, taking in the fire. Then she saw the bees.

Terror. Shock. Abandonment. All those emotions swam in her dark eyes before she squeezed them shut, blocking out the nightmare.

My chest ripped. Feelings I'd never known—and couldn't name—burst out. Her pain hurt me. Each sting on her skin, her fear, her abandonment. They'd become mine.

Three running leaps brought me close enough to throw myself over her. I knocked off the bees and rubbed, trying to transfer the repellant from my skin to hers while she fought me.

So much skin—too much!

And I stirred up the sleepy bees. Because of me, two more stingers marked her cheek. I abandoned my attempts and searched for protection in the trees. But the flame walls still licked too high to jump.

I felt a projectile's breeze as it whistled past. Again, I threw myself over her, but this time she didn't push back.

Heaviness slammed down on my back, almost breaking me. Groaning, I braced myself against it.

Had a tree fallen on me? Why had Jezebel stopped moving? I groaned again and felt my trembling arms give a little. No! I couldn't let them get her—not the bees or projectiles or this weird, crushing force.

Arms and legs grappled around me, and Wolfe's shoulder tried to bulldoze me aside. I discovered Stone's torso stretched across my back while he held onto Wolfe.

I arched my spine hard and bucked.

Miraculously, Stone rolled off. The wrestling continued next to me, but I ignored it and chafed Jezebel's skin. How brainless to not have kept my repellant jar on me.

My own layer had worn thin. I swiped at the bee stinging my wrist and started plucking striped bodies from the girl's tangled strands.

Why didn't she fight me now? Why didn't she move...or open her eyes?

More projectiles flew overhead, and someone banged against my legs. I kicked the invader wrapped in the blanket who'd tripped over me, but he stayed down like the others. Crumpled heaps around the smoky clearing. Only Diamond and another still paced the boundaries.

Through the haze, I made out the believers on the other side of the shrinking flames. Rebecca, Joshua, Hunter, and two more whose names I didn't know.

Reed leaned into the fire. "Get out of there, Stone! Let him go. We need you."

Open your eyes and be OK, I commanded the limp body under me.

"Jezebel!" Wolfe sprinted forward, then flew backwards. He sprawled yards away while Stone, who'd reared up in front of me, continued to crouch like a barrier.

"Reed! Reed!"

I'd forgotten Melody. And I couldn't see her around the oversized boy in my way.

"Extinguish the fire," Reed said. "Give me a two-foot entrance right here, right now."

Without waiting, he charged through the blaze but not fast enough. His pant leg streamed with fire as he raced out of my line of vision. He reappeared—still burning—staggering under Melody's weight. Stone beat the flames off his brother while a section of the ring went out. The three crossed to the other

Christians.

The swarm had moved off, and human forms huddled on the trampled ferns inside the dying fire ring. Farthest away, two defeated teens knelt with their hands up. The violet eyes were angry black slits.

I felt a push against my stomach. Jezebel's eyes studied me. Not scared now. But I knew I should comfort her.

"Well, Jezebel. That was a real brain dead thing for you to do, coming here."

She shoved me away with surprising force. "I," she glared up, "am going home."

She threw herself into my lap. I placed my arms in an awkward circle around her and felt warm drops running down my neck.

"I'm not crying."

"You better not be, tough stuff. You better not." I blinked against my own sudden achy-scratchy blindness.

Blue and green sleeves from behind lifted her off.

"Don't mess with me," Wolfe warned Rebecca, who jogged past with her hands full of rope. For the first time, I noticed the other Christians binding together ankles and wrists.

Wolfe removed a stinger from his sister's hair. "Your meds? You have 'em? Been taking 'em?"

She nodded and touched her bag's pink strap. Then curled against him with her face hidden.

Letting out a breath, he squinted at me. "Why'd you—"

Smack. A coil of braided vines landed next to me. I swiveled. Reed's leg was at my eye level. Ugly pink skin peeked through the singed deerskin hanging in tatters.

"Hurry up, Dove. After you restrain her, bring her to that enclosure. If you don't know it, go with Stone."

His brother paused, about to enter the midnight forest with three anchored-together attackers.

I brushed off dead bees. Reed's face strained tight under its ash and sweat. I focused on that. "Are you blind, Reed? She's a little kid. Not a prisoner. I'm not tying her up or making her go anywhere she doesn't want, and neither are you."

His eyes iced mine. "Fine. Stone?"

"Whoa." Wolfe sprang up. "Relax, Giant—I've got this. Dove. He's right. Jezzy and I should go with our friends."

I couldn't speak—could only watch him join his...friends, he'd called them. His sister's head bumped against his shoulder while he walked away from me.

"I guarantee when the brat is conscious, she'll be singing about how she's responsible for all this— spying on me with the homeless dude, ordering him to take her to me, rounding up Diamond and everyone, most likely with a bunch of made-up stories."

He turned serious. "But what I mean is they— we—accept defeat. My friends made a mistake, and we'll all leave as soon as it's light. You won't have to worry about them—us—again."

Reed snapped his fingers. "You've no negotiation rights, Heathen. You might live. Only God knows. Stone, tie 'em up. Both of them."

"What?" Wolfe jerked around to see Reed. A weak laugh escaped. "Oh, you're joking. But no. No, wait. You don't need to tie us. I told you we're not gonna give you trouble."

"Oh, come on." Diamond's teeth-clenched

demand rose from somewhere near Stone. "You're not going to be able to reason with a fanatic. So let him, come on, and we'll figure our own way out of here."

"Hey, not so tight, Giant. I'm carrying someone here."

The warrior blocked my path after them. "No." He studied me. "You'll stay with me."

Something clanked inside the sack he rummaged through. Before I could see what he held, an iron circle closed around my ankle—the kind my dad wore when the cops took him to jail. The other end he secured around his own uninjured ankle.

I folded my arms. "This is the dumbest thing you've ever done, Reed. Which is saying something. Give me the key."

He poured a trickle from his leather pouch onto his burn, breathing quick. "Cop misplaced these on the slope when he fell. At the time, I didn't understand the reason. Why'd God want me to have it? Now I know. And so *you* know, I consider my injury one-hundred percent your fault."

I fumbled my shackle mid-twist. "What? You're serious? That's not fair. Blame Rebecca. Fire was her job."

"And yours was to stand with Melody. You understood that."

"Is she OK?"

He ripped off the charred bottom of his pant leg and tossed it. The rest, he rolled above the burn damage. "Yet you abandoned her to aid an enemy who was at no real risk. Your gross overreaction drew her brother, who hadn't perceived her presence before. And, of course, Stone believed he should follow. And that, Dove, left us weak in our perimeter offense.

"Mercifully, God enabled us to win despite this. But the real point is that Melody became so upset by your desertion that she positioned herself to be hit by our slingers. She let two attackers use her as a shield. Yes, Dove. She'll live. She's recovering as I speak. But after your abandonment I had to rescue her. And so, because of your choices, I'm burned."

I shrugged. "Well, warrior. It's obvious, right? If you don't want to get eaten by the fire, move quicker through the flames next time. Don't drag your feet. Do it like how Stone did."

He choked while his fingers clenched the handful of moss.

"What's the plan?" His brother sidled up. "They want to know. And they're all pretty hungry."

"Yes." I tried to step forward but couldn't. "Food. Those greens and berries in your sack. Make sure the little girl gets most of them."

"Ignore her, Stone. You got them secured in the enclosure so they can't escape? Even the littlest?"

"Uh-huh." Stone noticed our ankles.

"Who's guarding them? Brother?"

Stone looked away. "Hunter."

"Not good enough. You and Mel are the only ones I trust tonight. Some of us may be turning traitor."

From under his bleached brows, light eyes lifted. Still, I read nothing.

Reed finished securing the moss to his calf. "You two are on guard duty tonight. If you can handle it?"

Stone nodded.

"Have Mel eat something, and she'll be fine. And let her know she's to give three peacock calls if that old, bearded guy—or anyone else uninvited—shows up. Dove won't be showing, but right now she applies as someone to give the alarm call on. Can you remember all that?"

"Yeah." His brother glanced again at our shackles before moving off into thick brush. "Yeah, I got it."

Reed led me towards the resurrected campfire where the others bedded down for the night, avoiding spots that still smoked. Before we reached them, he unleashed his ultimatum.

If I chose to stay true to the believers, I was free to continue on with them to the Council. But, if I went near the prisoners or aided them in any way, I'd be treated as an enemy myself. Excommunicated from the group. My prayer results would become worthless as the scraps of paper they were written on.

I laughed in his face that stayed too close since we were stuck together. "I can get to the Council with or without you."

As if it was *people* I relied on to guide me.

"So, that's your choice, Dove? Because if it is, I will accompany you back to the highway at dawn. You'll be bound and left with a note explaining you're a Christian involved in the police evasion last week."

I recognized the reality of his threat. Wherever Reed went, his brother and his Samson strength trotted obediently along.

With effort, I held my sneer. "Then you'd miss the Council's decision yourselves."

"Worth it." Reed gestured for us to settle at a piece of earth far from the fire. Keeping heat off his burn, no doubt.

"What's with the matching anklets?" Joshua craned his neck.

"So I can sleep." Reed gestured at me while I tucked the ends of my metallic blanket under myself.

The boy scratched his head. "And the plan? Are a couple of us staying behind tomorrow to lead those others back down to the highway?"

Reed yawned. "When the sun rises, we'll decide. Forget about them for a few hours. I promise they're fine, and you won't be harmed."

Joshua flopped down next to his sleeping sister and spoke to the stars. "I guess. But sure was a lot of bees."

26

The forest night pressed down, broken by the shifting noises of the hollow stump crumbling as it burned. Each time, Reed twitched beside me.

His kicks and ankle tugs didn't matter—I wouldn't sleep tonight. My head was too full, yet so brain dead, exhausted. My prayers and worries got all gummed together.

Oh Lord...

The key! He must have a key to this ankle trap. The cops had one for my dad's, and I bet it's in his sack under his head. Where's the opening? There. By his nose. Though he'll wake up if I try to dig a key out.

Oh Lord, tell me. Which side do I choose? The one with those you've chosen and blessed as your own? Or the other with the nonbelievers, with Satan's followers?

The answer seems obvious. But Wolfe and Jezebel...

Jezebel. Poor kid. Freezing. Not even a blanket. And all those stings.

I rubbed at my wrist.

Even if I escaped Reed's chains, Melody would sound the alarm when she saw me. I heard wedding vows every time they spoke to each other. And now that he'd rescued her? No. I couldn't trust her.

Fine. Tomorrow, then. In a few hours, I'd convince Reed to free me—that I was on his side. Then, I'd help brother and sister escape.

Escape. They had to escape to stay alive because the warrior didn't plan to let them go. Wolfe had thought he kidded about the 'you *might* live' bit. But I knew Reed better.

Under my glare, he turned and knocked my shin.

If only I'd been able to travel by myself from the start, then I'd have avoided all this. Messes like this didn't happen when it was only me and the Spirit. It was much less complicated with only one voice to listen to—

Rebecca's creeping feet traveled nearly soundless over the ash and trampled ferns. She put her finger to her lips and continued toward me.

For the second time today, it struck me how *different* she was from other Christians I knew. It had nothing to do with her height and skin tone, but by the way she wore her hair and clothes, similar to Diamond's style.

She sank to the ground a foot away.

What do I even know about this stranger? Fire. She liked it. And could handle it well. How could I have been so dumb as to trust a fire-loving stranger?

Cross-legged, she cradled her chin and studied me. Her grin pulled lopsided. "I'm freaking you out. Sorry. But we need to talk. I still agree with you about those prisoners. You called Reed's plan for them 'a sin' and I agree."

My hand hovered in the air—as if to wake and warn him. I lowered it.

She nodded. "But you'll convince the others better if you don't punch them in the ears with your words every time you open your mouth. When you speak, I want to duck and cover. It's that painful."

I opened my mouth and then closed it.

She bit her quivering lip. "So you agree. But I assume you're not actively trying to get people's hackles up?"

"Not my fault. I'm not used to talking with people so much."

"Yeah, Dove. I figured. But I've gathered despite your—umm—unfortunate manner of communicating with us humans that you're quite wise in heavenly things. I'm going to come right out and ask. You can hear God better than the rest of us, can't you?"

I shrugged and then nodded.

"Figured. The way you stop and listen sometimes, like you're hearing something the rest of us can't. And I bet when you talk to Him, your words come out better?"

I blinked.

"Right. That's the Holy Spirit interceding for you. It's an automatic phenomenon. It comes naturally for true believers. You do it without thinking. But see, Dove, communicating with people is different. There's a way of saying things so they'll believe you and agree with you. It's purposeful and requires skill. But don't rip yourself up over being a huge failure." She patted my shoulder. "You'll never be as good at it as I am. Because that's *my* gift. I'm a speaker—a people speaker."

"Speaking? That's an actual gift? Sounds made up." I wrinkled my nose. But what she said began to make sense—why I felt so ready to agree each time she opened her mouth.

"There you go again, Dove. Stabbing my eardrums. But yes. When I talk, people listen. Believe. And most often do what I want. Partly because God intercedes on my behalf, but also because I know how

229

to deliver myself to win people to my side.

"So when I meet someone like him," She stuck a thumb at the flushed warrior twitching in his sleep. "I soak him in. Who is he? How does he talk, move, respond? I adapt my ways so he'll respond in my favor.

"Sometimes I'm empathetic with an edge of humor. Or I merely listen and reassure. Or like your nemesis here, I exude pure confidence with a heavy dose of flattery. That way he believes I'm on his side, even if I'm not."

"Well, that's awesome for you, but I could never do that." I couldn't imagine the effort it would take to pull off something like that—the intricate untangling of words before they left my mouth.

She straightened, and the lines of her face hardened in the moonlight. Her warm irises turned cold. "You've never even tried."

After a moment, she softened. "But I feel similar to you about those others tied up. Even more for that clueless Wolfe of yours and his little one. They remind me of some of my neighbors and friends. Lost spiritually, but not bad people."

I gasped and, in my excitement, yanked Reed's ankle. "Neighbors? Friends?"

She waited until he stopped muttering. "Because of my gift I don't have to hide like the rest of you. Me and my brother and mom live in an apartment complex in Portland with five other families. Only two are still Satan's. Three we've brought to Christ. All those you see over there by my brother? They're from those families—their messengers.

"So, Dove, I know. I know most non-Christians aren't evil—only prone to evil because they haven't had a chance to experience Christ's transforming power."

I couldn't breathe. Couldn't speak.

A month ago, the idea of a non-believer switching sides had never entered my head. For two weeks, I'd driven myself to the edge of crazed annoyance, wondering if it were possible. And now, this girl promised it could happen. It *had* happened. And I believed her.

"Rebecca! Do you think you can—"

"Convince Stone and Melody to let their prisoners go? It's probable."

But instead of leaping up to do it, she melted onto the leaves with her hands tucked under her hair. "Yet, why would I risk your nemesis's wrath unless..."

"Unless?"

"Unless I'm convinced it's God's will—and not only my own. Or yours."

My body sagged. So, she'd do nothing.

She nudged me with her shoe. "That's your cue. Your moment to practice, Ms. Strong. Pray for the Spirit to guide your words so they're true and sweet."

I tried to swallow. My mouth dried up. My whirling head was blank.

She held out her hand, her fingers curling like mine had when I'd taunted Diamond. "Come on, chicken girl. Show me what you can do. Convince me."

27

Two hours. That's how long Rebecca had been gone—judging by the deadness of the fire and the charcoaling of the eastern sky—and how long I hadn't moved. Next to me, Reed hadn't stirred either, other than the steady rise and fall of his torso.

I fixed my stare on the sleepers nearest the black lump that'd once been a burning stump. My lips twitched, praying no one got cold enough to wake and build up the fire. Whoever did so would notice Rebecca's absence and alert the others, and I'd be humming down the blacktop in a cop car before sunset.

Leaves rustled, and I sat up. A tall, square-shouldered figure slipped out from between branches and scurried for the ash pile. Rebecca curled up close to her brother with her back to me.

"Hey, *psst*. Rebecca. What happened?" My every muscle expected a swarm of newly-freed, Satan-driven teens.

Or maybe it'd be Stone who'd show. Or Melody, shaking Reed awake to tattle what I'd convinced Rebecca to try to do. By sunrise I'd be shackled with a different set of metal circles and driven to the jail my father had had nightmares about. My prayer results would be confiscated. My purpose made obsolete. And Wolfe and Jezebel dead.

My heart lurched. Despite my pulse thrumming in my ears, I made out two distinct sets of footsteps by feet that didn't know the meaning of quiet.

Two bodies loomed in the darkness, hesitating. The shorter one streaked forward and landed on all fours by my head.

"I owe you," Wolfe whispered to Rebecca who lay unconscious.

Jezebel yanked on my arm. "Get up!"

"Shh," I cautioned.

Speak without fear. He will sleep.

God's outright provision left me speechless.

Wolfe knelt next to his sister, shaking his head in anguish. "Now the brat won't leave. Not without you."

She crossed her arms.

"Super dumb, tough stuff." I brushed back her dark hair. The sting marks weren't as bad as I'd remembered. "Dumb, dumb, dumb."

She stabbed me in the chest with her short index finger. "No, you're the dummy 'cause you're not using your dumb head to remember why I'm here. And him, why he came all this way. Know why? Because of you, dummy. So, you're coming. Woof, carry her."

I interrupted his stammer by pulling up my blanket. The metal circle glinting around my ankle shut them both up.

An owl hooted. It was a phony call, only yards away.

Wolfe rose, yanking the back of his sister's shirt. "Blow her a kiss, goldfish. Time to go."

Jezebel's face squinched.

I spoke fast. "I can't protect you if the others wake."

"You hear that, brat? Tantrum it up and you'll get

cuffed too."

I motioned at the trees. "Go. Both of you. Beat it."

Hoot. Hoot.

She cracked an eye. "OK. I'll go...if you pinkie swear. Swear to come to my house after they uncuff you. You know where I live, so it's no problem."

"C'mon, say it." Wolfe's fingers twitched in a coaxing gesture.

I don't lie. I looked away from his hand to her smaller one, waiting for my promise. "I want to."

Not good enough, I realized. Before she could yell, I yanked up my sleeve and peeled off the last pink strip. The others I'd abandoned that first night in the snake-infested garbage bin.

I didn't need this reminder of Jezebel anymore. I wouldn't forget her—like she wouldn't me. She'd gotten herself hurt to see me again. I was no expert, but that sounded to me like love.

How insane. The glaring, little Heathen loved me. I smoothed the plastic over a sting mark on her cheek until it stayed put.

Three more owls hooted and, for the first time, Reed stirred.

Then, sister and brother left me forever—sticks crunching under Wolfe's running feet, his sister flung over his shoulder in a backward flop so quick she didn't have time to make trouble.

They disappeared behind the rhododendrons.

"Just...don't die. Ever."

28

A blink later, Reed jerked me upright. With a thudding heart, I gazed blurrily at the cloudbank against the pearly dawn sky and around at the clearing.

What was his problem? I saw none. Our comrades were asleep. The fire dead. No animal. No attacker. He couldn't know about Wolfe's and Jezebel's getaway. Not yet.

Then I heard it—the reason Reed gripped the spear he'd slept with in a ready position. He aimed the tip at a lazy, tilted cedar. I nodded, and three men pushed out from behind it single file.

I exhaled. The strangers wore winter furs like Melody's.

"Please don't skewer me." The closest lifted his empty hands skywards. Behind me I heard the sounds of others waking. "We're from the Council—the one you can't find. We saw evidence of your fire last evening and guessed Christians had arrived and were searching for us. I'm Miracle and—"

My brow wrinkled in my confusion. "Why'd you have to guess? Why didn't you know? We've been waiting almost a week, so if you're from the Council, why didn't you listen to God when you wondered when we'd arrive? Don't you pray?"

Movement snagged my periphery, but Rebecca's

head shake came too late. So did her symbolic ear rub.

Ouch, Dove.

I anchored my lips between my teeth while Miracle's smile faded. His eyes narrowed at me. "Of course we prayed. God remained inexplicably silent in His answer until now. Perhaps He was waiting for the group of pagan kids to clear out first? Yes, that must be why. When I spotted them this morning I thought they might have caused you trouble, but I see now that—"

"You spotted...pagan kids?" Reed's first leaping step in the direction of the prisoners' camp didn't go well. Either he'd forgotten we were ankle bound or he'd expected me to run synchronized, like Stone would've. I grabbed at him when he fell so I wouldn't get dragged down too.

While he shook me off, Miracle reassured us. "Children, you don't need to be afraid. We sent two scouts after their group, and they made it to the foothills—"

"Keep up!" Reed flung at me.

"What's wrong this time? The Council people are here to lead us. Yay." Joshua yawned and waved an invisible celebratory flag, eyeing me and Reed. "Why is it always so many tragedies with you all?"

"Freeze, Dove." Reed bent over. Half a second later he straightened and darted off, leaving me behind with both iron circles, one open and laying in the dirt. The key he didn't bother to re-hide bounced on its vine encircling his neck.

When I caught up to him, he'd stopped. Arms crossed, he glowered down at Stone and Melody who sat next to a small cave or den. The creepers over its entrance still swayed from him peering inside at the empty prison.

The two guards appeared dazed, the hand-woven ropes coiled on their laps.

Had they both fallen asleep? Perhaps Rebecca had waited them out and then sneaked in and untied the prisoners. That would explain her two-hour delay in returning last night.

As I thought this, Stone's eyes flickered to Rebecca. She'd trailed me. His gaze remained on her for three blinks before dropping.

No, *he* at least knew the truth—he'd experienced Rebecca's gift full force. I couldn't tell from Melody's downcast eyes if she'd been awake. She might be as clueless as she looked.

Miracle and his men arrived. "Oh, I see. Two more. Yes, let's make sure we're all together before we leave for the Council." He turned a full circle. "Any more people we need to account for?"

"Apparently not." Reed hadn't taken his eyes off his brother since we'd arrived. Against my nature, I began to squirm a little for Stone.

"Righto. Well. Let's be off." The Council man made sweeping gestures in the direction we'd come.

Reed pivoted around to face me. "So, Miracle. Did this group of kids happen to include a lanky teenage boy wearing a dark blue jacket with a depiction of a hawk's head on it? Accompanied by a black-haired girl about six?"

The man rubbed his goatee. "Why, I don't know about a certain boy. But yes—they sighted a small girl. Did you have a run in with them after all? I'm sorry about that. But you don't need to be scared of bumping into them again. Our scout gave us the message Old Saul was guiding them down. So you can be sure they'll be at the highway soon."

"Old Saul?" Reed and I asked together.

"Jinx. Owe me a soda."

I tuned out the kid, Joshua. Again, that idea eluded me—something I should know...but not anything the Spirit nudged me about. This was from myself. Information wedged too deep, like a splinter I couldn't yank out.

The short, oldest Council guy cleared some gunk from his throat and flashed a no-teeth grin.

"You'd know if you'd met Old Saul." He pinched his nose between two rough fingers. His other hand waved as if wafting a bad odor. "Right, Cal?"

Miracle—Cal—laughed. "Yes. Saul's the most eccentric Christian brethren you'll ever meet. Or sense."

This irritated me. To stop the pulling waves of heat, I kept my eyes on Melody, who'd buried her head in her hands.

"Physical description please," Reed requested through what sounded like clenched teeth.

The third Council stranger, balding and droopy, sighed. "Skin and bones. Tattooed. Bearded. Carries a forked stick."

Reed's gaze pinned Melody, who'd peeked, to the mossy boulder at her back. "You, Mel. You called him 'Samuel' last night. The same man that you claimed rescued you from the snakes—but he's given you a false name since it's Saul. And now he's joined with our enemies. So..."

His voice dropped to a murmur, working it out while ignoring Cal's protests about Samuel's— *Saul's*— alliance. "So, it was all a setup. He's worked with the devil all along and has tricked everyone, all these Christians, into trusting him."

He pointed at his brother. "Why didn't you give the alarm call when he showed up last night?"

Stone gulped. "He...he didn't, Reed. I swear. We never saw him."

"Tell. Me. What. Happened."

The coils in Stone's hands made a small, fluttering noise against his pants.

I stepped forward. "Fine. I'll tell you, Reed. It was me. I let them go."

I hadn't planned on giving myself away so soon—or at all. But maybe I spoke because I had a hard time letting two innocents take the blame. Or because I alone knew Reed and *wasn't* afraid of him. Or because not claiming responsibility for the situation felt too much like lying.

I'd convinced Rebecca to do what I wanted.

I lifted my chin against the stares and Rebecca's gasp. "Me. All me. I'm responsible for the captured taking off. I told you last night I wouldn't sit by and let you hurt them, Reed. Unclog your ears next time."

Cal held his hands out to both of us. "Children, I'm confused in this conversation, but I am certain whatever the conflict is, we can resolve it once we get to our place of Council. As far as I can tell, no one's injured. So please. Let's make sure we're together, and I will escort you."

Reed's eyeballs popped when he stooped to examine the cuff still anchored to the outside of my pants. He tested the empty, open part he'd worn. His gray cells probably throbbed as he tried to figure out how I'd freed the prisoners when I was chained to him all night.

I gave no explanation. He deserved none.

He staggered closer to Stone, eyeing me.

"What *are* you?" His furrowed brow cleared. "Councilmen. I understand your eagerness for us to finish our journey. And believe me, I'm eager too. But we have a serious problem on our hands that must be addressed now.

"This girl—" Reed jabbed a finger at me "—claims to be a follower of Christ. She even claims to have a special gift of communication with Him. But since we've joined paths, I've experienced no proof of either of these claims.

"On the contrary, I've seen her actions work against us believers and in favor of the devil again and again. I'll admit I've always had my suspicions about her, despite my friend's vision that kept me waiting for her to start my own journey here. But this morning she's openly proven whose side she's on...and it's not God's. His purpose is now clear. I was to travel with her, so I could identify her as the snake—the enemy's spy—that she is."

A wave of icy numbness swept over me.

Cal laughed into the shocked silence—so hearty it startled the crow picking near the empty den into flight. As if catching, another of Cal's men began to chuckle too.

First, trampled by Reed's words, and now this.

I opened my mouth to deny Reed's accusation and let the councilmen know how idiotic they acted, but Rebecca prodded my spine.

Cal apologized. "I'm not so much amused as I'm relieved that this is the major problem keeping us at a standstill. So relax, everyone. Suspicions and accusations are as common as mosquitoes, routinely plaguing first-timers of this journey. Tension builds as the decision-making time nears, and it's not surprising for mature Christians to come to actual blows. Please remember, the Enemy is working hard to divide us.

"Yet, we can't ignore this accusation. The last thing we want in our midst while we determine God's will for the country is the devil's workers. Fortunately, we can resolve this now." He gestured at Reed. "You. Since you're the accuser. Tell me, do you believe everyone here—except for this girl—is a true Christian? Filled with light and not darkness?"

Reed hesitated. I could tell he was feeling out a hidden trap. "Some here are still relative strangers to me. But yes. Yes, I do believe they are all true believers."

"Fine, fine." Cal clapped his hands. "Then of the rest of you—you true Christians—will any of you testify on behalf of, what was your name?"

My teeth clenched harder.

Rebecca poked me. "Dove."

"On Dove's behalf? Will anyone bear witness to having seen her pray? And testify that her supplications have been fruitful? In other words, has the Lord answered her? Anyone?"

I stared at Melody, whose lips opened, came together, opened, and snapped together again—like the turtle my cousin found during the last rainy season.

With clamped lips, she appeared to lock her gaze upon a clump of ferns.

Melody. I itched to give her a shake. To haul her closer and make her see me—make her remember.

Memories of our journey stampeded through my brain: Our unspoken communication about danger. The shimmering cloak of comfort we shared in the garbage bin. All the times I waited for her, lifted her, protected her.

Coward. Traitor. Judas.

I felt another poke in my spine. Rebecca…asking my permission.

A cloud of gratitude washed over me, lessening the heartfelt sting of Melody's betrayal.

Rebecca would testify for me. Of course they'd believe her and, as a result, they'd believe me.

So with a feeling of free-falling twenty feet, I shook my head and refused her. Because Rebecca—an acquaintance—shouldn't be standing up for me now. The ones who knew me best should testify.

I zeroed back on my traveling partner who, a moment later, peeked up and gazed straight into the eyes of my accuser. She stopped fidgeting with the coils and sat up straighter, making her choice.

I shifted to Stone. But his decision showed in the slump of his shoulders and down-tilting beard.

Biggest. Coward. Ever.

The official squirmed. "Anyone?"

"No." I shook my head at the pressure Rebecca applied to my elbow.

Them. Not you.

This was a bad situation. And this was the moment for me to take off on my own—while Cal's comrades still raised their shoulders, uncertain of how to proceed.

"We cannot hastily deal with this situation…with you. Others wiser than myself must rule on whether you are God's child or not. And I promise the truth will be revealed." Cal nodded to Reed. Reed returned a nod that appeared disgusted. He turned to me.

You'll stay with me, Lord?

Always.

Because the people who'll be deciding this are the same ones who didn't have a clue we'd arrived on Mount Jefferson. They don't seem very good at hearing you. Or have a pine nut's amount of spiritual intuition.

I lead. You follow.

I swallowed hard. "Okay. Lead on."

And when Miracle chose to think, I spoke to him — and gave a satisfied clap — I didn't correct him.

29

I didn't wear the shackles anymore, but I might as well have worn them. The two guards at my back and my confiscated pack made it clear. Goodbye, freedom.

As I trudged single file behind Joshua, I imagined swinging into the branches overhead and staying there until the whole group gave up and moved on.

I stepped down more firmly. No one here could catch me if I climbed. Not even Stone, second in line behind Cal, who led. And never the geezerly Council guy breathing down my neck—the one with the four-year-old humor who'd sniggered about Samuel's—no *Saul's*— hygiene.

Saul. Of course he was Saul and not Samuel. Not that names mattered now, but the Bible passage he'd referred to when asked his name was about Samuel declaring Saul as king. Brainlessly, I'd latched onto the wrong name.

Reed craned his neck around, and I gritted my teeth when I met his gaze. He was probably checking that I hadn't left. He jabbed his walking stick into the ground until it bowed. He only had one prisoner now, rather than the eight who'd slipped through his fingers.

I lifted my chin and stared past.

Unfortunately, my sight line collided with the back of his brother's head. I jerked my eyes from the view of his ashy waves. *He'd* only spared me one dead-eyed glance—one—right before we'd started this hike.

A jerk—like his brother. No, worse. Because, unlike his brother, I'd thought...I'd thought Stone had...but it didn't matter now. Now I knew. He didn't care if I got branded as Satan's sidekick. He didn't even care if I fell off the edge of the cliff we hiked since he'd never checked to see.

And my original traveling partner? She was harder to find in our moving line, sandwiched between the brothers. But I understood. I was dead to her.

I swallowed against the tightening in my throat and refocused on the route I'd need to remember to backtrack home.

Since an obvious way existed around the thinning bushes, sticks, and nettles, my unchallenged mind began dwelling on what would happen at the Council.

Would the "wiser" people be wise enough to believe me? Or would I have to deal with some sort of test to determine my alliance?

I skirted some nettles, recalling one of my grandpa's history lessons on seventeenth century witch hunts and some of their "tests."

I released my lip. *You're a Strong, Dove. Act like one. Don't be so pathetic. Gran wouldn't worry and carry on like this.*

As we wound our way up Jefferson, patches of hard snow showed up in shady spots. Some I recognized, as well as the barren scree on our right, from an earlier scouting trip. Before Wolfe and Jezebel had tracked me down.

I gave up on not being pathetic. In my head, I accompanied them down the bluffs, through the foothills, and back to the pavement where their inevitable vehicle waited.

30

We halted once to rest. As soon as I sat, my sweat mingled with the breeze and became a herd of icicles. Shivering, I gulped my water, crammed the dried venison into my mouth carnivorous-squirrel style, and scrambled back onto my feet to keep going.

The sun dipped low when we abandoned the trees and stopped again. The others exchanged words, drank, and fidgeted. But I gazed around, pivoting in a slow circle. This made no sense. Where to from here? Where was our goal?

There was none. Unless the goal was the super-sheer wall of rock a few yards off that led to a mountaintop of snow.

Cal shattered my concentration. "OK, everyone. Now give your knots an extra tug to make sure they're secure. If we stay together, there's no reason we should lose anyone on this climb."

With a blink, I discovered a bright orange rope— the kind Heathen owned—anchoring together most of our group. The small end of the rope stuck out from the knot Joshua had tied around his waist.

The boy ahead of me noticed the problem when he tried to hand me the foot-long length of orange.

The toothless councilman at my back sniggered. "Happy climbing."

With a click, he latched his own climbing gear into

the silent man's behind him.

I forced open my clenched fingers and studied them. Strong or weak, they'd have to get me up this precipice. I had no other human help.

Bzzzz. A zipper hummed. Three young people tugged at outer layers of clothing, loosening jackets from under the knotted rope loops at their waists.

Wordlessly, Rebecca and the heavy-browed girl tossed their jackets to Hunter, who shivered in his shirt but held his own.

Reed objected. "There's no time. We need to move right now or Melody's going to be too frozen to make the climb."

I caught a glimpse of her bent, furry back as she hugged her legs. In front of her, Stone's was as straight as the wall he examined.

Hunter finished fashioning the bulky make-shift jacket rope with hard knots, and then he spat on them. Rebecca had untied her brother and now bound the orange rope together with the new one.

With a drum roll off his tongue, Joshua handed me the long length of knotted-jackets. The sound broke while I tied Hunter's jacket around my waist with a triple knot. Hunter's teeth chattered. Again, that weird sensation ripped me.

These strangers—nonbelievers, only recently converted— did this for me.

I blinked hard, still grasping the knot. "You know it probably won't hold. And I'll end up falling a million feet and getting smashed."

Rebecca rubbed her ear. But her purple-tinged lips pulled up into a lopsided grin.

~*~

I saw it now—the optical illusion. The reason we hadn't located the Council ourselves. What had appeared to be a solid slab of black bluff intersecting an even more sheer slab slathered with white, wasn't that at all. The two rock walls offset, and the gap between them was spacious enough for an entrance to the hidden Council below.

I teetered at the sharp edge of the first slab, next to Joshua, clutching my jacket rope and peering into the crevice. The canyon's floor was far below. The valley seemed to open up, but without signs of human life. I saw no shelters. No anything.

The Council would've built these under sections of undercut mountain. They'd be camouflaged to avoid detection from the nonbelievers' planes and flying machines.

With a glance at the lone hawk circling the snowy peak, I followed the slow-moving line down into the canyon. Cal demonstrated how to climb over and onto the giant outcropping boulders, using them as footholds to work our way to the bottom.

At the canyon's first shadow, my breath frosted my lips.

Before my fingers numbed, I picked at the jacket knot around my waist. I inched closer to the kid below me and undid the next one.

I didn't need a rope like the others for this descent. And if I did, I'd climb without it because I wouldn't be responsible for three messengers freezing to death.

The councilman's boot on the outcropping at my ear grated as it slid. "Keep moving your paws, girl. Move. It ain't the time to be changing accessories or adjusting your pretty outfit."

Joshua glanced up. I shoved the three-jacket bundle at him. I didn't survey further down the line to see if his sister and the others would accept their clothes back. Either they'd accept or Joshua would carry them.

A shower of pebbles rolled onto my sleeve.

"Move them paws!"

~*~

I sprang from the last foothold onto the crusted snow. Then I crunched over to join the huddle of messengers panting, shivering, and nursing crushed fingers and skinned ankles.

I'd survived. No thanks to my feet, which, like my brain, had been confused as to whether or not they'd wanted to reach the bottom.

No matter. I'd arrived with my prayer results. Melody had too. The grim red threat of my possible failure couldn't haunt me anymore. Best of all, I stood in a sacred place that welcomed Christians. Except there was always the chance I'd be disbelieved, rejected, and kicked out of this Council with my shredded papers fluttering around my soles.

In the twilight, Joshua showed anyone who'd pay attention the new bloody gap in his smile. He paused for a moment. "Wow. It's like I'm back home in Portland."

I scanned this gloomy world—monotone gray with patches of snow and impenetrable shadows. After some serious eyestrain, I located a row of crooked stone huts huddled against the cliff's base.

"You're serious?"

It was the first time I'd heard Melody's voice today. My stomach contracted as she turned full circle. "You're not joking? This is what Portland's like?"

Rebecca cuffed her brother's curls.

"Truth time." At my elbow, Cal gestured left toward the yawning darkness engulfing the narrow canyon. "Councilman Zeke will guide the rest of you to your sleeping quarters. Help yourselves to blankets, but we ask that you not make fires in this area, in case any of you brought in fuel. Zeke will explain meeting and eating times as well as other safety requests. Before you sleep tonight, your prayer results will be secured."

The man who'd trudged at the end of the line all day looked tired. He inclined his head and headed toward the line of crooked shelters.

Reed stepped toward me. "I'm ready to testify against her. Let's get it done."

Stone and Melody waited, watching Rebecca's group trudge after Zeke. Councilman Cal shook his head. "No. You three go with Zeke. The Governor won't need your testimony."

"But—"

"Yes, Bender. But only if she summons you. She won't. Now go."

I didn't dislike Cal, I decided, as we strode off into the darkness—neither of us gave a backward glance at the warrior fuming in the snow patch.

The uneven stones felt smooth under my aching toes, whispering through the stillness about all of God's people who'd walked here before. My uncle's feet might have pressed these stones. I shivered.

"Give it a week, Strong. In one week you won't be able to remember it like this. So silent. So empty. Calm.

You'll see. That is, if you're still here. It never fails to amaze me how small this place gets when we're all here together like sardines. So hoard up your peace now."

"Sardines?" I didn't recognize that word.

A rock-hewn bench loomed out from the gloom. He beckoned me to sit on it. He touched a lantern stuck in the slab wall at my shoulder. Cool light illuminated us and revealed my least favorite councilman. He had shadowed us.

Cal chuckled. "Something my daddy used to say. Fish, I think. Sounds like they must swim in tight schools, all crowded. Rest your bones while I go see if the Governor's up for this." He opened the stone door. Warm air and light rushed out through the gap. He slipped through and vanished.

I perched on the edge of my icy seat, craning to see the heavy, horizontal slab above my head. Some type of roof? From the shadows, I heard snatches of the toothless councilman's mutterings—stuff about a brimstone lake.

Then Cal reappeared in the cool light with a pile of fur, which he flung over my back. I wrapped the thickness around my clumsy fingers and studied the bundled woman who'd escorted him. Older than my mom. But fractionally less wrinkled than my grandma.

"First arrivals and already Satan's among us. Name?" Her charcoal hovered over her clipboard.

"Dove Strong."

Her gray head jerked up for an instant, and then the curtain of boredom dropped back down—the same one I used when I pretended not to care.

She began to question me. They were obvious questions directed at finding out whether my allegiance was to Jesus or Satan.

In my usual, super-articulate way, I choked out, "God is the Creator, eternal and perfect. He sent his only Son Jesus—God and man—to earth to live a sinless life and to die for me. Because He didn't sin, death couldn't keep Him, so He's alive. And because of this I'm allowed to have a relationship with God—and eternal life with Him." I stumbled to a stop.

"Do you pray?"

"Yeah, of course."

"To whom?"

Would Satan's spy be so easily tricked? I wondered. "Uh. To God."

"Do you love Him?"

"Would I be here if I didn't, ma'am?"

"Please answer 'yes' next time, Ms. Strong. Whom do you serve?"

"God."

"Where do you learn your truths about Him?"

"From my Bible. My family. And the Holy Spirit."

"Why am I standing in the snow, interrogating this obvious Christian child?"

I smirked when both men winced.

"I reiterate. What's the accusation?"

Cal's hands fluttered at the darkness and then at me. "This boy she traveled with—Reed, he calls himself—well, he...he testified that Dove here, well, I'm not quite sure what she did, but Old Saul brought up this group of pagan kids who got into a scuffle with them. I've been trying to piece it together, and as far as I can tell—"

"Reed accused me of acting on our Enemy's behalf."

Her unblinking stare shifted to me. "Did you?"

I shrugged—then realized that wasn't going to cut it. "I don't know. A group of unbelievers hunted us to Jefferson. Most of them wanted to start trouble. And I was sort of...merciful, I guess? Whether that pleased Satan, I wouldn't know."

I took a breath, thinking of Jezebel secure at home with her brother. "Reed's biggest problem with me is that I messed up his plan of attack when I protected a godless kid who needed help. I mean, there was fire and bees and rocks and that crushing weight, plus she thinks she's tough but..."

I shook my head. "What I did—protecting her—caused our self-proclaimed leader, Reed, to be burned a little. At least *he* blames it on me. Which is stupid."

The woman's mask cracked around her eyes and mouth. "And?"

"And I sort of made friends with two non-believers. They were the two who didn't want to attack anybody. And I don't allow my friends to be treated like prisoners. Or threatened with a death sentence."

Maybe my blunt honesty would get me tossed out. I imagined an unseen, giant catapult in the shadows that would fling me up and back into the ferns halfway down the foothills.

My chin rose an inch. "So I convinced someone on our side to release them and help them escape—not only my friends, but the whole captive group. I didn't trust Reed's plans for them."

The bored expression didn't shift when the woman nodded. "Miracle. Send out another patrol. Check for more Christians on the southwest side, hunting for their way to us. And keep your eyes open for any Heathen youth, just in case."

"Yes, ma'am. Yes, Governor." Both councilmen

backed away.

"Ms. Strong. Come get warm." She leaned against the door.

Heat came from all directions, everywhere. With sharp stabs eating my fingers and cheeks, I gazed around at the golden-lit space.

The giant slab roof from outside gave the room a buried, claustrophobic feel. Stone Bender would have to do some serious slouching to move around in here.

I checked that thought and focused on the carvings above my head, stretching the length of the long room. The Garden of Eden gushed its detailed lushness. Abraham and Lot divvied up their land. David hid from King Saul in the cave, clutching his telltale knife.

In the center of it all, Jesus dominated in His glorious ascension.

Oh, Trinity. You should be the one here seeing this. If by some miracle I make it home, you're going to strangle me for not being able to describe this well enough.

The whole place was chiseled to be holy. My eyes scanned the rows of polished stone benches filling the long room. The hundreds of birch-white candles in their pebble-formed sconces.

"And how is Sarah holding out in her tree home?"

My breathing froze. I took a backward step for the door.

"Hmm. I see you inherited all of Jonah's chattiness."

At hearing my dad's name, shock rendered me mute. Then, I realized she most likely referred to my grandpa if she knew Gran. Both he and my dad shared the name Jonah. Neither talked much.

"My grandparents. How do you know about

them? Governor." I tagged on the title Cal had used.

"Best call me Miss Ruth since we're such old family friends. Yes, I'd like that better. My title sits odd on me since my position is so new. I was elected Governor over the Oregon Christian Council only at the last Council meeting, and I'm still trying to fit it. Sarah ever recall me?"

I shook my head and dropped onto a warm bench. I kept my eyes on the stone Jesus.

"Your Grandma Sarah and I were classmates, almost sisters, up until the Purge."

Again, I shook my head. "I don't know, Governor Ruth. I don't know about you or what that means, 'the Purge.'"

"*Miss Ruth*. And that's what we Councils call the painful moment in our history when our nation decided to take a stand against us true Christians. And labeled us a domestic hate group."

My extremities no longer throbbed. Her words floated to me as if from a dream.

"As I recall, the only real hate I felt back then was being labeled *that*. Me? Part of a domestic hate group?" She shook a fist. "Ridiculous! But calling us that was the only way patriotic unbelievers could justify their actions.

"What it came down to was Americans not liking their sins called sins. For us believers to proclaim only one God and only one way to Heaven, and not to embrace the other blasphemous religions of the world. Well, it was unforgivable of us. Still is. It's only a matter of time now before the government rounds us up like wildlife to be eradicated in order to keep the 'civilized folk' undisturbed. Unless..."

She zoned in on a flickering candle a while.

"Sarah. She didn't realize her blessing back when it first happened, having Christian parents. I wasn't so lucky. And her engagement to Jonah. She was able to escape into hiding with his family on all that timber-rich land.

"She went southeast, and I came north. And here we are tonight—you and me. Still hiding from the patriotic unbelievers...yet, perhaps, with more hope?"

I slouched with half-mast lids when she abandoned the candle she'd been twisting in its sconce. "Sarah. Does she still receive visions? Dreams it was, I recall."

I nodded.

"Hmm. You resemble her, Dove. And if God sent you here rather than her, I'm supposing He's generously equipped you with a heavy spiritual arsenal as well?"

"I'm a lot like my gran."

"You blessed, blessed girl. And a bit like your uncle too, if you pardon me saying it. Your eyes—their expression."

I abandoned the fur cloak and leaned forward.

"My uncle? You knew him? Then he made it here to the Council before he died? We always wondered. Do you...do you happen to know how he," I swallowed, "went? Gran deserves to know."

Governor Ruth collapsed on a bench. "I can't believe, in all these seven years, he never returned home. Never visited Sarah." She shook her head. "No, Dove. He's not dead. Didn't Miracle say your uncle guided that group of pagans to you and your fellow messengers last night?"

A roaring darkness tried to swallow me.

"Head between your knees."

I obeyed, though it seemed pointless. I'd captured the idea that'd eluded me. That thing I knew I should remember...but couldn't.

Now I remembered.

I concentrated on my foggy childhood memories of my uncle. Uncle Saul.

Tanned. Lean and wiry, like my father. Introverted—almost as shy as my aunt. An artist, like his daughter Trinity who saw beauty in the weirdest things.

"Yes." She nodded. "Yes."

I *guessed* it fit. That my Uncle Saul was 'Old Saul'—the raggedy homeless creature.

But wait. No. It didn't. Because my uncle, unlike every male in my family, was *clean*. Super-hygienic. I remembered his smell—my nose hadn't forgotten. Soap and pine. Never sweat. Never stink.

And another thing. He shaved. My uncle kept his tanned face as smooth as any girl's.

And his immaculate clothes—not only clean, but carefully created too. He never wore his pants bunched at the waist with rope like the other males in my family. He sewed his own and taught little-girl Trinity about the 'right lines' of a tunic.

Most importantly, my uncle didn't speak in Bible verse. He was soft spoken, yes. But his brain was free and whole. Not damaged like that crazy guy's—the one who decided to stand in roads while vehicles mowed him down.

"No, Governor. You're wrong. It's not him."

"He's family, Dove, whether you accept it or not."

"The man's crazy. My uncle isn't. Wasn't."

She sighed. "Not crazy. Burdened. When Saul arrived seven years ago, he was tragic. He'd lost a young fellow believer on his way here but couldn't explain how. His words almost choked him when he tried. It's my opinion that he's still searching for the missing boy."

Melody's missing brother—I forgot his name. I cringed, not wanting to believe my uncle had turned insane with guilt he'd carried all these years. But no. *He* wasn't my uncle.

"No, Governor. He can't be—and it's more than the Bible talk and wandering around homeless. That Saul guy out there? He's got no self-preservation. He invites the pagan to hurt him. My uncle was too smart for that. He grew up avoiding them—outwitting them. Like me."

"Saul's burden is heavier than his sorrow for a single missing boy, Dove. I've no proof, but I've suspected for years Saul's mental change towards life and the Heathen population is God directed."

I blanched. "God directed? As in, God's responsible for his insanity and suicidal tendencies?"

I didn't like that. She shouldn't blame God for this guy—who might be my uncle—going crazy. I didn't want to talk anymore.

"Fine. I'll pray on it." But deep down, I knew. Old Saul was my uncle. Hadn't my subconscious been poking me since the dumpster?

She stood when I did. "You understand because you're Sarah's offspring and you admit to having some of her blessed gifting, it's your duty to join our prayer warriors?"

I frowned. "Only let me submit my papers first." My hand assumed its position over them.

She gestured at the shoulder-high, stone egg form I'd passed by the door. Seamless, but now I felt the hair-width slit near the more pointed end—an opening wide enough for one family's answer to eek through.

"Two?" Her brows shot up as I unearthed both creased papers from my worn bag.

"I wish. Three." I shoved in the second one. But how much easier to have simply carried the Brae's result paper instead of towing their back-stabbing daughter along with it.

"Then I expect Satan is none too thrilled with you now."

I shrugged. The lightness I'd expected at turning over my results to the Council didn't happen. The heaviness continued and my stomach began to ache.

Home. With an explosion of detail, the tanned, familiar faces of my family swam before me against a background of sunlit maple leaves and Douglas fir. They surrounded me in a circle of comfort.

I staggered forward, my fingers reaching for a treehouse ladder made of cedar. They pressed a frigid rock door.

Comfort vanished. I dropped my hand and screwed my face into a grin before Ruth could detect my homesickness.

"No. Don't celebrate, and don't think you're safe. You've made enemies here, Dove Strong. It'll spread like the flu that you've a soft spot for Heathen. I wouldn't wander off solo while you're here...and choose wisely who to trust. You understand?"

I understood. The sooner I shook Mount Jefferson's snow off my threadbare shoes, the sooner I headed *home*, and the better off I'd be.

31

I rocked back onto my heels and tried to balance.

When I could stand without keeling over, I abandoned the flat cushion that had become my home for the past few days. I wobbled my way around the others—still bowed and praying—to grab my food ration.

I'd blinked and now fifty others kneeled in the long, carved-out stone room with me. The first night only me and Supervisor Zeph, the guy in charge of us prayer warriors, echoed around in here.

I paused at the tiny, chopped-out window and hunted for green.

Quarry gray and matching clouds.

I narrowed my eyes at the familiar gigantic figure still waiting on the same boulder a couple yards off.

I squared my shoulders and kept walking. I wasn't scared. Only Governor Ruth's warning had become a seed that'd gotten jammed in my head. And sprouted.

Enemies. Not safe. Don't trust.

Of course Reed wouldn't do a physical job like this himself since he had such a capable big brother. Murder was bound to take some muscles.

At the table, I chose to eat bread over an apple so I could get back to praying.

Supervisor Zeph sidled up and almost knocked me down with his square-toothed grin. "Way to go.

You remembered to eat, warrior Strong. Grab some water too. Have you slept today?"

I aimed a glance at the line of six vacant cots at the far end of the room, half choking on my bread to answer. "When I need to I will."

He eyed me. But I knew I had at least a couple more hours of praying left in me before I crashed.

"Supervisor." A guy from the mats waved. "Got another one down over here."

"C'mon people. Eat. Drink." With a grunt, he bustled over and heaved an unconscious woman—my size and frame—off the floor and dumped her on the nearest cot. "Please, everyone." He screwed his fists into the small of his stout back. "Please. Take breaks before it's too late. My lumbar can't take many more of you."

As I chased the bread with an extra water ration, I watched the twenty-five stacked television screens next to the table. They were divided to show the other forty-nine prayer warrior groups in other states—other councils. Of course I'd *seen* a television before, but never one that still worked.

Through the small glass windows, I spied at people who seemed a few hundred yards off. Faint voices offered food and water—Supervisor Zeph-style—over the steady, low hum of prayers.

I saw sunshine. Firelight. Big, leafy tropical plants. And weathered wood similar to the sides of the barns I'd passed on my way out of Prineville. But most screens showed images identical to my own gray, dimly-lit room.

One screen I didn't understand. The background seemed normal—dull beige of a tent. But every believer in the tent wore bright clothing and flowered wreaths like crowns. A couple kneelers were stiff in metallic armor. The burgundy words *Kansas Renaissance Faire* fluttered on the beige like a banner. I guessed their clothes, flowers, and armor somehow disguised and kept them alive.

My fingertips trailed down the short length of glass where branches made the prayer warriors appear green. I turned and marched past the window without a glance at the occupied boulder outside.

I winced when my knees touched down on my mat. But I forgot them and the ache between my shoulder blades because I met my Lord again.

I begged for His clear will and that the leaders of our nation's Councils would understand. And for my family to be protected. No bloodshed.

I prayed for other Christian families' safety too and asked we wouldn't be tricked into hating and making rash, sinful decisions. No vengeance. No retaliation.

Then I prayed again for any stragglers still trying to find their way here.

Every so often I stopped pleading and listened for anything He wanted me to hear. Only yesterday, I'd become aware of a climber on our peak headed for an avalanche he'd accidentally triggered. A non-believer, not a Christian, as I'd told my supervisor. Still, he needed to be saved.

A soft scream interrupted my focus. I twitched in irritation. Muffled shouts reminded me that my knees ached. I shot a dirty look at the window—toward the outside where masses of non-praying Christians wasted their time being noisy. Supervisor Zeph wore a horrified expression.

The glass rectangle in the highest right corner of

televisions glowed blue—a color too fake for sky—a hard, unrelenting color. I tried to remember what'd been on that screen. A room like ours—rock hewn, bad lighting, but with only a couple dozen Christians kneeling.

A skinny guy next to me, with wheat-chaff hair and a sunburned nose, struggled onto his feet. "An attack! Satan's army! They're wiping out the Councils one by one. It's started. They fall. We all fall down." He chuckled.

Supervisor Zeph pointed at my neighbor. "Warrior Dahl, you are relieved of duty. Go lie down. People, you're taking a mandatory ten-minute break. A quarter—no, half—the food and all the water will be gone by then. That is, if you're interested in keeping your kneeling cushions."

Somebody groaned.

"After that, do your duty. Pray. Pray for our brothers and sisters on Mount Charleston. We've no way of knowing what happened to cut them off from the rest of us. The reason could be someone knocked over the camera giving us feed. Or Satan's forces shut them down." He frowned at my laughing neighbor. "It's not our responsibility to know. Ours is to pray. So do it. Dahl—you'd better be on that cot before I count to three. One."

~*~

Cal dismissed us from prayer duty at dawn. The high right screen still glowed blue. The Governor would announce the Councils' decision at noon in the holy hall. That left us five hours to sleep.

I stepped from the chilly room onto the frigid cobbles on unsure, grass-stalk legs. The boulder I lurched past sat empty, although some early risers clustered nearby. I caught their fragmented whispers that carried over the stones.

"*Where?*"

"She's right there, walking. That's the Heathen lover..."

"—heard she sent a group of our own people into an avalanche...a murderer."

"Can't be one of us... should get rid of her."

Even in my mindless stupor, I understood they spoke about me—and not about any of the other prayer warriors staggering toward the nearest shelters.

My hand reached for the first slate door and shoved it open.

The room could've been occupied, but no one tried to stop me. I zeroed in on the closest makeshift bed on the ground with a thick, rumpled blanket promising warmth. I collapsed under it. Done.

32

"Are you trying to get yourself killed, Dove Strong?"

I opened my eyes.

Another set looked into mine, looming, familiar ones, too big—despite being squinched up in anger.

"First, you up and disappear. And after hours of searching, I track you here. Here. In the guys' quarters. And now I find you didn't even bother to secure the door behind you?"

I half-glanced at the slate rectangle. A chain latched across its front. "Thanks, Melody."

She deflated. "I'm...I'm sorry. You know, for—"

"Forget about it." I'd lost my desire to shake her until her teeth rattled. And she'd brought along something in a bowl that made my stomach claw and purr.

I hugged her.

"Here." She shoved my pack into my arms. "You left it back where you were praying."

"Mmm." I gulped down the warm, leafy stew.

Melody apologized a million times more while I ate, and then she gave me a rundown on every meal.

I tried harder than usual to pay attention. Otherwise I would've missed the words she sandwiched between the fried opossum and potatoes. "...and the Council meets in the holy hall in twenty minutes."

~*~

Six or seven males huddled on the cobblestones on the other side of the door. Arms folded across shivering chests. "Well, well. Sleeping Beauty's awake."

A stubble-jawed guy whose muscles made the cocooning blanket bumpy lurched forward, his teeth knocking together. "We don't do coed. Dudes bunk with dudes. Chicks with ch...chicks."

I let Melody make the apologies and gazed around.

I was an ant in a colony.

Oregonian believers—most without wrinkles or gray hair—flowed out from the low buildings and shelters chiseled from the canyon's sides. Between these, I saw glimpses of a low, decorative wall that snaked between sleeping quarters. Shards of white and yellowish stones popped to create the illusion of wildflowers.

The cobbles vibrated with a door slam. I turned to find myself alone with my traveling partner. She'd sunk into a crouch, clasping a shaking hand to her forehead.

"Get a grip, Melody. They weren't going to pound us over borrowing their room for a couple hours."

She popped up and yanked my hood up over my hair. "You don't get it, Dove. Everyone here knows who you are, and most aren't fans. You're a Heathen lover, and everyone here's been hurt by Heathen. It was bad enough down in the trees acting how you did, but now—in the middle of this Council place—you had to go and start finding other enemies to save, risking our own people's lives?"

"It was one nonbeliever I knew about, Melody. One. He headed into an avalanche zone. And I can't help what God reveals."

"I know, only, I think you need to tone it down. And be more careful, OK? Try?"

I trailed her to the holy hall building with my head down. My eyes stayed on the smoothness under my fraying soles. I trod on fishes, crosses, and thorny crowns. And I learned, after careening into others a hundred times, to take miniscule steps and keep a slug's pace.

At the end of the valley ahead was the bench from my first night. A few more shuffles, and I shook off the surge that tried to carry me through the open doorway and into the carved holy room.

Melody clung to me, still trapped in the current. "Why are we stopping? Sorry. So sorry."

She waved to a cloaked bulk jabbing her with its walking stick.

I eyed my least favorite councilman on the bench, hunched over a waist-high, horizontal slab covered in stacks of papers. I craned my neck for a better look. Each bore a single black-inked word.

Althoff. Bayer. Carney. Dahl.

Names. And these were the Councils' decision to the Reclaim we'd carry home to our families.

I stepped forward until my legs pressed the slab table. "I'll take my paper now."

He batted away my outstretched hand.

"It will be right there." I jabbed my finger at the "S" pile. "The one in there that says 'Strong.'"

Wrinkled hands curled over the pile. "Now why

would you get yours before the others? No cutsies. No sneak peeks. No special favors. You'll get it the same as everyone else. After Governor tells you all the what's-what. Then you get in line and wait your turn. Yep, afterwards."

My steady hand didn't drop. "There is no 'afterwards' for us. Brae and Strong are heading home. Now."

Through the voices and footsteps of hundreds of Christians filing past, I heard Melody's surprised gasp.

I jerked my head around. She was shocked? To me, our leaving now seemed so obvious. And the Council's decision papers sitting here and ready? A blessing. One we should take advantage of.

She couldn't expect me to sit and wait with bated breath in this mass of people and not listen to the Governor announce an answer I'd known my whole life.

Peace was the whole reason I was here. The reason I'd been called. I wouldn't stay and endure the hours of questions from outraged Christians like Reed. Or the long, drawn-out explanations of why no war.

No one would force me into a pointless formality—especially one that might even be lethal.

Inside the doorway, a giant, stooping silhouette slipped past. The pull for home transformed into a sickening lurch.

I needed to go—to tell Gran about Uncle Saul and stop her being sad about him dying. I needed to be at her side to watch her unfold the white square from that pile and hear her read, "Peace." I didn't want Governor Ruth's voice. I wanted Gran's.

Didn't Melody know me after all this? How could she be so selfish?

The word slapped me.

I was selfish?

No. I bit my lip.

Well then, fine. What lit *her* fire, other than doing the obvious, expected thing, such as staying for pointless council meetings with murderers and upset Christians?

"Smoky...smoke-cured mole hash...with twice roasted turnips—no, potatoes." Which of her mother's recipes had Melody recalled the most? "Grub falafel with...umm...umm—"

"Blackened hazelnuts in a reduction of carob extract." Someone from the doorway finished. "A Brae favorite."

How ridiculous that the crowd of shoving people shifted to let Reed limp through.

Before the believers mashed back together, I sighted Governor Ruth inside. Her eyes met mine and then flickered to my outstretched hand. "Give it to her, councilman. And a radio. One of the good ones that gets a signal."

I wiggled my fingers at the toothless geezer and noticed the dark objects heaped under the slab. Radios.

After a pretense of hunting for it, he handed me my paper. "Strong."

I squeezed it tight and spelled "Joyner."

"B-R-A-E." Reed pulled back my hood. "Hope you're OK carrying three back solo, Dove."

I mashed my papers to my heart. "Melody? You're not coming home with me? But, but then when?"

Her face flooded red, and I knew the answer. Never.

"Your mom and dad and sisters?"

She shifted and lowered her gaze.

I tried again. "Micah?"

The last stragglers filed past. "Hey, Sleeping Beauty. Kiss any pagan princes today?"

"You can't do that to your family, Melody." I knew how Mrs. Brae would feel when her daughter never returned. A bruised heart. And a stomachache.

I kept my eyes on their intertwined fingers while Reed explained.

"Dove, she's staying where she's needed most—here. She's been given a rare gift that's one hundred percent wasted living buried in the earth the way her family does. You'd sentence her to a life of never feeling sunlight? Of never tasting fresh air? Bottom line, the Oregon Council needs her—needs *us*. We've been invited to stay on here. Permanently. Together, we'll use our abilities to protect God's land and His believers and prepare for our better future."

Arguments and questions whirled. I snatched at one. "But what about your family, Reed? You said how much the MTV relies on you to keep them protected. Can Stone do it alone?"

He grimaced. *Silly, Dove.*

Oh. Right. Together—and only together—would the warrior role be complete.

"My parents have always known me and Stone will be where God most needs us."

"Even if they die for it?"

"Even then. But I expect my third-in-command has stepped up to fill our shoes. He's gifted. And there's Darcy."

Numbly I clutched the three papers and nodded. His family's survival now depended on the whims of a giant, feral cat.

He dropped the radio into the bag on my back.

"Safe travels home, Dove."

Nice words. But his real meaning? Not so nice.

Dove, it promised, *you'll never make it alive.*

~*~

I'd only gone a few yards over the cobbles when Melody stepped on my heel.

"Tell them I'm sorry. And that I love them."

She was crying, so I agreed. I refaced the cliff.

She snagged my arm. "And a teeny favor?"

I braced myself.

"Since you're going home, Dove, and since you live so close, well, I was thinking. What if you could get to know Micah better? I bet you'd like him. And if you guys got married it'd be easier on my mom that I'm not there."

"Bye, Melody."

I finished traveling the empty cobbles and reached the valley's first giant foothold when I heard the tiniest *crunch* on the snow crust behind me.

I grasped the frozen wall. "Forget it. Me and Micah—we're so not going to happen. I'm not marrying him or anyone else—"

"Dove?"

My hand slipped off its hold—a mistake. I should've climbed hard when I'd registered no footsteps. A quick check revealed the worst. Stone and I were alone.

Yet, he didn't look like he was about to kill me. He seemed to have an impossible time looking at me at all. But that could be how he acted before he struck. Apologetic. Sorry he had to carry out Reed's order.

My palms pressed against the crag at my back, feeling for another grip. I could only hope to out climb him. "Did you come to say goodbye, Bender? Or that you're sorry."

"Neither. I mean, yes. Sorry."

He stepped forward with his hands out. I flinched away.

"I should've defended you."

My lids popped back open.

"You were up against us all, and I...I blew it. I knew from the moment I saw you that you're as pure and good as an angel from Heaven. I've never had any doubt. But what happened...that won't ever happen again."

Sky alive. How had I ever thought his face blank? It was intense with messages, all jumbled. Apology. Eagerness. And something that made my toes cringe inside my shoes.

"And you shouldn't be traveling home by yourself, Dove. Yeah. That doesn't seem right. Lots of stuff can happen to you out there. If you'll wait a little so I can explain to Reed, then I'll come with you. I...I get that you're tight with God, but that'll only get you so far when it comes to surviving an attack. But I can protect you. I swear." He offered me his right hand. "Always."

In his left, he held a skull-sized chunk of Mount Jefferson. He squeezed. After a tremendous *crack*, the solid mass fell into halves on the snow.

Oh, no. Oh, Father. Words. Give me words here.

He'd stooped for another when I stopped him. "You and my big brother are branches of the same oak."

He straightened slowly.

"My brother Gilead—he's strong. Unstoppable. And like you, he didn't think I had a chance of surviving my journey because physically I'm nothing compared to him. Or you. And I feel the same way about him as I do you. I love you both—but not..."

He nodded and turned away. "But not."

I watched his silent back. "Stone? Listen, Stone. You've got to do something for me. Promise me. Ditch Reed and go home. Don't let him tell you what God wants you to do anymore. Find out from the Lord yourself."

He swiveled so quick, I stumbled but didn't fall. His hands at my elbows stopped me.

"But that's why I need to go with you, Dove. I didn't say it before, but this week I've been thinking exactly that. The more I'm around you, the more you'll rub off on me. You can show me how to do this knowing-God-better thing."

I continued to shake my head. "It doesn't work that way. I'm no magical cure. Trust me. Sixteen years with my brother has done nothing. He needs to know God in his own way, so do you."

He released me. "So that's it."

"Yeah."

"You love me, but not like...like..."

"Yeah. Not like that." I gripped the rough edge of the wall we pretended to examine.

"You can handle this?" We both chose to ignore the break in his voice.

"I've never needed help climbing, Stone."

"Oh. Right." But he lifted and set me on the lowest ledge.

Taller than him now, I forced a half-smile down at him while thanking God I wasn't dead...and he wasn't sobbing.

He cringed away. A ray of sunshine must've escaped the cloud blanket behind me because light nailed him in the face. No matter how he shifted and shaded his brow, he couldn't focus on me. Weird, since I didn't think the sun ever reached this far down in the canyon.

"Huh." He gave up and shut his eyes. "Maybe you *will* make it OK after all." He lifted a hand.

I copied him in a goodbye he couldn't see. Then, I stood to face my next obstacle.

33

It was great to travel by myself. And camp by myself. And not have to wait for anyone at all.

Sure.

Sweat trickled between my shoulder blades, and I twitched the damp shoulder strap to the other side. I scanned the wooded terrain in my automatic, side-to-side way—more than aware I'd received no promise I'd make it home.

While I continued hiking the foothills, the part of my mind not on stay-alive duty hoped my uncle would appear from behind a tree and fall into step with me. Not my biggest hope, but the one I allowed myself to think on.

I was still hearing my aunt's imaginary gasps of joy, when way up ahead I spotted white. A wintery smear against a slope of broken, black scree.

By the time I reached the warped, bullet-riddled rectangle Reed had used as a shield, the sky's purpling clouds warned me of night. Both broken cars had vanished. The road was empty of everything. Everyone. No Saul, no—

I slid with the cartwheeling debris into the shallow gravel ditch and picked my way around the fragments of red translucent plastic and glass. The only signs left of my first—and last—car ride.

My gut ached. With my fingers pressing almost to

my backbone, I fought it and the disappointment.

"Keep going, Dove. Don't linger on the what-ifs and have-nots."

Still, I stayed rooted. Then I threw back my head.

"So, God, what was the point? I was fine before, back home in the life You gave me. Then You had to go and force me out into the world, among all those people. Believers. Non-believers—it didn't matter, You threw them all on me. And You knew they'd do something to my heart. Tug at it. Twist it. Break it. Why, Father? Why make me care about them? Because now I'm alone. Again. And it stinks."

My shoulders drooped, and I hung my head. "Stay with me. Help me remember I don't need anything—anyone. All I need is You."

~*~

A small, furry night hunter felt the warning before I did. It darted across the road behind me, into the ditch where I walked, and then it vanished. A moment later, I heard the engine. My shadow stretched long and misshapen in front of me.

I tried to copy the fox, but somehow I'd brainlessly allowed a towering wall of rock to come between me and my escape in the trees. The nearest accessible forest—without some serious backtracking—was on the other side of the road.

My body was too exhausted. My reaction time slowed. Before I made it across to safety, two beams of light bore down on me.

"So, what number on the jerk-o-meter does a guy win for ditching a girl, shackled to a creep, halfway up a mountain?"

"A ten," a higher voice shouted. "A million!"

I smiled and kept walking the yellow line.

A roofless, boxy vehicle—the kind that ends up dumped on our property—pulled up next to me and kept pace.

Wolfe leaned out. "OK. I give up. What're you doing?"

"Guess."

Something rustled near my ear. "I got chips!"

"No one cares about your chips, brat. Seriously, get in the vehicle, Dove. I'm not driving two miles an hour, watching you walk home. I'm not even touching the gas pedal. I'm actually braking."

I lengthened my stride, knowing I'd never keep it up. "Better?"

In response, the vehicle lurched forward and stopped. Hands gripped my wrists tight, and then my elbows, pulling me into the four-wheeled trap.

Wolfe settled down in front of me. "Relax. I can drive anything expertly. Tractors. Forklifts. Backhoes. Once even a firetruck. OK, fine, it was a brush rig. But Dove?"

"Yeah?" It came out a croak.

"You should still probably, you know, buckle up."

His sister crawled over me and pulled a strap across my rigid body as I perched on the edge of the warm seat. She clicked the strap's metal end into a plastic piece.

Even in my shock, I recognized Wolfe's driving ability. In the few seconds we'd moved, the car hadn't scraped a tree branch or thrown me off my perch. Not once.

The wind shrieked over and around as we flew

over the snaking pavement. Jezebel's greasy hand patted my leg. Then her whole body relaxed against my stiff arm.

"And so. Your home. It would be?" Wolfe flashed a grin over his shoulder. "Please, please don't say Arizona."

The buffeting twilight stole my air. "Head to where you live. I'm not too far from there."

Lights dotted the horizon in front of us, and I forgot to breathe. Next to me, Jezebel twisted, lunged up, and anchored my head between her hands. As I jerked away, I felt my hair coil come loose. It fell heavy onto my shoulder the same moment the approaching vehicle swooshed passed.

I clutched at my fast unrolling strands. "Are you insane?"

She slid back to her side with a smirk. "It's done, Woof."

Her brother didn't bother to glance back.

"Dove, you're a radical, and you look like one, which, so sorry, isn't a compliment. So unless you got another army of wasps in that bag to fight off anyone who gets suspicious, trust Jezzy and me on this. This?" He stuck his thumb over his shoulder at my head. "This is better."

I pawed through my straightening strands, deciding. Rebecca dressed different, worldly. And she was still a true Christian.

Jezzy's fingers helped mine comb while the night air whipped my hair around us and over us and behind us. She paused in her raking. "Wow. See this, Woof!"

His eyes showed up in a small mirror. "Hmm? Oh, whoa. That's...that's long. I guess it's better. But speak up if it gets snagged around the car's axle. Or if you start picking up roadkill."

I shoved handfuls of it behind, pinning the mass between myself and the seat. Even so, the eyes in the mirror kept reappearing.

I kept my own on the racing trees and rolling terrain, squinting against the wind and the escaped strands lashing me. Jezebel stuck her feet up on the black chair back in front of her. The one in front of me—its twin—had a big, vertical rip.

I followed its fluttering edges up to where they stopped at Wolfe's left shoulder. In the last of the sunset, I caught sight of inked, triangular lines marking his skin there. I shielded my eyes and for the first time looked at the tattoo.

My other hand muffled my gasp. And my laugh.

The triquetra. The Trinity Knot. His tattoo—this non-believer's—was my cousin's favorite symbol and namesake. Three elegant, interconnecting loops...representative of God the Father, the Son, and the Holy Spirit.

Wolfe's whistling warbled on like a songbird.

But why would he have...? *He doesn't know,* I realized. He has *no clue* what his tattoo means—that it's the believers' sign of the Almighty God.

But no. This tattoo wasn't a coincidence or joke.

I moved to the seat's edge, which released my hair. *No more wasting time, Dove.* Time to fight for a soul.

"Hey, Wolfe?"

Jezebel shifted in her sleep, her head pillowed on a red food bag that smelled like potatoes and grease. In the front, the whistling stopped. The alert eyes in the mirror laughed at me.

"Stop this thing, Wolfe. I'm coming up there. We need to talk."

34

Only two conversations starters came to mind. Both were lame. There was, "So, what's it like being controlled by Satan?" And the other, "It must feel horrible knowing you're going to hell."

"Stupid people-speaking gift." I remembered Rebecca and how she always got her way with her words.

Some words here, Father?

Wolfe glanced at me. "What'd you say?"

"Nothing."

"Nothing. Boy, you never shut up, do you?"

I hadn't spoken since relocating to the front.

"OK, OK, Dove. If I teach you to drive, will you please give my ears a rest?"

I blinked fast. "Maybe I already know how to drive."

He grinned and called my bluff. "Do you?"

I pictured myself behind the car's wheel, humming to a stop under my home. In the branches above, my boy cousins pointed at me while Gilead gawked from the shadows.

"I don't want to." I fingered my heavy braid I'd slopped together. My grandpa had admitted he could get at least one old, junker vehicle on our property running if he wanted. But he'd refused to do it for the same reason we're not allowed guns. He declared both worldly inventions invited sin.

"Driving would save you on shoes."

"No."

"What if knowing how to drive saved your life someday?"

I tossed away my braid. "I said, no."

"OK, OK." His hands drummed against the wheel. "I just want to do something. To make up for being the jerk who ran off and never said thanks. Thanks for saving us. I planned to, but then with all those flocks of owls swarming. Whoo-whoo."

My answering hoot was more realistic. We spent the next few minutes working on his, which broke the tension in my head and tongue. "It's Rebecca, not me, who gets the thanks. She's the one who talked Sto—your guards—into letting you go."

"Rebecca? The normal-looking fanatic chick? Yeah, I know. I heard her that night. But you were behind it."

He sounded so sure. Why?

He clucked his tongue. "Gotta tell you though, setting Diamond loose wasn't your smartest move. Not the most forgiving person, Diamond. And she'd never let radicals get away with what you—they—did. She talked revenge our whole first morning hiking back, and almost turned around to deliver it."

My hands squeezed pale in the gray light, clasping and unclasping between my pant legs.

He nodded. "But then *he* showed up."

I didn't ask who. Both Cal and Governor Ruth had mentioned Saul. Uncle Saul.

"Of course, he didn't say much. But his eyes...Dove, they had this scary warning in them. Like 'Keep moving and don't mess with no one.'"

I unclasped. "I know. It's a family thing. He's my

uncle."

"Ha! I told you he reminded me of you. And, well, after that, even Diamond wouldn't go back. But I'm still sort of drawing a blank on why you did all that—protecting the brat and putting your neck on the line to help us get away."

"You let me and Mel go that night at your home. So, for us Christians to be less merciful than non-believers?" I shook my head. "No, I had to help you."

He smiled. "Ah. I get it. We helped you, so you helped us. We're equal."

"No, Wolfe. I'm not talking about fair. I'm talking about mercy." My heart began to race while I tried to spit out the words before I lost them. "Mercy isn't what you've done, or what I've done. It's about Jesus, what He's done. Can't you understand? We all mess up. We sin. Me, you, everyone. And because of it, we're responsible for Jesus being nailed to the cross. But He allowed the cross and dying because He's God and He loves me—and you and everyone. If He can forgive me for killing Him and choose to show mercy so I can escape hell, well then, I have to have mercy for you guys. Don't you see?"

The night rushed around us while the tires hummed. He shook his head. "I don't buy it. What you're saying is the total opposite of the garbage that fanatic, Reed, spouted. Stuff about a war between radicals and normal people?"

I chopped my hands in an X. "Forget all that. No war—not now. That's sort of what I meant that night when I told you I had to get where I was going to save lives. I'm God's messenger...for peace."

He whistled slowly.

"Think, if I'd had you arrested?" He side-glanced

at me. "I caught that—no war now. Emphasis on *now*. So. What's up with that? Or is that secret, inside radical intel?"

I chewed my bottom lip. "No, and I don't think God's ever going to give Christians the OK to hurt others—at least not until the end-of-days battle. And when that happens, it'll be God's side versus Satan's—and spoiler alert, Satan's isn't going to win."

"Well, I'm on neither side, Dove, so you all can leave me out of that fun."

"By refusing Jesus Christ, you make your choice."

"Well, that's not fair."

"Then make a better choice, Wolfe. Be on the winning side, and then you won't have to whine."

"Wow. As easy as that? Just choose to be a fanatic like you?"

I ignored his sarcasm and ducked so low in my seat my nose barely cleared the glass window. "That's it."

We'd rushed past the painted *Welcome to Sisters* sign. Lines of wooden buildings with huge, staring windows replaced the trees. There were so many lights and flowers and colors. And people.

My fingernails stopped burrowing into my chair when he turned us out of the creeping line of cars and onto an unlit piece of pavement.

But I tensed again. The Enemy had been too quiet on this drive. Was he sitting back and letting me roll into this godless town like a worm crawling into a bird's nest?

I tried not to see the tilted, burned-out barrel in front of the boxy home we stopped at. Before the engine died, the home's light blared and its door opened. A lanky, black-haired woman charged at us.

"I got this. Wait here." He slid out with arms wide. "Grandma! Funny story…"

The woman threw open the car door behind me and stooped to unlatch the strap from around Jezebel. "And how do you expect to graduate when you're truant a full week of school? And you pull her out without telling me? No note. You don't return my calls…"

Wolfe maneuvered his grandma out of the way and eased the sleeping girl over his own shoulder. He dropped a kiss on the high cheekbone.

"You know why I love you most, Grandma? Because you forgive. And because you always know why your perfect angels should be excused from classes. You won't have any trouble with our unimaginative school system. They'll believe you. They always do."

She shook her head but unexpected dimples showed.

"Search and rescue." She spoke to his back that moved up the short cement path. "You joined up because a cousin of yours went missing in the Willamette."

Wolfe's shoulders shook. "Good news. He's been found."

I leaned forward for my last glimpse. One bare arm dangled against his white shirt.

Going, going…gone.

The moonbeams seemed to brighten, illuminating the two of us. I couldn't move. Held captive in the woman's dark-eyed stare.

She knows, I thought. *She knows I'm a radical*. I fingered my braid laying in a tangled mess over my shoulder and braced myself for her disgust…for her yell that'd bring Diamond and the others.

My eyes slid from hers—Jezebel's eyes—and located the tops of the forest over the roof.

A door slammed and Wolfe vaulted into the car next to me. "Sister of a lacrosse friend, Grandma. Ran into her camping and needed a lift. Be back in a few."

We bumped down the pavement backwards.

His grandma spoke again. "Did Jezzy get her meds?"

"As if I'd forget." He rolled his eyes. "The rest are in her Minnie Mouse bag on her floor."

At an empty stretch of trees away from city lights, we skidded to a stop next to the road. I reached for my pack behind me.

"Show me. Where?" He shoved his glowing electronic rectangle at me, and I gazed down at the bright map's lines on its screen.

I'm only relieved because I made it out of that godless town. And because I'm so dead tired and my feet ache and I don't have to walk yet. That's why I'm smiling.

I touched the edge of throbbing green labeled Ochoco National Forest near the Prineville dot. The corners of my mouth drooped. "It's too far. And you've worried your grandma way too much as it is. I'm walking."

He tapped my hair with his map. "Release the door and calm yourself. I'm not taking you to Kansas or nothing. Your home's like an hour away. I'll have you there by midnight."

That couldn't be right. It'd been a three-day hike. But, instead of arguing, I leaned back. "You should've told her the truth. She knows what I am."

"Grandma? Of course she knows. She's not a blind senile."

"Then why that lie about being a friend's sister? And camping?"

He moved us back onto the empty road. "I figured none of us wanted to get into all the *Q and A* right then. I know she didn't want to. She's much happier pretending you're a normal girl. And you hate personal questions, so...you're welcome."

The black pole pines flew by, and I shuddered.

"Thinking about those personal questions we avoided?"

I shook my head. Then nodded. "I've moved on to my own grandma's questions...if I do tell her about you. My answers are worse."

He cracked up, with his head all the way back and his mouth opened to the sky. When finished being an idiot, he reached in front of my knees and pulled open a hidden compartment. It was jammed with papers. One of these he threw on my lap, plus a fat pen.

"Then let's work on those answers. Write this down in caps and underline it, 'Wolfegang Pickett, a good person for your grandkid to know and why you shouldn't hurt him.'"

I shrugged but went along with it—at least scribbling down the first part— his name. Then, while I struggled to keep the flapping paper from flying, he threw out fluff like "chivalrous feminist" and "modestly witty." My own list remained solid earth.

"A nonbeliever. An older brother. Can drive. Decent whistler."

When I finished reading, he knocked his forehead against the wheel.

"Pitiful. And where's the argument for not dismantling me like how your boyfriend tried?" But his grin was back. "Decent whistler?"

I jammed the folded list into my shoe and tossed the pen. "Well, it's crow's cawing compared to my mom's, but..."

~*~

Wolfe's whistling lasted until he whispered, "You think we're getting close?"

I got why he whispered. I should've said "shalom" and started walking as soon as we left Prineville—even if I didn't recognize the terrain yet. I could only imagine the nightmare if he drove me too far.

The bell. The spotlight. The buckets of water. The bees. The big brother.

Our lights picked up something white ahead. It was the barkless pole of a tree with the eagle's nest on top.

He'd been right. Less than an hour.

"Stop. Stop, stop. Kill the lights. And noise."

He obeyed and craned forward to see. "So this is where you live, huh? I don't see a house. Should I take you a little further?"

"No." I pointed. "That white tree. It marks the corner of our property, so I'm good from here. And, uh...thanks."

"Yep."

My closing the car's door sounded like a hunter's shot. Wolfe had followed me out and put a stop to my objection. "Wild cats around, you know. Could be some pretty suspicious-acting squirrels around too, I'm thinking. I'll watch your back until you're closer."

Wild cats...Melody. I'd almost forgotten I got to deliver the news to her family that she wasn't coming home.

I strode forward. "Walk quieter."

"Should I quit breathing too? You're ridiculous. It's impossible to see where to step."

Then go. As fast as you can, get out of here and drive home.

"Grab onto my bag, Wolfe." I felt him take hold.

If we continued straight, we'd be at my front door in minutes. I led him off the rutted path and headed for the back of our property where trespassers never think to go and my grandpa doesn't watch.

My hands brushed familiar trees. *I'm* crazy. Why haven't I demanded he leave?

Because you want him to see what your life is like, the truth replied. And so he'll be able to find you again.

The truth was annoying. I quit asking dumb questions and focused on not tripping on tree roots.

~*~

I counted twelve purple cans up on the giant, tin-can rainbow. From the can's cutout side, I fished out the concealed lighter. Then I lit the lanterns on either side of the garden's entrance arch.

In the flash and glow, Wolfe's eyes bugged as he took in our garden's outer perimeter walls made from garbage.

"So long." I gave him a shove in the direction of his Jeep. "Keep the tallest firs on your left and you'll make it back fine." I didn't mind being called "radical" and "fanatic." But "freak" always stung a little.

"Are you kidding?" He shook me off. "I'm seeing

this."

I threw up my arms. Then I folded them and waited for him to hurry and finish gawking.

Holding up the little light on his keys he examined the sculptures in the wall. His light loitered the longest at the front half of a black mustang poised in a full gallop. You could tell by the way its mane flew back in gusts—hundreds of jet black wires that had taken my cousin a week to hand bend.

"Are these all CDs? There must be a thousand." His light swung at an eight-foot-high tidal wave made out of blue and white colored discs. Under its crest, a miniature dolphin balanced on its tail.

Without warning, Wolfe shoved past me and the rows of googly-eyed tin owls perched at the wall's top. "The other side." He plunged through the rainbow arc. "I've gotta see the other side of this."

"Stop!" I ran after. Passing under the arch, I sank up to my ankles in soil and stopped. "And get off our bean plant." I lifted the lantern from its hook so he could see the green stalk he crushed.

He pointed at me instead of looking. "That's made of bike chains. You have a chandelier lantern made of bike chains." He began to laugh but stopped when he saw my anger.

"No—no. This is all so...so...cool, Dove. But I can't see it all. It's too dark. Tell me about where we are."

After a long moment, I held the lantern higher. "Since you're still murdering a bean plant, you won't be surprised that this is our garden. Our hives are along that wall over there—near the flowers." I shoved the light at the pitch blackness where a couple bees sounded awake. "The catapults for organic waste are on the other side of the wall, and my home's up in those maples ahead. You'd better go."

"Dove?" A hopeful but cautious voice called from the maples. "Dove girl? Is that you?"

"Mom!" I let the lantern fall with a clatter. Instinctively I dashed between vegetable beds to where she waited in the tree canopy.

Ringing thundered. Familiar voices shouted my name, swallowed in the bell's call. I scrambled up maple limbs, too impatient to climb up the normal way.

I swung myself onto the platform but never touched the planks. Gilead had me. My ribs creaked in his squeeze while my mother imprisoned my hands in hers. Smaller fingers dragged at my clothes and hair. Even my shoes. Each cousin found a part of me to hang onto.

Under the platform's covered area, my grandma sat straight-backed in her rocking chair. So impatiently patient.

She coughed. In two strides, Gilead set me down in front of her.

She eyed my messy shoulder braid. "Took you long enough."

"I was the first to leave, Gran. I promise." I ripped the plastic bag with the Council's decision papers from my belt and handed it over. My bag, with its radio, I flung at my brother.

Now unburdened, I leaned down and hugged her, feeling huge like Stone. I'd forgotten how tiny she was. I let go. "Gran, I have to tell you, he's not dead! S—"

I pitched backwards as Trinity grabbed me from behind.

"Get off, idiot." I tried to shake Trinity off my back. I laughed, struggling in a circle until she released my neck.

She hugged me like a sane person. "Was it beautiful out there, Dove? Tell me."

The ringing died. My grandpa now stood behind my grandma, his gray beard hiding his mouth, his eye creases crinkled. "Well, now. It seemed like we were short a blonde. You'll do."

My mom squeezed my fingers. Happy tears trickled down her tanned cheeks like I'd known they would. After another squeeze, she melted away with my aunt, down the ladder to get my dinner. I could taste my pie and squash.

Squash. From the garden.

My heart lurched, and I took a ho-hum step nearer the platform's edge. I forced my lips to hold their smile. "I...I'm going to make sure Mom—"

"Let her go," Grandpa said as I reached the second limb down.

I paused on the last and held my breath. My mom's and aunt's silhouettes approached the bed where squash grew. Behind them, the two lanterns glowed symmetrically from either side of the rainbow arch—including the one I'd dropped.

I almost toppled from my perch in relief. The replaced lantern was Wolfe's signal. *Goodbye, Dove.*

With a glance up at the home I'd spent months dreaming about, I made my decision. I slipped off and headed away from the garden, onto the washed-out path. The Jeep, if it was still there, was a five-minute walk away.

I walked, and then ran, past black masses in the darkness—monstrous piles of rust still holding their identities as cars and trucks. Other piles had grown too while I'd been gone.

Somewhere between the skunked-out camper and the smallest maple on our property, a silhouette detached itself from the maple's shadow. In the dim light, Wolfe surveyed the mounds of garbage.

He gave a dry chuckle. "My people dump this junk on your doorstep to annoy you...but you use it. So, in fact, we're delivering you radicals everything you need for a comfortable, money-free existence. Which is funny. And nauseating. But still funny."

Funny? Sure. Whatever.

"Of course, God has an amazing sense of humor." He seemed in no hurry, so I tried to shove him toward his vehicle.

He planted his feet. "I don't get why you talk about God that way. Like you love Him? Or are in love with Him? I have to be honest, it's a little freaky."

"I do love Him."

"You love Him...like how you love people? Or more than people? More than Jezebel? I know you love her. Don't lie."

"Yes, yes, she's great. You need to go, Wolfe. It's not safe."

He let me bulldoze him another few steps. "But you think Jezebel's a lot better person than what you expected a normal person—a Heathen—to be, right?"

"Yes, yes. Of course. Move it. My mom—"

"You are, too." He seemed oblivious I was using my last ounce of exhausted muscle strength to move him. "You're a way better person than what Jezebel thought a Christian would be. I mean, you haven't attacked or set fire to a single person."

I paused to wipe my brow. "Because your—her—assumptions were ridiculous. Move your feet. I don't think you understand my whole family is—"

"I'm not an idiot, Dove. I get I'm not welcome here. I'm going."

He hugged me.

My family doesn't hug much. I've been carried over my brother's shoulder plenty, and squeezed a few times until my ribs cracked. But this hug was different. My body instinctively went rigid.

His breath touched my ear. "Thanks. For letting me into your world. You've blown mine apart. And I will be back. Argh..."

His arms spasmed while he lurched forward, taking me to the ground with him.

Too surprised to shout, I struggled out from under.

"Dove!"

I turned toward Gilead's bark from the camper, where another familiar voice shouted, "You're OK now, Dove Strong. We're here. You hit him, Gil, but I don't think he's dead. See? He's moving. What now?"

"No!"

My brother breathed too hard to hear my muted cry.

"Finish him, Micah. Then we find his family and finish them too. We end this vile line of—"

"Gilead! Micah! Sons, that's enough. Don't move."

I groped for my grandpa's shout. His light, the force of the sun, times ten, hit me square in the eyeballs.

I peered through finger cracks. Wolfe's body lay twisted in the leaves, one hand clawing at his shoulder blade. Gilead and Melody's brother flinched in the brightness behind him. Micah's skinny blade reflected in his upraised hand, but Gilead's hands were empty. His knife glinted from the back of Wolfe's jacket.

"Now, Brae!" My brother darted to my side and lifted me. "Now! Quick. Finish him. Before my grandpa..."

As I struggled, I saw Micah's eyes mirror Gilead's excitement. He fingered his knife.

"Hurt, little sister?" My brother's arm tightened and held me in place.

I twisted and kicked.

Oh God! Intercede! Save him! He can't die. Please, oh please. He can't die. Not him. I love him!

God must have heard my prayer and answered. Micah froze, his knife hovering inches from Wolfe's Adam's apple. Suddenly breaking free of my brother's hold, I ran over, grabbed Micah's knife, and chucked it to the ground.

God hadn't stopped their attack—I had. My silent prayer still rang loud, not silent. Stunning Gilead and Micah.

I loved Heathen.

My grandpa strode into the blaring light, a hand to his heaving chest. "Gilead. Grandson. Will you never learn to pause? To check with the Spirit before lashing out? Is that what's in your heart...such violence?"

"He attacked her, Grandpa. Micah and I—we both saw it." But doubt crept through the shock in Gilead's voice.

"Rot." I heard my grandpa jam the fallen knife blade into the maple while I kept my gaze on the scary white face drenched with sweat and tight with pain.

Micah sidestepped behind my brother. "Sir? Sir, your grandson's not lying. I promise you."

Grandpa's knees cracked as he knelt and laid a hand against Wolfe's heaving chest. "You both saw what you wanted to see. What I saw was a young man drive Dove to the edge of our property and escort her to the garden. That she came to see him off the property would be clear to any lamebrain numbskull who paused and watched a moment."

"Nice, Dove."

I hunched a shoulder at Gilead's sarcasm and glanced over at the shadows. Someone impatiently crouched there. "Is he going to die, Grandpa?"

Jonah Strong stood. "No, thank the good Lord. The knife missed his lungs and everything major as far as I can tell. Don't pull the weapon out, so he doesn't lose more blood. Where'd you find him, Dove?"

"Sisters." I told him the numbers on the home and described what I could remember of the roads we'd taken. I took a deep breath. "It's at least a three-day walk there, Grandpa. What...what if I drive him?"

My face flamed at Gilead's curled lip.

"Leave the driving to me." My grandpa gestured at the camper. "Boys, get that sheet metal leaning there. And keep him off his wound when you carry him. Since you caused this, you will deliver him to his mother yourselves. With an apology."

"No mom." Wolfe spoke for the first time. While my brother and Melody lifted him onto the make-shift stretcher, he gripped my fingers until they numbed. "Only my grandma."

Grandpa bent over him, his face etched. "I'm sorry, son. Truly. For you to have to face this world without a God and without a mother. And now...this thing we've done to you. I'm sorry."

Wolfe's fingers slid from my grasp and dangled.

I trailed after his unconscious figure, but my grandpa motioned at the spotlight. "Go home, Dove. Tell Sarah I'll be back before first light. Celebrate your return, but remember to pray continually and keep watch. Satan may use this night to his advantage. If this turns into a Dead Night, keep to the trees and use the buckets. Don't be afraid. The young man will live."

I wanted to go with them. "Yes, Grandpa."

The trio moved down the road, working to keep Wolfe from sliding off. At the bend where the path wound into deeper forest, Gilead told Micah to wait.

"We thought he was hurting you, Dove. And if he had, I promise his whole family would've died for it. But whether he dies now doesn't matter so much, does it? He's going to die in a few months anyway."

"What?" My nails pressed my cheeks.

"I saw the Council's decision. We're going to war." They rounded the curve and disappeared.

War.

The silent forest became loud with red.

I'd flown. And failed.

Over the Jeep's engine, words I'd once heard—and shrugged at—now repeated themselves in Stone's thoughtful tone.

"Maybe the answer is more complicated than any of our puny human brains can understand. Maybe you're both right...just...only God knows how."

I squared my slumped shoulders. Then I dragged myself past the heaps of garbage to where my homecoming squash and crow pie cooked.

Melody. Saul.

The war would come and maybe the red. But I had messages to deliver first. Then my brain would be free to decide...to choose my side.

We hope you enjoyed Dove Strong.
Here's a sneak peek at what comes next,
Fanatic Surviving

1

Thunk. Gilead's blade sank into the X scratched on the pine. Dead center. A breath later, Micah Brae's steel nicked the trunk's bark and scuttled, disappearing in the frozen groundcover.

My brother's grunt of disgust reached me up in the crow's nest where I huddled out of sight. "Pathetic, Brae. Keep your knife horizontal to your target until you release it. Like this."

Thunk.

I focused on the sunlit branches overhead instead of my brother's and neighbor's knife-throwing session—their way of preparing for the Reclaim. The war's first attack on the godless Heathen was broadcasted for May 15, a month and a half away. And they thought this would make them ready?

Next to me on the snug lookout platform high in the maple, my grandpa surveyed the tree-filled horizons in his systematic way. I leaned my elbows back on the woven blanket, evidence he'd slept up here, despite the biting Central Oregon nights. My mom said he slept in the tree to be extra cautious—with the war between us Christians and Satan's people approaching. But that wasn't the real reason. Grandpa was obsessed with sighting his missing son, my Uncle Saul, who I'd discovered back in September, alive, crazy, and nearby, roaming the Oregon Cascades.

"If Uncle Saul wanted to come home, he'd have done it years ago, Grandpa. You know that, right?"

He grunted.

My frown fell on the barkless, white pole in the distance. A dead tree with an eagle's nest on top, marking the corner of our property. Next to it ran the rutted path on which Wolfe Pickett had driven me home. Wolfe, the Heathen teenager I hadn't seen in six months, two weeks, and five days, who'd changed my mind about the nonbelieving population.

My frown deepened into a squint.

Under the third bleached branch from the trunk's bottom, a woodpecker had whittled out a bird-sized hollow. Did another note wait for me there? Could I check before sundown without my family noticing? Wolfe had already left me two secret messages in this hole.

Hey, Dove. I'm better and up for a visit. How about next Saturday? Su casa. Let me know. Wolfe

And then...

Dove, I know you got my note. Is this about the bean plant I killed? Tell me when it's good for me to come see you. No killing this time. Wolfe

I'd taken the notes but left no response. *Stay away, Wolfe.*

He wouldn't shed any more blood because of me. Last September my brother had stabbed him on our property for hugging me. Gilead would have killed him if I hadn't blurted out that I loved this unsaved guy and his intense little sister, Jezebel.

I rested my warm cheek on my knees.

So what if I loved a couple of pagans from the town of Sisters? Didn't *love* mean I didn't want them to die? At least the Spirit reassured me it was fine to love nonbelievers even if my family didn't applaud this.

"Being equally yoked in marriage is God's will, Dove. It's biblical. You marry a lost soul, and you'll bear a burden you won't be able to carry."

"Amen," my aunt had agreed.

Why did my mom keep blasting me with this spiel? Marriage? How dumb. I was only seventeen. Gilead's nineteen. Had she ever cornered him to give the "equally-yoked" talk? I was willing to bet my year's quota of honey-roasted squash she hadn't.

I grabbed a promising pinecone and cracked it against the platform. After a few taps, its nuts knocked loose.

"Here, Grandpa. Eat."

With a grunt, he picked out a couple from my palm. We sat in the sunshine, chewing and spitting hulls while knives clattered and thudded below. Maybe this squirrel food would hold my stomach until dinner. Then I wouldn't have to leave this hidey-hole or my grandpa, the one family member who never referred to my unexpected relationship with nonbelievers that kept me awake at nights.

"Dove!" My cousin Trinity's voice sang from close by, no doubt from inside our tree home, since it was too clear to be from the junk piles. "Dove, Gran wants you!"

Grandpa extended his hand for the rest of the pine nuts. Making sure not to knock against the giant emergency bell that hung within reach above our heads, I climbed on branches to my home's larger platform.

Once in our main living space, I took a backward step toward the open doorway. I should have taken my time in the branches and not rushed to get here. I took another step back.

My grandma faced me, spider-web fragile in her willow chair. Mom stood behind her, clenching the chair's straight back, an odd, tight smile pulled across her sun-stained face.

I braced myself for the marriage spiel.

Gran heaved herself to her feet, revealing bulkier homespun apparel than what she usually wore to shuffle around on the platforms. "Dove, child, go find your backpack. We're going to fix the blasphemous mistake. God wants peace and not war. He knows it, you know it, and I know it. We're heading back to the mountain to get it straight with that Council. Obey, child. I have no time for your gaping at me. Go get that pack so we can leave."

The mountain? The Council? My past failed mission came crashing down so hard I staggered.

Last summer, I'd been commissioned as God's messenger for peace. I'd traveled to Mount Jefferson, Oregon's Christian Council, and carried my family's and a next-door neighbor's prayer votes for peace. And on September 15, the fifty Councils had tallied America's Christians' votes. Despite my best effort to obey God, a decision for a war we called *the Reclaim* had been made.

A human mistake. God didn't want a war.

Before I'd left last summer, Grandma's vision revealed me reaching Mount Jefferson, and my own dream later showed the importance of halting the startling red that flooded the nation. I wasn't brainless. I knew what the growing crimson color meant. The red meant massive bloodshed—specifically our people's blood. And as God's special messenger for peace I should have stopped this bloody threat by getting to my Council. But my journey's successful arrival at the mountain with votes, my arguments against violence with fellow messengers, and all the hours on my knees among other prayer warriors hadn't stopped it. The Councils had announced war.

And now I had to make the trek again.

I glanced over my shoulder to the green, fuzzy canopies beyond our property and then squeezed my eyes shut.

Travel back into the devil's territory? My hands shook. But not because I was scared of his attack. Satan would strike—using snakes and hunters to do his evil deeds— and I would handle them. Bring on the snakes! No. I trembled because of a secret knowledge—an unknown threat—that kept me awake at night.

Lord, there's a pull I'm too weak to fight, even wearing Your armor. Part of the world out there draws me—like a heaping pile of compost draws a fly. Will the pile collapse on me this time? Trap me so I can't escape? Will I choose not to escape? Is that what happened to Uncle Saul? Almost eight years ago, he left on the same journey to the Council. Maybe I'll end up haunting the nonbelievers' roads and towns too...maybe Sisters? Will I never return to my family if I leave?

Should I tell Gran no?

I sighed at His reply. My feet traveled two steps forward.

"Yes, Grandma."

2

"You murderer! Look at your hair! You massacred it." Trinity pounced and gathered my now collarbone-length strands into a short tail and attempted to coil it. I'd left the rest of my blonde hair on the floor near my hammock next to the ancient scissors and family mirror.

I sniffed. It didn't look that bad. But I glanced down at the factory-made blue pants and black, zippered jacket I wore. Should I have not...?

I squared my shoulders, which were weighed down with my bag, and returned my mom's and aunt's stares. "It's smarter to blend in out there. So we're not spotted and attacked so easily."

I spoke the truth. My last trek into enemy territory had taught me the safety of blending in. Not that I was about to offer to search the junk pile for some castoffs for my grandma to wear instead of her homemade clothing. Or suggest she cut off her long, coiled hair like I'd done.

Mom drifted nearer to me, holding out her hands. "Dove. Daughter. You want to be a...camouflaged Christian? And look like a...a worldly woman? I don't think it's wise—"

A *thump* sounded, and I crossed my arms.

Gilead stepped onto the platform trailed by Micah. "Whoa!"

A crowd of chattering, little-boy cousins swung in from different limbs. At least my grandpa, following in back, didn't react to my changed appearance. Instead, he scowled at the black radio dangling from his hand. The bottom half was missing except for some wires, which he jiggled so they danced. "Radio. Seems to have got broke. Somehow."

I shrugged. Other than the initial news of the Reclaim date, our radio hadn't announced anything worth hearing. The radio had been a gifted provision from the Council to each departing messenger so families could receive important information and stay united. It blurted out news of sporadic attacks cropping up in Portland, where I assumed the Christians who broadcasted were stationed. Last week a believer hurled a rock into an enemy's truck. The projectile had struck the pagan driver and caused the vehicle to flip. But the radio reported no more Council news.

Gilead slouched closer. "The radio was the first casualty of war. My bad. Almost as bad as...this." He flicked my zipper and started to hum.

Micah, glancing at me every third word, stuttered about how the electronic got crushed during his and Gilead's sparring practice. It had been an accident. A freak gust of wind that had knocked it into their path was the real culprit. And all the while, Trinity watched him with a satisfied smile, as if she'd finally discovered a person too perfect to improve upon.

I gagged behind my palm. How could my talented, artistic cousin fall for our skink-boy neighbor who'd shown up a few months ago and wouldn't leave? But I'd spotted her newest piece of artwork at our garden's perimeter. The sculpture depicted a familiar, angular face with dark, Brae irises and spider-leg lashes.

Grandma cut Micah off with a slashing hand motion. "Gilead, you do realize that this demolished radio is our only communication with our people about the Reclaim? This is no humming matter."

He jerked up as if surprised at her scold. "What's left for us to know? We attack May 15. That's what the radio people said."

"Don't be so sure, Grandson. Dove and I are going to see that the decision is changed. We're heading back to the Council at Jefferson for the true ruling, and it may take us longer than mid-May to return. So how will you know what to do come May 15?"

My brother's brow cleared. His lip twitched—almost a smile. "If God wants me not to fight, then He'll have you home before the fifteenth with the good news. Or He'll fix the radio. I still have faith, Gran. Even if some of your other grandkids have lost theirs...and want to dress up like Jezebels." He knocked my zipper again.

I bit my tongue because Gran brought her knuckles to her hip. "Gilead Jonah Strong. You will not fight in sin."

We Strong kids don't argue with the adults, but Gilead did...and almost crossed the line of disrespect this time with his typical, pigheaded fierceness. He wouldn't be the only Christian not to fight on Reclaim Day. Gran and I would make it home before then with a changed answer if God's will was for peace. He wouldn't even agree to wait for us in case we were a few days late.

In the charged silence that ensued, my aunt whimpered. My grandpa stepped forward with a straighter spine than was natural for him and cleared his throat twice. But what could he do? If only he was the powerful grandpa he'd been years ago. Back then, he could hold both me and Gilead in place with one arm. Or if only his son, Jonah, had lived. If he hadn't been murdered, my dad would still be scrappy enough to knock some sense and respect into my hulk of a brother.

"You're a lamebrain, Gilead." I moved to the top of the ladder and began to climb down. "But it's a deal. We return with the Council's new answer for peace...and you lay down your knives and leave the godless alone. Now come help Gran down so we have a chance to get there and back before you make yourself a dead lamebrain."

~*~

Mount Jefferson filled the horizon faster than it should for an arthritic old woman and a homesick seventeen-year-old. How had we come so far in four days? Last August it'd taken me weeks to get this close.

The painstaking length of that summer trek must have been Melody Brae's fault. Melody, Micah's twin sister and the Braes' family messenger, empowered with her spiritual gift of being ultra-alert to danger, had led us on zigzagging detours through the farmland and high desert country. Her panic had dragged us off course and wasted time.

But I wouldn't lie and pin the whole difference in journey on Melody. My grandma and I weren't making a pit stop at Mount Washington this time for a

Christian "warrior" to accompany us. We would stay far away from the mountaintop villagers—or MTV—and avoid the closest town of Sisters with all its godless citizens, including the Picketts.

"Good," I told the cicadas' electric buzzing in the sagebrush. "The last thing I need is to run into Wolfe or Jezebel now."

"Amen." Four shambling steps ahead, my grandma picked her way straight through the piles of red lava rocks, as if following an invisible beacon.

"Keep away from the unsaved, Dove. Especially the male ones. I always knew you had brains somewhere in that skull of yours."

My toe scuffed against the rocks, and I faltered. "Well I don't plan to pick up any males of our kind either, Gran. The last ones about killed me."

She didn't reply. She probably understood that I referred to Reed and Stone Bender, the macho Christian brothers from last September who'd tossed around violence as easily as throwing around pinecones. Although Stone had disobeyed his warrior brother's last orders to silence me. And he'd made a kind offer...

I trudged toward the snow-capped peak. It towered as a sky-reaching reminder of how I'd failed my last mission of peace, of how the prophetic red grew. I glanced behind, eastward, toward home.

"What are they're doing now, Gran? At home?"

"Praying."

"Even Gilead?"

She didn't reply to my stupid question. It was daylight. He'd be running drills and doing target practice.

"You think we'll make it home with a new

decision in time? To stop him and Micah from attacking?" Why couldn't I shut up?

My grandma plunged into a stream's weak current without seeming to notice it. It was the only response I got.

*Look for **Fanatic Surviving** and **Sent Rising** where books are sold.*

Thank you…

for purchasing this Watershed Books title. For other inspirational stories, please visit our on-line bookstore at www.pelicanbookgroup.com.

For questions or more information, contact us at customer@pelicanbookgroup.com.

Watershed Books
Make a Splash!™
an imprint of Pelican Book Group
www.PelicanBookGroup.com

Connect with Us
www.facebook.com/Pelicanbookgroup
www.twitter.com/pelicanbookgrp

To receive news and specials, subscribe to our bulletin
http://pelink.us/bulletin

May God's glory shine through
this inspirational work of fiction.

AMDG

You Can Help!

At Pelican Book Group it is our mission to entertain readers with fiction that uplifts the Gospel. It is our privilege to spend time with you awhile as you read our stories.

We believe you can help us to bring Christ into the lives of people across the globe. And you don't have to open your wallet or even leave your house!

Here are 3 simple things you can do to help us bring illuminating fiction™ to people everywhere.

1) If you enjoyed this book, write a positive review. Post it at online retailers and websites where readers gather. And share your review with us at reviews@pelicanbookgroup.com (this does give us permission to reprint your review in whole or in part.)

2) If you enjoyed this book, recommend it to a friend in person, at a book club or on social media.

3) If you have suggestions on how we can improve or expand our selection, let us know. We value your opinion. Use the contact form on our web site or e-mail us at customer@pelicanbookgroup.com

God Can Help!

Are you in need? The Almighty can do great things for you. Holy is His Name! He has mercy in every generation. He can lift up the lowly and accomplish all things. Reach out today.

Do not fear: I am with you; do not be anxious: I am your God. I will strengthen you, I will help you, I will uphold you with my victorious right hand.

~Isaiah 41:10 (NAB)

We pray daily, and we especially pray for everyone connected to Pelican Book Group—that includes you! If you have a specific need, we welcome the opportunity to pray for you. Share your needs or praise reports at http://pelink.us/pray4us

Free Book Offer

We're looking for booklovers like you to partner with us! Join our team of influencers today and periodically receive free eBooks and exclusive offers.

For more information
Visit http://pelicanbookgroup.com/booklovers